INDIA GRAY

INDIA GRAY

HISTORICAL FICTION

SUJATA MASSEY

IKAT PRESS
Baltimore

"Bitter Tea" originally appeared titled *"The Mayor's Movie"* in the short story anthology *Politics Noir: Dark Tales From the Corridors of Power*, edited by Gary Philips and published by Verso in 2008.

The Ayah's Tale was originally published as a standalone novella by Sujata Massey and Ikat Press in 2013.

Cover Design by Deranged Doctor Design
Interior Design by Sue Trowbridge

Table of Contents

Outnumbered at Oxford

OPENING NIGHT

Perveen and Alice had made excellent progress with a bottle of Madeira by the time Maude opened the door. They hadn't done as well with Perveen's Roman law essay or Alice's geometry proof. It had been a lark, breaking the rules with a few tiny drinks as they studied by the fire on a cold February evening in Perveen's third-floor room. But the thrill was gone.

Maude surveyed them with narrowed eyes. "The principal's compliments, and she would like to see you at once!"

Perveen's scout was the eldest of the entire college: a stout country lady somewhere north of forty who had firm opinions on the behavior of Oxford's female students. Those opinions had rattled Perveen during her earliest months. But Alice, the daughter of a lord, insisted that the scouts assigned to the students at St. Hilda's Hall were paid for service and cleaning, not bossing. Maude was supposed to build fires, bring tea and the post, and tidy during set hours. This was why her unexplained arrival at 9:15 p.m. was a shock.

"Surely you didn't bark on us, Maude!" Perveen said, trying for a laugh. She was keenly aware of St. Hilda's own laws. House Rule 7 read: *No wine, spirits or opiates to be kept in bedrooms without special permission.*

Maude shook her head at the two college friends hunched over a table cluttered with books, Alice's special Belgian crystal glasses and the illegal bottle. "I didn't. But Miss Mistry, you'd better wash your mouth with carbolic because Miss Burrows wants you in her drawing room now. And she's got the Master of Balliol College in with her!"

"They want to see me?" The sweet taste in Perveen's mouth had gone sour.

"What on earth, Maude?" Alice asked. When the stone-faced scout said nothing, she swung her blond head around to address Perveen. "Do you have a secret beau at Balliol?"

"Don't be daft!" Perveen snapped. She'd come from Bombay to study civil law, and as one of a minuscule population of Indian females, she had no intentions of bringing shame onto this community.

"What could it be about?" Alice capped the Madeira bottle, looking at it with regret. "Balliol's Master, Professor Alistair Mason, is the eldest mathematician in the university. He's rumored to be ghastly; I'll go with you as a support."

"They called for Miss Mistry." Maude's voice was starchy. "If I was you, I'd stay out of it. If I was 'er, I'd step right quick."

Reluctantly Perveen rose and went over to the washstand, where she reached for her Colgate Dental Cream, wondering what could have gone wrong. Perveen had rarely been inside Balliol, because of St. Hilda's ordinances forbidding unsupervised coeducational fraternizing.

Five minutes later, Perveen was hurrying downstairs while her stomach headed upward to her throat. The Madeira had been a mistake, but she'd never expected this summons. Perveen knocked lightly on the door of the principal's drawing room. It was opened at once by Lucy, the shy maid who served Miss Christine Burrows, the college's head. Lucy motioned her inside and hurried off toward the kitchen.

Miss Burrows might have been petite, but she was a formidable lady with silvered hair she wore in a coronet that made her a touch taller. The sight of the principal's hair—so perfect even at day's end—led Perveen to nervously touch her own wavy black hair, which she'd taken down from a complicated bun because it was after supper and close to bedtime.

"Professor Mason," Miss Burrows said, "may I present Perveen Mistry, our young lady from Bombay?"

Sitting by the fire was an elderly gentleman with a half crown of white hair, leading Perveen to guess his age upward of seventy or even eighty. He looked vaguely familiar.

Through round, gold-rimmed spectacles, the professor scrutinized Perveen, who was wearing a green-and-blue-patterned sari with a long-sleeved white blouse and a gray wool cardigan. The combination was odd, but it was the only way she knew to keep from freezing.

"Miss Mistry." Professor Mason indicated his head toward the tufted velvet wing chair across from him. Perveen looked at Miss Burrows, knowing this was the principal's favored chair.

"You may take it," Miss Burrows said. "I shall be nearby."

The principal settled at her wide mahogany desk a few feet away. Her head was bent over papers, although she was probably listening closely. This was how she typically performed chaperonage: remaining in a room whenever males were present, but not participating in the conversation unless something truly unacceptable was said.

"I hear you read law, Miss Mistry. I don't typically speak with students in your field. My area is mathematics."

"Yes, sir." She could not think of anything better to say.

"I've come regarding a situation with Charles McAslan, an undergraduate candidate for mathematics. He's older than most—he left us to serve in the war and has returned."

She didn't know him, so she'd have to offer her regrets that she couldn't be of service. Trying to look somber, she said, "Sorry, I'm not acquainted with Mr. McAslan."

"No matter. He is served at his rooms in Balliol by a scout named Subramanian, who is a native of your country."

"Really! Do you know the rest of his name?"

Clearing his throat, he said, "Just—Subramanian. Our scouts generally go by surnames only."

Subramanian could be either a first or last name, but explaining this might be more than the don cared to hear.

Mr. Mason said, "I understand you spoke with Subramanian recently."

Blood rushed to her face. Was the Master accusing her of going up to the student bedrooms at Balliol? "No, sir, I did not! It must have been someone else."

The professor stiffened in the straight-backed chair. "But you were one of the chief organizers of an Indian Student Society party held in one of our halls. I am certain I saw you there."

"I issued you a pass to attend that party," Miss Burrows chimed in.

"Why, yes, I do remember the party. But I'm afraid that I wasn't introduced to anyone named Subramanian."

"But others recall you two chatting; apparently Subramanian spoke to you at length!"

Perveen paused, trying to summon the memory. Yes, she recalled the Balliol Master. He'd been ensconced at a table, surrounded by sycophantic Indian mathematics students during the society's last event during Michaelmas term. It hadn't been a real party—at least not by Indian standards. Rising to the challenge of an Asian gathering, the Balliol cooks had prepared a few plates of cheddar-and-chutney sandwiches and iced gingerbread. Wishing for something a bit more Indian, Perveen had slipped into the kitchen with her little bags of spices and supervised the making of Parsi chai, a milky, cardamom-and-mint-flavored tea that was the favorite beverage of her own home.

After the scouts had served chai to all of the partygoers, she'd returned to the kitchen and poured out a few cups for these men. Although a few scouts hesitated, proclaiming they couldn't tolerate spices, most of them liked the sweet tea. She remembered one man, darker skinned and smaller than the others, who'd taken the cup and raised it to his nose for a long inhalation. She warned him to wait a moment because it was still boiling hot, but he'd sipped quickly, as if he'd be called back into service in a minute.

"Thank you. It's different from my mother's chai, but still very good," he'd proclaimed.

"Your mother must make delicious chai." Perveen had looked at him more closely and realized he had Indian features.

The scout had begun to say something more, but a senior law student, Anand Patel, interrupted. "Come along now, Miss Mistry! I've someone for you to meet."

Wordlessly, the scout put down his own cup and took the tray from Perveen's hands. She'd smiled apologetically at him as Mr. Patel steered her over to speak with Miss Chatterjee, a shy fresher from Somerville. Miss Chatterjee had recently come from Calcutta and was miserable. The scout who liked chai had slipped straight out of mind.

Perveen explained the course of events to Professor Mason and Miss Burrows, adding, "I'm afraid I don't know anything else, as I didn't see him again."

"Subramanian began working at Balliol in 1914, serving another man who graduated in 1918. Then he began the work for Mr. McAslan, who had returned to his studies after serving with the army for two years. Five days ago, he did not arrive as usual to light a fire in Mr. McAslan's room. The student naturally assumed that his servant had fallen ill. He asked another scout about him, but that fellow said Subramanian hadn't slept in the scouts' quarters that evening. The porter investigated and concluded that the man's suitcase was gone from the storage room and so were most of his clothes from his cupboard."

"Perhaps he's left his job," Perveen said.

"Indeed! But after Subramanian left, Mr. McAslan realized his own papers were also missing."

Perveen's interest was piqued. "What kind of papers?"

"Academic papers involving an original mathematical proof. I shan't trouble you with details that you cannot understand, but his tutor, Mr. Edward Flynhall, says it is brilliantly complex and would have been finished Trinity term."

"Sorry, sir, I'm still not understanding! For which reasons might one relate the disappearance of the proof and Subramanian's leaving Oxford?"

"We will have the answer if we could find this Indian and question him!"

"But . . . " Perveen trailed off. The logic seemed specious, but how could she say that to such an important, elderly don?

"For the sake of our college, I'm requesting your assistance in finding out whether anyone in the colleges or in town has knowledge of Subramanian's whereabouts. You will be able to speak with Indians more easily than our proctors can."

"Forgive me, Mr. Mason," Perveen began. "I gave Subramanian a cup of tea, but I am hardly his confidante. Surely some of the male students in residence at Balliol College must be better acquainted."

"I've queried the six Indian undergraduates currently studying at Balliol. However, they claim not to have spoken with him. It surely is a matter of caste discrimination." Mr. Mason's moustache drooped lower, accentuating his frown.

"Perhaps." Perveen guessed that Subramanian was a high-caste name, but not being a Hindu, she didn't know for certain.

"And I will not ask undergraduates to proceed further. They are here to earn degrees. It would be improper."

"As a St. Hilda's student, you have studying privileges at Oxford but stand outside the university community and its regulations," Miss Burrows said. "There is no conflict of interest."

Mr. Mason spoke again. "The matter is sensitive. Subramanian is the first Indian to be employed as an Oxford scout. We wish to solve the crisis without public notice. Nothing that would reflect badly on any of your people."

Perveen felt desperate. "Professor, am I understanding correctly that you wish me to make inquiries throughout the town about the location of a missing Oxford employee—someone whose face I saw so briefly?"

"You shall obtain these and any more details from McAslan and his tutor, Mr. Flynhall."

"Has anyone considered whether the academic papers were misplaced?"

"Mr. McAslan and his tutor have turned his quarters upside down looking for them," the Master answered. "At this point, I have not involved the police, but if Mr. McAslan chooses to ask for their assistance, we could have a minor scandal."

"But it's the middle of term." Perveen heard a tremor in her own voice, the evidence of her difficulty in contradicting the powerful administrators. "Unfortunately, I attend lectures every morning and spend the afternoons and evenings studying. My essay on Roman law is due in two days, and honours examinations are ahead."

The professor's eyes blinked furiously behind his glasses. "With Miss Burrows' agreement, I shall notify your department head that you may have an extension."

An extension. Perveen thought how relieving it would be to have just a little more time with Caesar's law. By now she also felt sorry for Subramanian. Regardless of what he'd done, he should know his legal rights before anyone got a choke hold on him.

"Very well," Perveen said. "But what if he's gone away? He might be living somewhere in the towns around here or even gone to London."

"You shall have a pass for entry into town and beyond. I'll have a word with the bursar about recouping any costs for train fare."

"Mr. Mason!" Miss Burrows' voice was cool. "St. Hilda's ladies never go into town without an approved chaperone. As college head, I am the one who signs every pass that is issued. We are not subject to Oxford University regulations."

The elderly professor blinked, as if utterly surprised by this information. "Of course, Miss Burrows. You shall select the chaperone."

Miss Burrows cleared her throat. "Regrettably, I only assign our hardworking tutors to chaperonage during short visits on Saturday and Sundays afternoons. I've pledged my support, but Miss Mistry cannot go anywhere beyond academic buildings without a chaperone."

"Might the Honorable Miss Alice Hobson-Jones accompany me?" Perveen knew her friend would be thrilled by any chance for freedom.

"Miss Hobson-Jones is a student—not a tutor," Miss Burrows said.

"Of course, madam, but she's much older than I am—she's twenty-two! Did you know that Miss Hobson-Jones is daughter of a Balliol graduate? And she happens to be reading mathematics."

Looking thoughtful, Professor Mason nodded. "If she reads mathematics, she may already be acquainted with Charles McAslan or his tutor. Miss Burrows, it would be a great kindness to our college if you would appoint this senior student as a chaperone."

"It's irregular." Miss Burrows paused. "I will permit it for this instance, but both of you must return by nine o'clock every night. Let me see you to the door, Miss Mistry."

Perveen said good-bye to the Balliol Master and went to the door. As Miss Burrows opened it, her voice was low in Perveen's ear. "And you must not go anywhere outside of your room with your hair in such a state. Have I made myself clear?"

"Yes, Miss Burrows."

THE SEARCH BEGINS

That night, in the narrow bed in her small room at St. Hilda's, Perveen dreamed. She was no longer in Oxford or even Britain: she was huddled against the smudged window of a third-class carriage that reeked of coal fumes and garlic. Outside, India was passing: rice paddies, fields of mustard, long clumps of undeveloped jungle. A cluster of peasants stood at a junction: Perveen watched as the train grew closer, then was shocked to see they weren't unknown. Each person staring at her was someone from her past: first, Miss Vaccha, her geography teacher from J.B. Petit High School for Girls; then, her parents and her brother, Rustom. All these people, looking disapprovingly at her as she ducked away from the window.

In the next instant the train compartment was filled by a stern ticket collector. Perveen reached for her ticket but found she had Miss Burrows' pass instead. Feeling sick, she began explaining that she'd not had time to buy a ticket. But the ticket collector had caught sight of what packed the interior of her silk-lined bag: the heavy pearl choker, the set of pear-shaped diamond earrings, all the gold-and-ruby bangles and the rest of her wedding jewelry.

"Thief!" the ticket collector yelled and began blowing his whistle. Suddenly she realized all the other passengers in the compartment were looking eagerly toward her half-open bag.

"It's *mine*," she said, clutching the beaded bag against her stomach. "Yes, I'm a runaway, but it's *mine*!"

"Up with you!" the collector shouted, and as he shrilled his whistle, Perveen knew she was doomed.

"Up with you, miss! Another minute and you'll be late for chapel."

The voice was different: it was Maude. Perveen opened her eyes to find she was no longer in a hot train compartment of the Bombay Mail but in her own small college room with a coal fire burning in the grate. And the jewelry was all gone: it had been sold for her travel to England and three years of tuition and expenses.

"What—what time is it?"

"Half-eight. I've been calling you every five minutes."

Perveen gazed around the room, simply furnished with just a desk, chair and bureau. No devils or angels of her past were here. Nobody at Oxford knew about her brief, failed marriage or how she'd got to Oxford on a passport that wasn't in her proper name.

"You'll tell me later about the goings-on with our Miss Burrows and Balliol Master," Maude said. "Not enough time now."

As Perveen slid her feet into her slippers, her gaze alighted on a small folded paper between the sheets. It was Miss Burrows' pass, tightly folded up. How odd. Perveen remembered placing it in its original, unfolded condition on the nightstand, along with the one meant for Alice Hobson-Jones. Her friend's pass was still untouched.

• • •

Given the alcoholic revels of the night before, Alice Hobson-Jones was suffering from headache. She peered with half-open eyes at the pass that Perveen laid next to her breakfast plate. They were sitting at the end of a long table in the dining hall and had enough space around them that Perveen felt the situation was private.

After Perveen explained the situation, Alice said, "You're putting me on. That can't be Miss Burrows' signature—it's a forgery!"

"Alice, I swear to you that she wrote it out in front of me."

"And you believe this pass will allow me to miss classes and go all around town with you?"

"Yes, indeed. Hopefully we can get just a bit of information to satisfy the professor and be done with the matter quickly."

Alice laughed. "Of course I'll join you. When do we start?"

"This morning. I think we should meet Mr. McAslan at Balliol. I saw Subramanian so briefly that I probably couldn't recognize him if he were standing in front of me."

"But he's Indian!"

"Are you saying we look alike?" Perveen mock-swatted her. "India comprises many different kingdoms and people who arrived from various places—"

"Just like Oxford!"

"No, much more complex. As I've said before, I'm Zoroastrian—but everyone calls us Parsi in India because our ancestors arrived from Persia to escape religious persecution between the eighth and ninth centuries. My Persian heritage is probably why I've got my strong nose—and such lively hair," she added.

Alice rolled her eyes. "But what has this to do with anything?"

"I'm saying that we Parsis coexist in India with Sikhs and Muslims and Christians, Jews and Buddhists and Hindus. We're all quite different."

"Mind you, I was born in India too." Alice put her hands to her head as if Perveen had just given her the worst headache.

"Yes, but you were shipped off to school at seven—so you require education. Returning to my point, Subramanian is a South Indian name particular to Hindus. There's a common assumption that South Indians are all of Dravidian origin with sharply defined features and dark skin. If Subramanian had such striking looks, I would have noticed it straightaway—which I did not. I'd like a description of Subramanian's appearance and manner from Mr. McAslan before proceeding."

Alice nodded. "And this meeting will give me a chance to hear more about this supposedly brilliant paper. Charlie McAslan's a foul-mouthed wretch, so it rather surprises me his classwork is valuable enough for a don to become involved."

"So you are acquainted with him."

"We've been in a few of the same lectures. After I made a comment the other day, he called me a bluestocking. Thought he'd get a laugh out of his lads, but he's damned unoriginal bringing up that tired old insult."

"Do you think he's corrupt enough to have either lost or hidden his paper and then blamed it on his scout?"

"Honestly, I've no idea. But putting him through a few questions is something I wouldn't mind."

"Don't be too wild, Alice."

"Oh, I won't."

But Alice's lazy smile made Perveen nervous.

• • •

Balliol College lay at the heart of Oxford. It was about a mile from St. Hilda's, which had been built up out of a country house on the southeastern edge of Magdalen College. But the morning was unusually sunny for February, and after a brisk walk, Perveen and Alice reached the massive men's college dating from the thirteenth century. A dour-faced porter emerged from the lodge to dissuade them, but after seeing their passes and reading the Balliol Master's letter of introduction, he relented and told a scout to take them to the library, where he would send Mr. McAslan and his tutor, Mr. Flynhall.

Perveen found the Balliol library quite different from St. Hilda's own library; chiefly, it had many more bookcases and a smell that was virtually unknown at St. Hilda's: tobacco. Also, the furniture here was much grander than the secondhand pieces gracing St. Hilda's. Perveen was admiring the medieval relics when a clatter of leather-soled shoes returned her to 1919.

Striding in was a slender blond man with aquiline features and violet-blue eyes. He had played up his looks by dressing in gray flannel trousers and a well-fitting Norfolk jacket. A plum silk cravat was tied just so at the neck of his starched white shirt. His oxblood-colored brogues gleamed with a mirrorlike shine.

The fellow next to him was taller: about six feet, and strongly built. However, his reddish-gold hair was unruly, and his tweed suit lumpy. Perveen imagined Mr. Mason rarely bothered the men about their appearances.

The blond fellow assessed Perveen and then smiled. "Good morning. I'm Edward Flynhall, a tutor of mathematics at Brasenose College. Miss Mistry, isn't it?"

"Yes." Perveen put out her hand. Mr. Flynhall's cool, pleasant grip felt almost sensual; she pulled her hand away, not wanting him to think she found him attractive. "Mr. Flynhall, may I introduce my chaperone, the Honorable Miss Alice Hobson-Jones?"

"I know her already." The other man spoke in a voice laden with a heavy Scottish burr. "She's appeared at a number of mathematics lectures. Last week she was speaking about the finite."

"Finite equations," said Alice, who was now shaking Mr. Flynhall's hand vigorously. Perveen knew the tutor's attractiveness and insinuating grip would not affect Alice. The only person who made Alice swoon was a first-year girl, Jemima St. Clair, who was utterly oblivious.

"Miss Hobson-Jones and Miss Mistry, will you permit me to introduce my student, Mr. Charles McAslan?"

Charles McAslan kept his hands in his pockets and nodded curtly at the women.

"The Master of Balliol said you wished to speak to us before undertaking a search for the thief." Mr. Flynhall delivered another practiced smile. "I daresay you consider this plan as irregular as we do. But thank you for being willing to help."

"I need a proper detective—not schoolgirls," Mr. McAslan said gruffly.

Nodding at Mr. McAslan, Perveen said, "Sorry, but this is not how we expected to spend our time, either. Miss Hobson-Jones and I won't keep you overly long. We've come to learn just a bit more about your scout. Have you a photograph of him?"

"A photograph?" echoed Mr. Flynhall. "It's not often that a student keeps a memento of his scout. Mr. McAslan, have you any photographs, etchings, watercolors or paintings of Subramanian?"

"Indeed, no. And why should I be photographing my scout?" Mr. McAslan glared at Perveen. "He's darker than you, for sure, and a wee thing. He's got rabbity teeth."

"What does that mean, exactly, about the teeth?" Perveen asked.

"They jut out in front—you know, like a hare."

Perveen began taking notes in her diary. "How old is he?"

Mr. Flynhall shrugged. "I've not the slightest. Did he ever tell you his birthday, Mr. McAslan?"

"About your age," McAslan said to his tutor.

"Early thirties, then," Perveen said. "What was his daily costume?"

"I don't know," Mr. McAslan said. "I never noticed."

"Male scouts wear white aprons," Mr. Flynhall said. "Underneath they wear a white shirt, a dark cravat, usually a woolen weskit, and trousers of similar material."

Charles McAslan added, "He also had a black wool jacket—he wore it often, as he found the building cold."

Perveen considered the five cardigans she owned: cream and dove gray lamb's wool for spring, and black, gray and brown mohair and cashmere for winter. Such dull, non-Indian colors, but all that she could find in the ladies' shops in town.

Edward Flynhall spoke again. "Tell me, is there a place that Indians take shelter together, either in Oxford or London?"

"The only places I've heard of are in London: the Northbrook Indian Society, which is a club for Indian students and interested British people, and the Asiatic Seafarers' Society, which concerns itself with destitute laborers," Perveen said.

"You two have a difficult road ahead of you." Flynhall looked directly at Perveen. "My worry is that this scout absconded with Mr. McAslan's most important academic papers."

"I'd like to hear more about that," Perveen said. "But before I do, Mr. McAslan, did Subramanian ever chat to you about his personal life or friends he might visit when off duty?"

The undergraduate shook his head.

Perveen continued, "He didn't mention boating or sport or the pictures?"

"Always had his nose in a book," Charles McAslan said.

"What types of books?"

"Just—books. I never asked."

"What were things like between you? Was it a cordial relationship, or was it more . . ." Perveen trailed off, wondering if a male student could feel as nervous as she did around her scout.

"Yes, he was a good help to me. I trusted him," Charles McAslan said. He blinked his eyes rapidly, and Perveen thought she saw a glimmer of moisture.

"Servants withhold their true emotions," Mr. Flynhall said. "Someone like Subramanian would find a trusting student an easy mark."

Alice jumped in. "An easy mark for what?"

"Subramanian might sell the papers," Mr. Flynhall said. "It

would take just a bit more work to bring the proof to a brilliant fruition."

"What kind of proof is it?" Alice didn't hide her interest.

Flynhall answered, "It's rather complicated for others to understand—"

"I'm a third-year honours mathematics student," Alice said sharply.

The tutor smiled. "Very well. It relates to one of the twenty questions posed at the 1900 International Congress of Mathematicians in Paris."

"Professor David Hilbert's questions," Alice clarified. "Perveen, he's a very famous German mathematician—the fellow who created the axioms that explain geometry."

McAslan squinted at Alice, as if he couldn't believe what had come from her mouth. "Yes, that's the man. I'm working on his seventeenth problem."

"Oh. Are the earlier ones all solved, then?" Perveen asked.

"Oh, no! It's all so complicated," Alice said. "Many scholars are diving in willy-nilly, wouldn't you say, Mr. Flynhall?"

"That's not quite true." Mr. Flynhall's voice was silky. "Hilbert's seventeenth problem is not as abstract as some of the earlier ones and therefore is likelier to be solved. Number seventeen is concerned with expressing a nonnegative rational function."

"Yes—as a quotient of sums of squares," Alice said.

Mr. Flynhall's patronizing smile vanished. "Miss Hobson-Jones, are you working on the problem as well?"

"Oh, no. I'm much more interested in the merging of physics and mathematics," Alice said with a laugh. "But I certainly know about Hilbert."

Perveen felt the two were missing the point. "If people haven't been able to solve this particular problem since it was unveiled nineteen years ago, what might an uneducated scout do with it?"

"He couldn't understand it," said Mr. Flynhall. "But it might be finished by someone at Cambridge or the University of London."

"Oh, that's intriguing!" Alice said. "Who could do it? Have you a particular scholar in mind?"

"Of course not," Mr. Flynhall snapped. "I'm only suggesting that Mr. McAslan's missing proof has tremendous value."

"Perhaps Mr. Mason could send a letter to various mathematics deans warning that important work by an Oxford student has gone missing," Perveen suggested.

Flynhall laughed lightly. "Other academics would make him a laughingstock for sending out such a letter."

"And how do you feel about it, Mr. McAslan?" Perveen asked.

Charles McAslan remained silent.

"Please, won't you tell us what you think should be done?" Perveen asked again.

The tutor spoke, filling the silence. "As you can imagine, we don't want anyone else knowing about the calculations until Mr. McAslan has completed his work."

"I'm curious about something," Alice said. "Is Mr. McAslan working on a proof to which you—his tutor—don't know the answer?"

Flynhall sighed. "As his tutor, I will vet the proof for accuracy, and then, of course, it goes to Mr. Mason. If the mathematics faculty agree that the work is sound, Charles will submit an article about it for publication."

As his tutor spoke, Charles McAslan stared at a fixed point beyond them, as if wishing himself away. *So he is a genius,* Perveen thought. This explained his awkward, disheveled state. He had no time for daily concerns like soap and combs. The tutor, on the other hand, already had earned a master's degree and might be working toward the D.Phil. degree the university had recently introduced. And perhaps he dressed so formally because he was gunning for an administrative post. It would be quite a boon for a tutor to have directed the scholarship of such a brilliant student. From a purely cynical perspective, Perveen could understand why Flynhall was concerned about the missing proof.

"Who is the current scout caring for your room?" Alice asked McAslan.

"Jeffries. He was pulled from another college after Subramanian left."

"And has Jeffries cleaned your room yet this morning?" Alice continued.

"I suppose he's doing it now."

"Splendid! May we all go there together to speak with him?" Perveen chimed in.

"To all our regret, ladies aren't allowed in a male undergraduate's quarters!" Mr. Flynhall said with a chuckle. "If you wish to speak with the scout, he can be summoned here for an interview."

"Shall I call him, then?" McAslan looked at his tutor for guidance.

"Yes, but do remember to come back!"

McAslan hurried out of the room without saying good-bye.

Mr. Flynhall looked after him, then turned to the ladies with a soft, serious expression. "I'm grateful for the privacy. There are things you must know."

"Do tell!" Alice said.

"Mr. McAslan is most awkward in his conversational skills, but he's a good young man. During the war he acted with such tremendous valor that he earned several medals."

"How did the war affect him?" Perveen asked, thinking about the many grim-faced veterans who'd returned to Oxford.

"Like most veterans, he speaks seldom of the war. Returning to Oxford was a dream that kept on through the hardest of times. That's why I'm livid about what's happened. The mathematics faculty and I devised this opportunity for him to do more individual work than sit examinations, because those settings are unbearable for him."

"That's most compassionate," Perveen said.

"We don't widely publicize this practice, lest the other students become aggrieved. But the situation's become grave. For Mr. McAslan to rework this proof on his own from the very beginning would be most difficult. He has problems with memory and endurance."

Perveen decided to bring up what she'd been thinking of since the previous evening. "There's a chance that he's lost some of the papers in his room, don't you think? Or he could have dropped them elsewhere . . . a scout cleaning up in a college room or lecture hall might have thought the papers were discarded and just thrown them in the bin."

Mr. Flynhall's expression was rueful. "I searched the room with his new scout, but our efforts were in vain. And in response to your other question, he wouldn't have taken the papers anywhere else except for my own study."

Perveen asked, "Mr. Flynhall, how many other students might have visited his room or yours?"

"I shan't dare venture as to how many men may have visited Mr. McAslan—he stays here in Balliol, and it's a sociable college.

In my rooms on the third floor of Brasenose, half a dozen mathematics undergraduates regularly come for tutorials and other consultations. But no student could possibly submit Mr. McAslan's work to their tutors or professors without being caught red-handed."

"Although someone might have kept the paper as a prank," Alice suggested. "I don't know if you're aware of it, sir, but your student isn't terribly popular."

"Perhaps *you* dislike him, but I don't know about problems with any others," the tutor said, looking quizzically at Alice. "He's got a small circle of friends, most of whom he knew before the war. They study together often at the Bodleian."

"Who are these friends?" Alice sounded skeptical.

"He studies often with Mr. Ian Little and Mr. Roger Campbell."

"All Scottish names!" Alice said with a laugh. "I suppose it's a case of blood brothers staying close?"

The creak of an aged door made Perveen turn. Charles McAslan had returned alone. Looking down, he said, "Jeffries can't come."

"What a shame. Why is that?" Perveen asked.

"Slops," said McAslan.

"And what does that mean?" Perveen continued.

"He takes my chamber pot for washing. I know that's where he must be, because I couldn't find the pot."

Perveen gasped, and Alice shook with inappropriate laughter. The women's colleges, which were always being lambasted by the men as architecturally insignificant, at least had modern lavatories. The fine antiques in Balliol's library didn't seem as enviable, if the private quarters still had characteristics of the Dark Ages.

"We're drawing close to luncheon, and I'm expected at the High Table today." Mr. Flynhall stood up and shook hands with each of the women. "Thank you for coming, Miss Mistry. Tell me again the name of your academic dean?"

"Dean Robertson, in the school of jurisprudence."

"A good man; I know him. And I trust that if you hear anything about Subramanian's whereabouts, you'll let me know first. I'm willing to go to Subramanian, wherever he might be, to help you convince him to speak to the Balliol Master."

"We will do that, should the need arise. Good day, Mr. Flynhall; and also to you, Mr. McAslan," Perveen said.

"Are you returning to St. Hilda's now?" the tutor asked.

"Not yet; we're headed into town," Alice said. "We've been issued special passes that give us almost the same freedoms as Oxford men."

"Ha. I still don't think you'll find him," Mr. McAslan said with a glowering look.

Mr. Flynhall's expression wasn't as clear. The smiles he'd showered upon their arrival had dwindled. Perhaps he hadn't liked Alice knowing so much about David Hilbert. Or had he sensed Perveen's secret sympathy for the accused?

QUESTIONS AND CAKE

Perveen and Alice stepped out of the gloomy college and into sunshine. This was a rare occurrence for February, and Perveen was determined to enjoy the walk. She barely heard a woman with a rural accent pointing her out to a group of children as "a real heathen." This had happened to her before. Surely it had also happened to Subramanian.

From Broad Street, Perveen and Alice turned into George Street and onward to the Oxford General Railway Station. Several ticket windows were open, so Alice and Perveen asked at each whether any agent recalled an Indian man recently buying a train ticket. One clerk did recall an Indian, but from his height, and a description of his beard and turban, Perveen guessed the man was Jaswinder Singh, a senior student of law. She would see him in a seminar in a few days' time and be able to ask.

"If you really know every Indian studying at Oxford, Mr. Mason did right by putting you on the case," Alice said when they'd finished their station visit and stopped in at Smitherton's, a pretty tearoom in Park End Street. Scones, lemon curd and cake seemed a necessary fortification.

"There are fewer than twenty of us," Perveen said, eyeing the almond and jam confection known as a Bakewell tart the waitress was just setting before her. "I want to learn if it's really true that none of them ever spoke to Subramanian."

Alice's fork slid smoothly into a Victoria sponge topped with a quarter inch of icing sugar. "He surely had friends amongst the scouts. We could try to chat them up."

"But getting into the student rooms is forbidden—remember what Mr. Flynhall said? And Miss Burrows gave me a severe caution about everything this morning. She said that any misbehavior while on pass creates repercussions for every female student." Spooning more sugar into her tea, Perveen added, "Let's think about where Subramanian may have gone. If he stayed in service, he could be working in a household within a few miles."

"Unless he ran off to London for a chance at something better," Alice said. "Or he's gone back to India—that would be topping."

"I know *you'd* like to go to London or India," Perveen answered. "But that can't happen today; there isn't enough time to get past Paddington Station and return before the door's locked for evening."

"True—but let's not return to college too early," Alice said, chasing after the crumbs on her plate. "Being outside of St. Hilda's is as much a treat as that scrumptious cake. At least let's see a picture or shop for some books!"

"Alice, we've no time for fun."

That wasn't exactly true, but they compromised on a bookshop visit, remembering what Mr. McAslan had said about Subramanian reading English-language books.

As Perveen turned into High Street, she thought about how her standards had changed—she'd been born and raised in a bustling city full of colors, scents and sounds. Now, a day in the city meant walking the underpopulated streets of a picturesque town filled with old gray and honey-colored colleges and a few shops and monuments in between. She wondered how Subramanian had felt. Had he grown up in a big Indian city, the small scale of the British Empire's academic hub would have been surprising. On the other hand, he might have been born and raised in a simple village, so Oxford would have felt like a city of castles.

Inside the bookshop, Alice lost herself in the bookshelves, while Perveen asked at the counter whether a small Indian man had ever come through shopping.

"Are you looking for your brother or husband?" the clerk asked nosily.

"No; an employee of the university. A man named Subramanian."

"Sounds Indian," the clerk said. "The new books we sell are too dear for most of your people. We recommend they buy from the Jew who goes about with a used-book cart. Nothing wrong with that, mind you."

Blood rose to her face. She'd heard too many snide things about Jews since coming to England, and this time, the comment was a slur against Indians, too. Most Indian students held Rhodes or other endowed scholarships. She was one of very few students whose father was paying tuition out of pocket.

"Subramanian wasn't a student; he would have worn a suit without a scholar's gown."

The man just shook his head.

The friends enquired about Subramanian at a dozen other

establishments, including restaurants, two chemists, three provisions shops, and a haberdasher, but nobody seemed to recall a small Indian man who was not an Oxford student. She even found the book-selling Jew, who turned out to be an olive-skinned Catholic from Italy.

"Yes, many foreign students buy books from me—best prices here and I treat them kindly," the bookseller said proudly. "I carry recent textbooks, novels and travel guides. Baedeker's guides to England are most popular, but recently one Asian student bought everything I had on Germany."

"Did you ever see an Indian wearing a black suit?" Perveen asked.

"I have encountered gowned students only. Is it your husband or brother you seek?"

"No. Thank you anyway."

• • •

"I'm fairly confident that he isn't in Oxford anymore," Perveen concluded to Alice during the walk back to St. Hilda's. "But would he really have set off without giving a hint to anyone in his daily life?"

Alice plodded alongside her, slowed by the weight of two carrier bags containing new books. "Maybe the porter who guards Balliol's entrance could persuade some of the scouts to come down and talk."

"Why would they do it? Chances are, they've got better things to do."

"My first choice would be luring them with Madeira, but that might be misunderstood," Alice said. "We could return to the tea shop and buy a dreadfully tempting cake."

The tea shop manageress boxed up a large pink-and-white-checked Battenberg cake, as well as a similarly sized Victoria sponge they planned as a surprise for the other students in their hall. There had been some envy over their passes into town; this gift would sweeten the situation.

The sun was sinking by the time they reached Balliol. Owen Blake, the porter in charge of entry to the college, told them that the scouts were unavailable due to their early evening work serving the students and dons their evening meal in Hall.

"Might anyone be available afterward? We only seek the few who knew Subramanian," Perveen said.

"I'm thinkin' who that might be . . . Oh, it's a Battenberg?" Blake had already opened the lid of the box and eyed the thick marzipan coating.

"Yes, from Smitherton's," Alice said.

Blake ran his tongue over his lower lip as he looked at the cake. "Right you are. I'll spread the word and they should be here sharpish after Hall's cleaned up. Is it possible for you to come around eight?"

• • •

Back at St. Hilda's, Alice presented the Victoria sponge in the common room to an appreciative audience.

"I hear you met Mr. Flynhall from Brasenose College this morning," purred Sylvia Gooding, a girl from down the hall.

"How do you know?" Perveen asked carefully. She was mindful of Mr. Mason wishing the whole business remained confidential.

"A little birdie told me. He's too handsome, isn't he? He broke many hearts at Somerville, I've heard. I wouldn't think he'd be interested in you . . ."

Perveen's face flushed, and Alice said sharply, "We're neither of us interested in such a fop. And you haven't answered Miss Mistry's question. Who's the bird chirping nonsense to you?"

"He called in at St. Hilda's during the early afternoon," Sylvia said. "Requested to see Miss Burrows about you—I overheard him speaking to Lucy. Our dear principal wasn't available, so he departed."

Perveen was determined not to give any material to Gossipy Gooding, but she couldn't allow false rumors to start, either. "Mr. Flynhall was involved in a group meeting earlier today. Miss Hobson-Jones was present, as well as another person."

"Cozy," Miss Gooding said with a little laugh.

Perveen left Alice to slice the cake fairly while she went to her room to write a quick note to Professor Mason. In it, she asked if his secretary might be able to enquire at the various shipping companies to see if anyone with the surname Subramanian had sailed for India. If he'd already left, she doubted the university could ever settle the matter. She was annoyed by this, as well as the knowledge that Mr. Flynhall had come to see Miss Burrows. She imagined he'd come to reassure the administrator that he would provide oversight and guidance during their efforts. Such behavior was just a bit too patronizing for her taste.

Perveen and Alice appeared at Balliol's lodge at exactly 7:55. Because of the darkness, they'd hired a hansom cab. The driver had agreed to wait for them near Balliol's gate during their interviews and return them to their college before nine.

Perveen had worried that nobody would come—but she found

three fellows laying a small table with plates and rather dainty cake forks. A kettle whistled on a small hob. Mr. Blake also was measuring out small cups of a dark liquid, perhaps ale, for the scouts still dressed in the daily uniform of trousers, vest and tie.

The two younger scouts who had been chatting became quiet; the elder man, who had a gleaming bald head, greeted them.

"And a good evening to the both of you. Are you the Indian student?" he asked Perveen.

"You couldn't tell?" Perveen laughed.

"If you're Miss Perveen Mistry of Bombay, my sister works for you."

"Goodness! Maude never mentioned her brother worked at Oxford."

"Yes, indeed. I'm Willie Atkins. I started a few years before her in '90, when I was just eighteen. She's been at St. Hilda's since the first residence hall opened in '93. Our father was here before us—retired ten years ago—and my younger brother's working over at Merton."

"Oxford's a tradition for many families," Perveen said. "My chaperone here—Miss Alice Hobson-Jones—had a father and grandfather and great-grandfather who studied at Balliol."

"Charmed to meet you," Alice said. "I do see your resemblance to Maude. Around the ears, wouldn't you say?"

All the scouts laughed, and one of the men shyly glanced at each of them. Perveen thought he might be in his late twenties; he had a full head of reddish hair and skin that was pitted from acne. She wondered what it would be like to make a choice so early on in life to work as a manservant to Oxford students, if one could call going into service a choice.

Perveen's household in Bombay had six or seven servants. She couldn't recall the exact number because someone was always on leave and her mother was always hiring. Rural villages were full of people whose choices seemed to be working the land for almost nothing or going into service in a far-off place. The large bungalow—with its high-ceilinged rooms, wraparound verandas, cooling ceiling fans and larders full of good food and large urns of cold, sanitary water—became the servants' new home. Perhaps to be in service at Oxford, where the buildings were magnificent and the Cherwell River offered the chance to row during free afternoons, was better than the British rural life.

"That's Robbie Jeffries, Mr. McAslan's new scout." Willie Atkins introduced the shy-looking man. "And this last gent is Vince Shepherd, who serves the young man who's bunking in the room next door."

Vincent Shepherd looked about forty years old; his eyes were sunken, and his nose an unhealthy, telling red. Perveen recalled the spree she and Alice had with the Madeira and decided it would be a good thing if Alice didn't keep getting bottles delivered by her cousin, an old Oxonian who called on her once a month.

Alice had already accepted a glass of ale that the lodge's porter, Monroe, had offered her, and was settled around the table, where Monroe was cutting the cake.

"It's most kind of you all to be here." Perveen glanced at her watch. The pleasantries had already eaten up twenty minutes of time. She didn't want to rush, but they would have to return by nine o'clock. "I should like to begin with a question for Mr. McAslan's current scout. Mr. Jeffries, did Mr. McAslan tell you about Professor Mason's request that we learn what happened to Mr. Subramanian?"

"He said nothing about any ladies," Jeffries said in a rich Yorkshire accent. "He's only speaking of his papers. I've been sorting out his room, looking for any and all papers with numbers, but not come up with the blasted papers."

"I imagine his room is a proper mess," Alice said.

Jeffries stiffened, and Perveen realized that he could take such a comment as a criticism of his tidying abilities. So she said, "She means to ask whether he is orderly by nature or the type who often misplaces things."

"Gentlemen don't ever put things away," Mr. Jeffries said. "That's why we're there. But Mr. Flynhall helped me turn the room upside down, even looking under the bed. Nothing was found. It was then that Mr. Flynhall said to Mr. McAslan that Subramanian probably lifted it. Mr. McAslan didn't want to believe it."

"And what's your opinion of the matter, Mr. Shepherd? Do you think this scout might have stolen?"

"No reason to think that, Miss Mistry. He was a helpful soul. But I didn't know him so well. He said little."

"What did you talk about, then?"

"Oh, whether the coal was running low for the fires . . . could he borrow a broom right quick . . . that sort of matter. Sometimes he had trouble understanding English; I explained to him."

"Was his accent quite strong?" Perveen stretched her memory back to the party.

"Subramanian spoke posh—more like the students here. No offense, miss, but you should be sounding regular in a few more years."

Perveen smiled to herself. While an Oxbridge accent held

status in India, the last thing she wanted was to lose the long vowels and sharp consonants of Gujarati and Hindi.

"About his manner of speaking," Alice said. "If one were to close one's eyes, could one think an Englishman was talking?"

"No. Like I said, he had some Indian about him. And he was brown—no chance of hiding that."

"And his appearance?"

"He's about Shepherd's height," said Mr. Atkins, who was clearly the group's leader. "I'd put his weight at eight stone. But here, you can see in the picture." He motioned toward the cracked plaster wall near the door. "We take a picture every year at the scouts' picnic. A celebration that comes as we're ending Trinity term."

The men, dressed in light shirts and trousers, stood in formation on the grass, each holding his hat. In the second row, off to a side, was the man Perveen remembered speaking to about the cup of chai. The photograph was taken on a very sunny day, so his complexion appeared darker than she remembered. His delicately molded face and deep-set eyes were the same.

"Is this Mr. Subramanian?" she asked, tapping the glass.

"That's right, miss."

"Mr. Atkins, what else can you tell me about Subramanian?" Perveen turned to her own scout's brother. "You've been working inside Balliol the longest."

"We greeted each other in the morning. He was a quiet one. I usually made a night of it before he did. He stayed up late in our break room with his books."

Perveen thought about it. "Do you mean that he often read?"

"No, he was scribbling. From what I saw of it, it was lots of numbers and such."

"Was he working with a text?" Alice added.

"No, but he had lots of papers kept in a black portfolio. Made a point of not letting people see them."

"I don't suppose . . ." Perveen hesitated, knowing that it was much to ask. "Might we be admitted inside the scouts' quarters to look for that portfolio?"

"A visit from ladies would *never* be allowed." Mr. Blake, the event's host, spoke firmly.

"I'll tell you that we all searched," Atkins said. "Subramanian left behind his summer suit and hat, but all else was gone, including that portfolio. Maybe that's where Mr. McAslan's paper is."

Perveen was thinking about something else he'd said. Light clothes, such as the ones worn in the previous year's picnic portrait, would have been what a man would pack for India, especially in springtime. Subramanian hadn't taken those clothes, so it was unlikely he'd gone home. The fact he'd packed woollens supported the notion that he had gone somewhere in Britain.

"This is quite helpful. Anything more?"

There was a pause.

"He was quiet," Atkins said. "But it was more than that. He didn't want to speak to us. He didn't seem to realize what a good straw he'd drawn working on the first storey."

"Mr. Shepherd and Mr. Jeffries, you are on that floor," Perveen said. "Do you find the work easy?"

"It's better'n going up and down from floor three as Atkins does with his gammy leg," said Mr. Jeffries.

Perveen had noticed that Atkins had seemed to list slightly to one side when he came in. If he had a bad leg, and was considerably senior to the others, it seemed strange that he'd been assigned to a much higher floor. Especially if—she shuddered, remembering—bringing chamber pots down for cleaning were a daily duty.

"Do scouts ever exchange duties with each other?" Perveen asked.

"We generally stay with our particular young man all their years here. I was specially requested to take care of Mr. Little, because I served his uncle twenty years ago."

Alice was raising her eyebrows at Perveen, signifying something. But Perveen didn't really have time to ask. She'd just glanced at the clock; it read quarter to nine.

"We must leave, but are ever so grateful for your information. If anyone should hear from Subramanian, or think of something else, would you be kind enough to send a message to me at St. Hilda's?"

Perveen withdrew an engraved card from the slim brass case she kept within a pocket of her satchel. Her calling card had been made at Bombay's best stationery shop just before her departure. It carried her St. Hilda's address on one side and the address of Mistry House on the other. "It is important for people to understand your place," Mrs. Mistry had said—as if anyone holding the card would know about the landmark Bombay Gothic stone building where her father kept his law practice.

Mr. Blake studied the card intently, and the other men crowded around to look.

"It's odd to see your name written out like that," Mr. Atkins said. "Hearing it all these months, I thought it was a bit different. I thought it was spelled like 'mystery'—you know, one of them penny dreadfuls."

Mr. Shepherd and Robbie Jeffries chuckled, too.

Perveen said, "Yes, it is an unusual name when written in English. We've got to rush before the doors are locked at St. Hilda's. Thank you kindly for speaking with us."

They had only ten minutes. As they scrambled toward their waiting cab, Alice almost careened into an elderly don.

"Terribly sorry, sir!" Alice called as he shot her a reproving glance.

When Perveen saw the man's face, she almost yelped. "Oh, dear! That was Professor Mason. I don't know if he recognized me with you. He looked rather shocked."

Alice groaned. "I'm such an oaf."

"Back to St. Hilda's College as quickly as your horses can go," Perveen instructed the cabbie as they seated themselves.

"Almost 'eaded out of here. Thought you wasn't comin'," the cabbie grumbled.

"Thank you for waiting." To Alice, Perveen remarked, "I wonder if the professor received my note about checking names on ships bound for India."

"If not, he shall see it by morning," Alice predicted. "It's the oddest thing, but going about today has given me some energy. I think I'll finish those equations tonight."

The taxi jolted into motion. Perveen asked Alice, "Was this desire to return to your equations the only reason you kept giving me those looks?"

"Oh, no. I was thinking it was interesting that your maid's brother came to speak to us. I mean—he didn't have much to do with Subramanian."

"He came only because he was curious about his sister's student," Perveen said.

"He mentioned working for a Mr. Little. Flynhall said that one of McAslan's good friends reading maths is named Ian Little. I'm tempted to find him tomorrow and ask some questions."

"That would be good," Perveen said. "Someone's got to know something about what might have happened to the proof."

"If any part of the proof could be found—or even notes about the equations—I could help sort it," Alice said. "Really, the more I hear, the more suspicious it all sounds."

"And what do you suspect?"

"That McAslan gave up on Problem Seventeen. It sounds too bloody difficult for an undergraduate, let alone one who's got war damage."

Perveen didn't like this idea, but it couldn't be ignored. "Do you think he's hidden it?"

"I think it's more likely he's burnt it to bits or thrown it in the river to disintegrate. If it's gone, he can blame someone else. He won't be held accountable."

It was dark inside the cab, so Perveen couldn't see Alice's expression. She said, "I know you don't like McAslan. Do you think your emotions are coloring your perception?"

Alice sighed. "I wouldn't like to think a student would do such a thing. But who really knows?"

BLOOD BROTHERS AND COUNTRYMEN

The next morning, Perveen awoke to the sound of rain running through the gutters. She could practically feel the chill that was to come, the wetness that would seep over her hands clutching her umbrella and satchel. She sighed. She had no ideas about any other place to search for Subramanian within Oxford, and she had no inclination to travel to London in such weather. And if what Alice had suggested was true—Charles McAslan had thrown away his own work—they'd never succeed.

Watching Maude Atkins poke at the fire in her grate, Perveen said, "Good morning, Maude. I didn't know you had a brother working over at Balliol."

"Yes indeed." Maude looked over her shoulder and gave an uncharacteristic half smile. "How did you come to know?"

Perveen hadn't informed Maude about the search for Subramanian, but she'd likely hear it from her brother. So now she told the briefest details, while the maid sat back on her heels, listening.

"I heard of that scout," Maude said at the end. "But I didn't know he was Indian—just heard there was a foreigner come to join the others at Balliol. All these years my brother's been wanting to work on the first floor, and this boy comes in, what, five years ago, and gets a prime spot."

"Your brother said he was assigned to serve the nephew of one of his previous students staying on the third floor. Apparently he felt he couldn't refuse."

"Because the first Mr. Little was a gem. The second, not so much."

"What's wrong with the current Little?" Perveen asked, her interest rising.

"Very messy," said Maude. "Inconsiderate. No tips at Christmas or at the end of Trinity term."

"I see."

"All that matters for us scouts is a bit of kindness and good manners. Which—I'll say—you've got, miss."

"Based on the usual criteria, I suppose your brother wouldn't think much of Mr. McAslan. He's not terribly courteous. But I've heard that he was wounded during the fighting and in hospital for months after that. The men who came back from the war are supposed to be different, aren't they?"

"Bad nerves, shouting, hiding their faces sometimes," Maude agreed. "I'm only too glad my brother's leg and age kept him from joining. Now, miss, you'd best be getting on with your day. The Honorable Miss H-J is going back to her classes this morning, so you might as well do the same."

At ten o'clock that morning, Perveen's tutor, Mr. Forrest,

presented on a routine subject, the origins of parliamentary law. She found it hard to keep her mind from wandering. Maude's brother Willie had plenty of reason not to like Subramanian—could he have had something to do with his disappearance? If so, she couldn't imagine how it could be proven, except with the aid of other students living in the hall.

Anand Patel, a Balliol College student, was sitting nearby but was ignoring her in favor of the three Englishmen present. How differently Anand had behaved during the time of the party, when everyone around was Indian. People did that—they shifted styles, wanting to blend with the others. But Perveen could have told Anand there was no point; he could not change the color of his skin, or the vibration of his Gujarati vowels.

"Mr. Patel, could you wait just a moment?" Perveen asked as the group went down the stairs to gather up their umbrellas. Mr. Mason had specifically asked her to interview the university's Indian students because he thought she'd make better inroads. And here was an Indian who'd been at the party where Subramanian had served.

Anand Patel seemed not to hear, so she called out to him again. When he strode out into the quadrangle without looking back, she switched languages.

"*Bhaiya*!" She had yelled out the common word for "brother," which was often used to informally address a man on the street.

A few English students looked curiously at her, and then him. Anand Patel got the message. He went rigid and waited for her to catch up. No doubt he feared his continued progress would bring a full cascade of Gujarati upon his shoulders, attracting more attention.

"What?" He wiped rain from his face and glared at her when she'd caught up to him.

"Mr. Patel, I've a few questions about the Indian scout who worked at Balliol."

Scowling at her, he said, "He is not my scout."

His attitude made her feel even more cross. "Why did you tell Professor Mason I know Subramanian? You and several other Indians live with him. I certainly don't."

"Ah, but you are the only one who ever shared a cup of tea with him. Remember—I rescued you?"

As Perveen shook her head, she had the unsettling feeling of her hair beginning to unravel. Not again! "I was in no danger—he was courteous and grateful for the tea."

"And he was getting above his station, as he typically does," Anand huffed.

"Is that what other scouts said? Willie Atkins, perhaps?"

He looked confused. "Is that Mr. Little's scout?"

"Yes, he's a man in his forties who's bald. A very talkative chap."

"But not with me." He coughed. "Look, it's cold and wet. I've no time for this."

"Did Subramanian ever try to make conversation with you?" Perveen asked, continuing to follow him.

"Yes. He asked where I came from—not just the city but my college. Then he had the audacity to say he didn't know undergraduates from Poona College could go up to Oxford."

"That must have felt unpleasant," Perveen said, thinking it was rather similar to the way the students in her hall asked questions of each other, trying to fathom who was really top-drawer.

"I'd even see him sometimes in Radcliffe Camera, seated at a table with books and papers. Just like any student," Anand added in a bitter tone.

"Are there rules against scouts studying in the libraries?" Perveen recalled what the scouts had said about Subramanian scribbling numbers late at night in their quarters. He was clearly a self-taught intellectual.

Anand Patel adjusted his umbrella, nearly poking Perveen in the eye. Without apologizing, he said, "If there are none, I recommend they be added."

The rain's surge increased, forcing Perveen to raise her voice. "Am I correct in thinking you dislike him?"

"It's not a matter of liking or disliking. It's a matter of behaving with an understanding of this world!" When Perveen showed no reaction, he charged on. "The English are politer to us in this country than in our own. But the situation will worsen if there are Indians working at menial jobs in the very same places where we stay. It confuses people." He sighed. "I sorely wished Subramanian weren't at Balliol. It was tiresome having to pretend I didn't see or hear him."

Perveen was struck by the way the St. Hilda's girls spoke to their maids; how she herself had tried to copy their authority. How many times had she done something that hurt Maude's feelings? Perhaps the woman's strictness was the result of too many slights. Slowly she said, "To be kind doesn't hurt anyone."

Anand Patel looked down at her, shaking his head. "I suppose those things matter more to girls."

"What do you mean?"

"You're here for social reasons, aren't you? A credential that makes you suitable for marrying the top Parsi lawyer of your parents' choice. No, don't look at me so! The truth is that you can study all you like, but you won't leave with a degree. Nor can you sit for the bar examination. You're not on the same level as me."

"Actually, I've risen to the challenge here without as much anxiety as you have," Perveen answered evenly. "And who says I won't be the first woman to appear before the London Bar?"

"Say what you will. But I doubt you'll ever plead a case beyond that of the scout."

Perveen took a deep breath before going on. "Mr. Patel, I'm very sorry that you're so fearful of the competition!"

"Hardly! Let's see how well you do at mock trial next week. And . . ."

Thunder drowned out the end of Anand Patel's words, but Perveen could guess he was boasting about something else. The Gujarati student was short, but he had a powerful voice and a lot of bluster. She also knew, from being at lectures with him, that he had a good memory for legal precedent. But if he didn't understand the idea of human rights, he wouldn't be able to craft a strategy to win such cases. In her opinion, he'd be a better solicitor than barrister.

Drenched in the downpour, Perveen watched Anand shoot off, his vigorous steps splashing water. She continued at a normal gait toward St. Hilda's, reveling in personal conviction.

BRIDGING THE PAST

"The principal's calling for you again," Maude said, taking Perveen's wet coat to wring out over the sink.

"Oh, dear." Perveen had just come in from her soggy, splashy walk and had been looking forward to a warming lunch. Swiftly, she pulled off her sodden sari and swapped it for a practical, dry skirt and English blouse. She brushed out her wet hair and braided it swiftly into a coronet.

"You look almost English," Maude said approvingly as she helped her with the last few pins.

Perveen's talk with Anand Patel had raised her awareness that she didn't want to be English; nor should she remain in the country too long. Oxford had been her parents' idea of a sanctuary after all the trouble, when what she wanted was to be home in her childhood bedroom, reading her favorite books and teaching new words to the parrot who lived on her balcony. Reluctantly, Perveen recollected how she'd abruptly left Calcutta to go home to Bombay, the route retraced in her recent nightmare.

Perhaps her own sad experience was why she felt such kinship with Subramanian. Wouldn't he also want to be in India?

When Perveen entered the principal's office, the strength of character she'd felt whilst challenging Anand drained away like rain in a gutter. She could see from Miss Burrows' drawn expression that the lady was disturbed about something.

"Yes, Miss Burrows?"

Miss Burrows spoke in a low, deliberate tone. "Mr. Mason reported that you're misusing your pass to socialize during the evenings at Balliol. I deserve an explanation."

Perveen felt like a child to have to plead with the college head. Nerves made her voice quaver, embarrassing her. "It's true that he saw us—but we were not actually inside Balliol College—"

"He said the two of you were, and I quote, waltzing out of the college gate. That is behavior beyond decorum—"

"We were only at the porter's lodge, interviewing some scouts about Subramanian. And we weren't dancing; we were hastening toward our cab."

"And then why didn't you report it?"

"Because we're still learning things. Miss Burrows, forgive me, but it's not even been two full days since we received the Master's request for help."

She shook her head. "Miss Mistry, I'm counting on you to bring St. Hilda's modest praise, rather than turning into fodder for gossip. Our women must be considered unimpeachable in the Chancellor's eyes. I've expelled women before who were noncompliant with college rules. It's all for the sake of St. Hilda's reputation."

"Yes. That's understandable, Miss Burrows."

"And will you tell me why a certain gentleman keeps coming to see you? Mr. Edward Flynhall was here yesterday when I was out and has since returned."

"Mr. McAslan's tutor," Perveen said. "Miss Gooding mentioned he'd come. I gather he must have something important to share."

Miss Burrows gave her a measured look. "If so, we both shall hear it."

• • •

Edward Flynhall was sitting in one of the wing chairs before the fire in the principal's sitting room: he got to his feet when the two ladies entered. This time, Miss Burrows settled in her favorite chair and indicated that Perveen be seated on a settee some distance away. This created a rather odd dynamic, with Edward Flynhall craning his head to speak to her.

"I called here, Miss Mistry, to offer assistance with the search."

"That is most kind," Perveen said, mindful of Miss Burrows' watchful eye.

"Have you learned anything of note?" he asked.

"In town, nobody seems to remember seeing any Indians who weren't students going into shops. Nobody fitting his description rode a train. It seems as if he wasn't around Oxford lately."

Flynhall nodded. "I reckon that could be the result of scouts keeping to themselves and not having much money to spend elsewhere. Have you learned anything from the Oxford community?"

"I spoke briefly to an Indian student today who believes that Subramanian behaved in a manner not befitting his station. Apparently Subramanian made an insulting comment about this student's prior education in India. Also, Subramanian was seen studying at the Bodleian. The student thought Subramanian was pulling rank and sought to distance himself. I haven't spoken to any other Indian students yet, but I imagine they might have had a similar emotional reaction."

"And what do you think of that?" Flynhall was gazing at her in the same intent manner as when they'd first met. Perveen longed to tell him to quit it: it was unsettling and would make Miss Burrows all the more suspicious.

"I believe in kindness to others. It's part of my religious tradition—and that of many others," she added hastily, seeing Miss Burrows' quizzical expression. "Now, Mr. Flynhall, did you have some knowledge to share with us?"

"It's rather a small tip. I overheard a group of Indian students talking in the Bodleian yesterday. One of them said that an Indian had been pulled from the Thames River in London!"

Perveen felt a chill run through her body. This was not the resolution she'd hoped for. "What else?"

"I attempted to find out more from them, but they scattered when I approached—rather clannish behavior."

"I'll have Lucy bring the daily newspapers," Miss Burrows said. "Surely we will see mention of such a tragedy."

But there was nothing in the *Times* or the *Guardian*.

"I could look for more newspapers at the library in Brasenose," Mr. Flynhall offered. "Although there's a chance it won't be in the papers because it wasn't considered a death of significance."

"Anand Patel knows everyone—he's a real gadfly—so I'm rather surprised he didn't mention this when we spoke."

Flynhall raised his eyebrows. "Perhaps your Mr. Patel didn't connect the dead man with Subramanian. I also noted the chaps talking about this in the library didn't speak of Subramanian."

"Let's not become enamored with an unproven idea," Miss Burrows said. "The drowning victim could very well be a waterman or drunken vagrant. However, it was proper for you to reveal what you heard, Mr. Flynhall."

Edward Flynhall rose gracefully from his chair and went to shake the principal's hand. "Principal Burrows, I feel it my duty."

Perveen rose to walk him to the door. As he shook her hand, he bent his handsome, fair head down toward her. In a whisper he added, "And anything to do with *you* is my pleasure."

• • •

The hair was still standing on Perveen's arms when she arrived in the dining hall a few minutes later. Had the tutor dared to flirt, or was a foreigner misreading things? The only person she trusted to ask was Alice, but she feared she could not get a straightforward opinion, since her friend had declared the handsome tutor a fop.

Alice had saved a seat for her away from the chattering masses. One of the hall's other scouts, Adelaide, took a pitying look at Perveen and filled her bowl with hot soup: mulligatawny, the uniquely British concoction of chicken, flour, apples and curry powder. Still, she liked it better than the mutton soup that was served at least once a week.

Alice regarded Perveen's plain British clothes. "What happened to the charming sari you were wearing earlier?"

"It was soaked through. I had to change into something warm, and I just had the most awful conference in Miss Burrows' sitting room."

"Bring coffee," Alice instructed Adelaide. To Perveen, she said, "What happened with Miss Burrows?"

"She informed me that Professor Mason did notice us yesterday evening. He thought we were running around Balliol to socialize. After I explained about only being in the Porter's Lodge, she announced Mr. Flynhall was waiting in her sitting room. She suspected he was calling for romantic reasons."

"So what did Flynhall say?"

"He said an Indian man drowned in London. Apparently he overheard some Indian students chattering about it at the Bodleian."

Alice's eyes widened. "How awful. What are the press saying about it?"

"Today's *Guardian* and *Times* hadn't any mention. The drowning could have been in an older paper or, as Mr. Flynhall said, considered too insignificant to warrant mention. He said he'll study the earlier papers at the Bodleian."

"Most kind of him," Alice said. "So you've got a new direction to investigate. I have as well."

"And what is it?"

"Did I ever mention that Charles McAslan's friend Mr. Little is part of my geometry tutorial?" Without waiting for a response, she continued. "I approached him during a break. He was startled that Charles McAslan was composing a brilliant mathematical proof. In his opinion, Mr. McAslan struggles with abstract reasoning. Mr. Little said Mr. McAslan becomes so confused that sometimes his scout helps him before he brings any work to Mr. Flynhall."

Perveen put down the cup she'd been about to bring to her

lips. "Actually, that could be true! I heard from Anand Patel that Subramanian frequented the Bodleian Library to study."

"My goodness!"

Perveen was forming a theory. "What if Subramanian understood mathematics as well as any undergraduate? And what if he was undertaking to learn more to help McAslan—and perhaps better his own situation?"

"In that case, Mr. McAslan must be suffering, now that Subramanian's gone."

"The friends spoke of the scout offering help." Perveen sipped her coffee, thinking some more. "What if McAslan ordered Subramanian to do the reasoning for the proof? Subramanian could have been distressed enough to quit his position. It's not right for a scout to do intellectual work and a student take credit."

Alice stared at her. "No, that wouldn't be cricket. And if your hypothesis is correct, the proof might be Subramanian's property."

Perveen drained her cup. "I don't know if we should go to Mr. Mason with this information. It's all hypothetical, isn't it?"

"I say that we test Mr. McAslan first to determine his capability for abstract reasoning. Then we will have a number of good points for the professor."

"I don't see how he can be tested. Mr. Flynhall said Mr. McAslan has been exempted from examinations due to his nerves."

"I've a different test in mind." Alice chuckled. "Messrs. Little and Campbell have invited us to the Oxford Bridge Club this afternoon. Charles McAslan should be there. He's a beginning player."

"And we're both sharp at bridge." Perveen paused, considering things. "The only problem outstanding is that this bridge club isn't on the 'approved' list for St. Hilda's posted by Miss Burrows."

"That's because there probably aren't any female students and chaperones involved," Alice said.

"How can you sound so casual? That means our involvement could be misread again if Balliol's Master notices us spending time with gentlemen!"

"The club meets at Brasenose College, not Balliol," Alice said. "And the Brasenose Master, Professor Layton, is much younger than Mason, which means he's likely more tolerant. I did ask about whether women students played bridge with them, and Mr. Little says they often come from Somerville with a lady tutor in attendance."

It sounded straightforward enough, but Perveen had an uneasy feeling. "Mr. Flynhall lives inside Brasenose. I don't want it to appear . . . oh, I don't know!"

Alice scrutinized her. "You appear rather conventional in those clothes."

"No. I'm concerned it might appear to strict administrators and gossiping students that I've gone to Brasenose to chase Mr. Flynhall. I'm also nervous because Mr. McAslan was so impolite to us before. Anything could happen at the bridge club."

"That 'anything' is exactly what I'm hoping for!" Alice's voice rose. "You shall put whatever he says and does in your report to Mr. Mason. You might also suggest that he himself examine Charles' mathematical acumen by giving him some first-year equations to solve."

Perveen shook her head. "Don't you realize it's tantamount to claiming that a war hero studying at Balliol is a plagiarist? Mr. McAslan might be jolly good at mathematics but anxious when put on the spot. The administrators are more likely to strike back at me for the audacity of the suggestion. Miss Burrows said—"

Alice interrupted, "Have you ever heard Miss Burrows recite the St. Hilda's motto? You haven't? It's *non frustra vixi.*"

"You know I'm weak at Latin," Perveen grumbled. "All I can guess is that it means 'don't do something'!"

"It means 'I lived not in vain.'"

• • •

The rain was still heavy, so Perveen and Alice hired a hansom cab for the trip to Radcliffe Square. The long, Gothic expanse of Brasenose College stretched across the square's west side.

The Porter's Lodge was built into an arched entry of the building. Upon entering, Alice declared herself Perveen's chaperone, and Perveen showed the pass. Their passport to freedom was severely creased, and exposure to damp had caused Miss Burrows' signature to blur. Somewhat reluctantly, the porter led them through the Old Quad and into another section of the college. The bridge club was held in a large common room where the walls were hung with tapestries and aged portraits of medieval men. A line of recent framed photographs of undergraduates was the only similarity this place shared with St. Hilda's cheerful, casually furnished common room.

Five men jumped up with alacrity to greet Perveen and Alice. Then they began arguing with one another about reshuffling the table assignments. Everyone wanted a lady at the table, and there were just Perveen and Alice, since the Somerville students had not come.

"Are you afraid to play against me, Mr. Little?" Alice challenged with her most winning smile.

With private amusement, Perveen noted that Mr. Little was a small man. He was a tousled, cheerful fellow who appeared delighted by Alice's challenge. He showed Alice to a seat across from him, close to where Mr. McAslan was already dealing out the deck. Just like that, Alice had set herself up as McAslan's partner, without anything being stated.

Perveen seated herself at the very next table, where Mr. Campbell, a raven-haired Scot, humbly requested the honor of being her partner. The other two men—Mr. Sandringham and Mr. Lee—inquired if she would like a practice game first, in order to learn the rules.

Perveen warned them that she and Alice were regarded as the most formidable bridge team at St. Hilda's, and no accommodations were needed. Although she intended to keep watch on Mr. McAslan, she was quickly drawn into the competition. Mr. Campbell was surprised and delighted by her assertiveness. The other players moved faster, not offering her any breaks.

After the first round, Perveen and Mr. Campbell were slightly ahead. But then a cry came from the other table.

"No. It's not—I had—" Mr. McAslan was standing up, cards in hand. His face twisted in an odd expression that Perveen suspected was rage, given the slitted eyes and set jaw. If a man could explode, he would.

"It's their turn," Alice said calmly.

"You made too many fool choices!" McAslan hissed.

Perveen's skin prickled, because she was certain Alice would do something rash intending to get a reaction.

"I'm terribly sorry," Alice said in the same annoying, girlish tone.

"Charlie, you shouldn't have played the three of hearts," Mr. Little said. "But it's all right. You're a new player."

Charles McAslan flung his cards on the floor and swore an oath that would have been rude on the streets of North London, let alone in an elegant room inside Brasenose College.

"Charlie, you mustn't," Mr. Little said warmly. "Not before our lady guests—"

"Oh, we've heard it all," Alice said.

Perveen blushed because her companions were all looking at her. They wanted to see if she understood what the vile word meant. Although Mr. Little and Mr. Campbell appeared horrified, she sensed malicious excitement among some of the others.

"Damn all of you!" McAslan swept the cards off his group's table. He rose to his feet and towered over Alice, who was still sitting and sorting her cards. Perveen rushed over and took a protective position beside her friend. Perveen had seen a man in such a rabid emotional state before. She knew how fast a punch could be thrown.

Perveen's movements triggered an uproar. Most of the men ringed the ladies, but Mr. Campbell and Mr. Little approached McAslan, who bellowed with rage and swung out.

"I shan't be taken!" he said. With a jab of his elbow, he sent Mr. Campbell stumbling a few feet. Then Mr. McAslan stormed out of the room.

"And you were the one who wanted ladies to play!" An Oxford upperclassman gave a withering look to Mr. Little.

"Our guests weren't at fault," Mr. Little protested. "Charlie just went into one of his moods.

"I believe he was frustrated by our making decisions at high speed," Alice said.

"Please don't leave. We can resume," said Mr. Campbell, who had regained his composure. "We'll resume and get a new partner for Miss Hobson-Jones."

As the men picked up cards from the floor and vied to play alongside Alice, Perveen and Alice moved away. Perveen looked at her friend, wondering if it was wise for them to remain. They'd be safe with this particular group, but the violence McAslan exhibited had frightened her. Had he been this way with Subramanian?

While Alice studied the pictures along the walls, Perveen sank down on a handsome high-backed chair by a medieval window and stared out into the driving rain. What if Subramanian hadn't run away, but died at the hands of furious, frustrated Charles?

"Of all the things!" Alice exclaimed. Perveen glanced up as Alice beckoned her over to the wall of photographs.

"Look at this picture, dear. Third row."

It was a large framed photograph of Brasenose's College population of 1913 titled *The Mathematics Society*. Three rows of men, all of them pale except for one sitting dead center.

"He clearly resembles the man in the photograph the scouts showed us," Alice said, pointing at the darker student in the photograph. "But the caption underneath says V.S. Iyer."

"The scouts always just use one name . . . could the *S* in the middle stand for Subramanian?" asked Mr. Little, who'd come up behind them.

"Possibly. Like Mr. Mason, I'd assumed that Subramanian was a surname. But South Indians typically have three or four names honoring their father, family, town of origin and caste. In this case, Subramanian might be a middle name. His first name is something unknown that starts with a V." Perveen continued reading along the captions, and nearly choked.

Edward Philip Flynhall. Perveen's eyes moved from the caption to search the rows of white faces. There he was, two rows behind V.S. Iyer, looking a bit younger—and even more beautiful.

OUTNUMBERED

Mr. Little and Mr. Campbell had been right behind Perveen and Alice. They'd also met Subramanian and Mr. Flynhall, so it was impossible to keep them from marveling at the pictorial revelation.

"Why wouldn't Flynhall have told this to us?" Mr. Little wondered aloud. "They weren't just in the same college; they were in the same club!"

Perveen gave Alice a stare that warned her not to say anything more. However, it seemed wise to accept Mr. Little's offer to lead them to the Brasenose Master for further discussion.

Mr. Little swiftly led them through a long passageway and out past the chapel and into the New Quad. The principal's residence had a heavy door with a brass nose-shaped knocker, which Mr. Little rapped.

"The college's original twelfth-century nose-shaped knocker hangs over the High Table in Hall," Mr. Little said, noticing Perveen's fascination with the knocker. "This is one of very many.

You can't have a college called Brasenose without a lot of brazen noses."

"Serpents are part of the college symbol at St. Hilda's," Alice said. "I don't know what is more repellent: a brass nose, or a coat of arms with a snake. What do you think, Mr. Little?"

"We should discuss it later," Perveen said as a butler opened the door. "Mr. Little, thank you for the escort. I think we'll be fine on our own."

Mr. Little appeared crestfallen. "But—surely you'd like me to introduce you to our Master?"

Perveen regarded the friendly young man she'd met so recently—someone who was also being tutored by Flynhall. *Too close for comfort,* she thought. "We are on private business for our own principal. We don't need any more help, thank you very much."

Perveen showed her pass to the butler, who didn't hide his shock at the arrival of two lady students whose names were not on the principal's agenda.

"I'm the chaperone," said Alice, who straightened into her full five feet ten inches. "Dispatched by Miss Burrows of St. Hilda's College."

"I'll ask if Professor Layton is available," he said, giving the two a disapproving look as the rain dripped off them in the vestibule.

Professor Layton came out to the hall. The middle-aged man was dressed in a severely tailored suit, although his expression was neutral. Looking them up and down, he said, "What is this?"

"Good evening, sir, and my apologies for the interruption. I'm Perveen Mistry, a student at St. Hilda's College. My chaperone and I have come on confidential business. This is at the request of Professor Mason from Balliol, and Principal Burrows from St. Hilda's—"

His expression warmed. "Take their coats, Dobbins. And bring us all a pot of tea."

Seated before a roaring fire, the girls were served cups of good Darjeeling. As the three sipped, Perveen discussed their interest in the Brasenose student named V.S. Iyer.

"I can say with assurance nobody by that name is currently enrolled," said Mr. Layton. "However, I was promoted into my position as the college Master in 1915. I shall check for a record on Mr. Iyer in the year 1913."

Mr. Layton rose from his armchair and went to a bookcase. Taking down a leather-bound portfolio, he settled with it on his lap. He put his monocle to his eye and began paging through. After a few minutes, he said, " Mr. Vanu Subramanian Iyer, a candidate for honours mathematics. He was a Rhodes Scholar who arrived in 1912."

Perveen kept quiet as he turned the page. "Mr. Iyer left Brasenose in 1914 during Trinity term. A curious decision; he had a very fine record and had completed nearly all the work for a bachelor's degree with honours."

"Maybe he left because of the war," Perveen said.

"The war didn't start until August," Alice cut in. "It can't be that."

"Dobbins!" Mr. Layton called out.

The butler appeared. "Sir, what do you require?"

"In the anteroom, the shelves closest to the door contain a set of brown folios containing correspondence from the Overseas Student Office. Please bring the folio for the year 1914."

The three made conversation while the butler carried out the

Master's request. Professor Layton was startled to hear that V.S. Iyer had become a scout at Balliol College. Shaking his head, he said, "I don't know what would be a greater difficulty: simply laboring with hands instead of mind, or for a Brasenose man to handle the refuse of Balliol?"

Dobbins returned with such a large book that Professor Layton was obliged to review it at his desk. Perveen yearned to creep out of her chair and peek over his shoulder but realized that the contents of whatever he was looking at might be confidential.

"In April 1914, the Overseas Student Office recorded that they'd received a letter from the Rhodes people stating they cut V.S. Iyer's scholarship due to a conviction of plagiarism." He looked up at them. "My goodness."

Perveen sucked in her breath. She didn't believe it.

"What evidence is there of plagiarism?" Alice demanded.

"Their evidence was a letter from Professor Mason. He never mentioned this to you?" Professor Layton popped the monocle from his eye and regarded them with surprise.

"He did not," Perveen said. "Of course, he did not know the scout called Subramanian was the former student known as V.S. Iyer."

"But they were at the same holiday party with the Indian students!" Alice said. "You told me that you had a cup of tea with Subramanian, and Professor Mason and his wife were chaperoning."

Perveen thought some more. Professor Mason was elderly and wore spectacles, but he should have remembered an outstanding scholarship student. Then again, Subramanian might have avoided him.

Alice continued, "If Subramanian was a plagiarist, he would

have gone before some kind of university court and been formally expelled. His leaving should have been prompted by that more than an inability to pay his bills."

Professor Layton paused. "One would hope so. And now that I consider the facts, I would have known if a Brasenose student had been expelled over the last few years. Expulsion is a major dishonor for the entire college."

Perveen asked, "If you didn't know about it, does it mean he might not really have been expelled? Despite what the Rhodes letter says?"

Mr. Layton slapped the book closed. "There's nothing to do but speak to Professor Mason about it. Don't worry, my dears, I shall find the answer."

They'd come so far that Perveen did not want to lose control. "You are most kind to help. But before we leave, I was wondering whether you're acquainted with Mr. Edward Flynhall, the mathematics tutor?"

"Certainly. He earned an honours bachelor's degree the year I came in."

"Does he tutor many students?"

Mr. Layton hesitated. "I don't know the exact number, but it's not many. He's carrying a light load because he's hard at work on his D.Phil. Why do you ask about Mr. Flynhall?"

"Are you aware of the topic of his dissertation?"

"I'm an historian, so the two of us have not yet spoken of its specifics. I do have a record book with brief summaries of our scholars' projected work . . . Dobbins!"

When the book came, the Master opened it and began flipping pages. He stopped and confidently tapped his finger. "Here we are.

It's about an old question posed to the mathematics community. I'm not sure any of us would understand."

"I'm reading mathematics," said Alice.

"All right, then. His work is a response to a question posed years ago by a German mathematician named David Hilbert."

Alice laughed aloud. "How coincidental! Charles McAslan was working on something related to David Hilbert. Mr. Flynhall was very hush-hush about the whole matter, and it seemed tremendously ambitious for an undergraduate. Does it strike you, sir, that they might be working on the same question?"

"It could be. Students often follow their tutors," Professor Layton said.

And tutors might follow scouts. Perveen asked, "Regarding Mr. Flynhall—what are his strengths?"

"He's a confident and mature fellow. The students like him very much, so I'd say he's a born administrator."

"Does he publish much research?" Alice asked.

Mr. Layton paused. "I'm not aware. Perhaps Professor Mason knows? He's his advisor."

• • •

"We must call on Mr. Flynhall before he gets word from any of the bridge players that we know about his long-lost classmate," Perveen said after they'd thanked Mr. Layton and were shown out to the cold hallway, where their sodden coats hung like giant sleeping bats. To their surprise, Mr. Little was still there; he had been sitting on a small bench.

"It's just as well you didn't go," Alice said. "Any idea where we might find a tutor from your college at this time of the day?"

"If you're after Mr. Flynhall, he usually has sherry in his room before Hall. I can show you where the tutors' rooms are," Mr. Little said. "It's up one of our many staircases."

"Splendid!" Alice picked up her umbrella.

"Just a moment," Perveen cautioned. For female students to enter male residential quarters—rooms with beds—was unthinkable. In fact, it was so beyond the pale that it hadn't even been codified as a St. Hilda's rule.

If no rule was written, could it technically be enforced? Perveen thought they had two arguments in their favor: the fact that Mr. Flynhall occupied a respected teaching position, and the granting of chaperone status to Alice. Such meetings commenced throughout Oxford for academic matters. Yes, that would be the line she'd take, if Miss Burrows found out.

"We would be grateful for directions, but please do not accompany us; that would muddle the picture of what we're doing," Perveen said. "We've a pass to travel inside the colleges relating to an administrative matter, but we don't want to be perceived as misusing it for student fraternization."

"Don't you sound like a principal in training!" Alice said with a smirk.

"Very well," Mr. Little said. "I'll show you to the ground floor and explain about the staircases. Walk up one storey and there will be a name card on his door." There's another door, but that's another tutor."

"It sounds simple, but if we're confused, we'll ask a scout," Perveen said.

"Should you see one," he rejoined. "Most will be downstairs helping organize Hall for supper."

It was the same case with the scouts at Balliol; Perveen

remembered they hadn't been available for interview until eight o'clock.

Mr. Little directed them away from the New Quadrangle and back past the chapel and the Old Cloisters into the Old Quadrangle. The ancient stone staircase leading to the tutors' quarters was already wet with rain shed by other scholars. As they carefully proceeded up, Perveen began thinking about how to confront the deceptive Mr. Flynhall.

Perveen knocked lightly on the closed door that was labeled "Mr. Edward Flynhall, Tutor."

"He may not be in," Alice said.

Perveen knocked more insistently.

"Look! You pushed the door open with your knocking," Alice said.

"Mr. Flynhall, are you there?" Perveen called as she stepped inside the quiet, dark chamber.

Inside, she lit a gas lamp and discovered two adjoining rooms: one for sleeping and one for study. The walls appeared to have been plastered many times over the centuries; they appeared pleasantly golden in the gaslight. Arched windows with wavy glass had been bordered with modern green and gold paisley curtains. The chairs around Mr. Flynhall's small oak table had stylish, exaggeratedly long backs.

"Charles Rennie Mackintosh designed those—or someone made a good copy," Alice said knowingly, as the girls hung their coats and umbrellas on a stylish stand. "And look, Mr. Flynhall must fancy Japonism. Those must be Japanese woodblock prints on the wall!"

Perveen glanced at the woodblock prints of scenes in faraway countries, but looked more intently at the mahogany drinks cart with a full array of decanters. It was like that for her and alcohol; she feared it due to some bad old memories, but at the same time would have enjoyed a glass of sherry and a moment to discuss with Alice their investigation strategy.

Professor Mason and Mr. Flynhall both had prior doings with V.S. Iyer—but did that mean they were complicit in setting up the search? She had the horrifying thought that perhaps the request for the search was a ruse to draw attention away from the truth that they themselves had something to do with the scout's disappearance. And they'd asked women students to look into the matter because they were sure to fail.

What had they done?

"I don't think we should stay in this room. Or even this building," Perveen said.

"But we could find something important!" Alice insisted. "This is a bloody good opportunity."

"To glance around quickly while we wait for Mr. Flynhall is one thing, but if we were to open desks and drawers, we could be faulted."

Besides the woodblock prints of Japanese ladies and snowcapped mountains, the tutor's wall was hung with framed degrees: his Oxford bachelor of arts in mathematics from 1914, the master's degree from 1918. Alice lifted each picture and looked behind it.

"Alice, be very careful!" Perveen warned.

"That's where villains hide things: under beds, too."

Alice worked her way around to a large slate hanging on the wall over the table. "Oh, look. He must have been teaching integer theory to his students."

"Really?" Perveen looked doubtfully at the scribbled numbers, which made no sense to her. "Are you doing the same with your tutor?"

"Second year. So this is a review, or the start of something much more complex." Alice picked up the chalk lying in a saucer near the board and scratched a few numbers on the board. "Yes, that's the next step. And then—"

"Oh, dear!" Perveen said as Alice's chalk split into fragments. This was a problem. Even if she erased Alice's small bit of work, a broken chalk would alert the room's owner that someone else had used the board. They could take away the fragmented chalk, but he might notice that, too.

As Alice bent to pick up the broken chalk, her head bumped against the board. It shifted and two papers spilled out from behind the blackboard.

"What the devil!" Alice swore.

Perveen came over to help her lift the three-foot-wide slate board from the wall. Turning it, she saw a cotton strap fitted tightly across the back, and an array of pages covered with rows of penciled figures. "Why would academic papers be tucked behind the board?"

Alice whooped. "Do you see the initials on the bottom of the page?"

"C-M-A," Perveen read aloud. "Maybe—Charles McAslan? How do Scots write their initials if they're Mc-something?"

"All of the pages have C-M-A!" Alice said. "And it's clear that one page leads into another. I can hardly begin to understand this; it's a very complicated proof."

"Our proof!" exclaimed Perveen.

THE FINAL SOLUTION

"We can't leave it here," Alice said. "It's exactly what Mr. Mason wanted us to bring him; leaving it here's a terrible risk."

"If we can trust Mr. Mason," cautioned Perveen. "I never thought I'd want to go to Miss Burrows about anything, but I think her study is distant enough to safely hold these papers."

"I'll ask her to lock them in her desk. Perhaps tomorrow she can ask both Mr. Mason and Mr. McAslan to come," Alice said.

"First, let's erase what you were calculating and hang the blackboard," Perveen directed. "Then promise me you'll go straight to St. Hilda's. I'll make a stop at Professor Layton's residence to alert him about our discovery. Better to be frank straightaway so we do not face theft charges from Mr. Flynhall. I'll just clean this little bit of carpet—no, don't bother trying to help! You're so accident-prone I don't know what might happen next."

"Are you certain you'll be all right?" Alice said as they hefted the blackboard into its former position.

"Go on, my dear. And do keep the papers underneath your coat so they don't get wet!"

As Alice hurried out, Perveen went into the bedchamber and wet her handkerchief using the half-full jug on the washstand. She hastened out of the bedroom and back to the white spot near the table. As she rubbed away at the carpet, she heard footsteps coming up the stairs outside the room.

Had Alice come back?

"Why, Miss Mistry!"

Perveen recognized the voice of Edward Flynhall. Feeling sick, she looked from the oxblood-polished brogues and up along the impeccable gray trousers and Norfolk jacket to the chiseled, unsmiling face.

"I didn't think that members of the women's halls were allowed to visit gentlemen's rooms! What are St. Hilda's rules, Miss Mistry?"

All Perveen could think was that Alice must have vanished down the staircase just moments before he'd come up. She'd escaped his notice, which meant the papers were safe. But Perveen was thoroughly alone.

Hiding the damp handkerchief in her pocket, she stood up with as much grace as she could muster. "As you know, Professor Mason and Miss Burrows issued me a special pass, and I'm still within the hours that St. Hilda's students are allowed to be out of college."

"That's irrelevant. You had no permission to go through my rooms."

"I came to speak with you!" Perveen felt desperate. "Do ask Mr. Little about it; he'll confirm giving me directions to your room."

Glancing around, Mr. Flynhall asked, "He didn't come with you, then?"

"No, I . . ." Perveen trailed off. Likely this was the wrong revelation to make.

Mr. Flynhall was slowly walking around his room, looking at everything. Approaching his desk, he tested the drawers, which were all still locked.

"If you'd prefer, we could speak downstairs in the library, or within Principal Layton's home." Perveen kept talking, aware she needed to distract him from the blackboard.

"But you seem quite at home here. By the way, what were you doing down on the Axminster?" Mr. Flynhall asked.

"I accidentally knocked something onto your lovely carpet. Your scout wasn't here, so I took it upon myself to wipe it up."

As Edward Flynhall stepped closer to the damp spot, his shoe crunched on an errant chalk fragment. Inclining his foot, he examined the white residue on his shoe's leather sole.

"Do law students use chalk? Or . . ." He stared at the blackboard, which hung just a bit askew on the wall. He lifted the wide blackboard easily and flipped it around to look at its back.

Perveen's heart began hammering. She could plead ignorance and say she'd not touched the blackboard, but he'd never believe it. Not when she'd been discovered cleaning up chalk.

Flynhall left his blackboard and advanced toward her. "Where?"

"What are you asking?" Perveen wanted him to admit exactly what he was looking for. This would give her something precise to recount for the Oxford authorities.

He spoke slowly, enunciating every syllable. "Where did you put what you found behind my blackboard?"

"I don't know what you mean." Perveen's eyes strayed to the small doorway. Flynhall followed her gaze, walked casually to the door, and drew the interior bolt.

Turning back to Perveen, he said, "Return my papers now, or you shall regret it forever."

"Your papers or your student's papers?" she challenged, hoping he didn't hear the shake in her voice. He was much more dangerous than she'd believed.

Slowly, he looked her over. Perveen still wore the high-waisted wool skirt and had covered the blouse with one of her cashmere cardigans. She'd felt cozy before, but now she felt naked and cold. She felt as if Mr. Flynhall was undressing her with his eyes.

Instinctively, she crossed her arms before herself, just as Mr. Flynhall's hand shot out and tore at her cardigan. A button popped, and Perveen shrieked as she recoiled.

"Open it yourself, then," he demanded. "And there's no need to raise your voice again. We're absolutely alone."

Perveen never thought she'd disrobe before a man again. Shakily, she unbuttoned the cardigan and showed him there was nothing underneath but her thin muslin-and-lace blouse. "As one can see, there are no papers. Nothing to worry about."

"And underneath that blouse?" His voice was cool.

"I wear a *sudreh*, a garment that is traditional for my faith." Suddenly she felt a surge of courage. "It's been proven, over the centuries, to provide spiritual protection against evil."

He snorted. "Religion—or heathenism? You'd best tell me where the papers are, or I've no use for you anymore."

"I don't have anything of yours. I'll be saying good-bye, if you don't mind—" Her shouting was interrupted as he dragged her toward the other room—his bedchamber.

"You mustn't—" She lost the rest of her sentence as he knocked her onto the bed. This was what he'd meant when he'd said she'd regret not giving up the papers. What was about to happen would have nothing to do with seduction; it would be worse than the most awful cautionary tale told by Miss Burrows to the St. Hilda's women.

"There you go, face in the pillow . . ." His murmur was low, as if this was a seduction and not an attack. "You don't want to see me. It will be easier."

He was not touching her skirts, but she felt a new horror. He was pushing her face into the heavy down pillow because he intended to suffocate her. And this bloodless, quiet method was perhaps the way he'd rid himself of V.S. Iyer.

Perveen managed to twist both her arms toward one side and grab something: a long bolster. It was not soft like the pillow she was sinking in. She had no ability to turn and strike him, but she did manage to tug it underneath her, creating enough space that she bumped hard against Flynhall. He cried out as her head hit his mouth, and she took advantage of the moment to rear up further.

She was halfway to sitting, and her face was clear of obstruction. Flynhall still had a hold on her, but at least he hadn't started to beat her. She shouted, "You had it in for Subramanian since you were an undergraduate."

"He was too competitive," Flynhall said, pressing his body down over hers. They were face-to-face. "That thesis wouldn't just have put him first; it would have gained him the tutor's position I have now. He had to be stopped."

"So you did that," Perveen said. "By writing a letter accusing him of plagiarism to the Rhodes Committee."

"There was never any such letter signed by me," Edward

Flynhall said. His violet-blue eyes had a curious light. In earlier days, Perveen had mistaken it for flirtatiousness. Now she realized it was smug challenge. He didn't think she'd ever put together what he'd done.

"Then this letter was a forgery signed with Mr. Mason's name. You see, if a college head were faced with a situation of a student's plagiarism, he would have brought it to the university's attention. We know that never happened. However, you sent a letter to the Rhodes Committee, pretending that the student had already been tried and convicted."

"It's not such a big matter," Flynhall snapped. "He couldn't pay the fees, so he had to leave."

Perveen realized that although Mr. Flynhall kept his body pressed over hers, he hadn't done anything to hurt her any further. He must have wanted her to understand the depth of his frustration with Subramanian. Trying to sound sympathetic, she said, "But he did not leave. Do you know the reason he began work as a scout?"

Flynhall wrinkled his nose. "Good God—it's such an easy job! Scouts have unscheduled time during the afternoon and in the evening, leaving him time for intellectual pursuits. I don't know how long he was doing it; I only caught him when I called on Charles in his room during Michaelmas term."

This was when Perveen had seen Subramanian working at the Indian Student Society party. Trying to appear helpful, she said, "Subramanian has been serving Mr. McAslan since he returned from the war."

"Well, it was futile—most of the boy's brains are gone, although I was fooled by the strong work that he presented to me for the first few months I taught him. I can't think of why Iyer chose to aid him, unless he hoped to be discovered as a lost genius and have the past forgiven."

"Forgiven? The poor man did nothing wrong. On the other hand, I've heard your dissertation is on one of Hilbert's problems. Why is that?"

"I became interested while helping Charles. Many mathematicians are working on his problems, as your friend aptly noted."

"My question is why you didn't want Subramanian to stay on assisting Charles? The longer he helped your student, the more you'd benefit. Why did you feel the need to drown him?"

"The drowning?" He laughed shortly. "I fabricated the rumor to divert you—although I think the Thames would indeed have been a good resting spot for Iyer. But the truth is that I never touched the chappie. He ran away."

Perveen shook her head. "No. You wanted him gone because you feared he'd reveal his past experience with you to Charles."

"I'm not afraid of anything." Flynhall smiled unpleasantly. "However, Iyer should have been more cautious. He looked at me with insolent eyes and even called me by my Christian name. But how dense he was to keep supplying Charles with equations that I was able to keep for my own purposes."

"That was shrewd. However, you couldn't present the proof to the faculty with him nearby: that was too much of a risk."

His voice lowered. "Miss Mistry, when your large and expressive Asiatic eyes regard me—I almost feel something. What are you trying to communicate?"

"You had to rid yourself—and Oxford—of V.S. Iyer. Where is he, Mr. Flynhall? At the bottom of the River Cherwell, or stuffed down an unused coal chute?"

He chuckled. "Your rhetorical skills are vivid! The truth is that all I did was give Subramanian some money. That would seem to be one of the kindnesses of which your faith might approve."

Perveen shook her head. "Mr. Flynhall, you appear to be a man of means, but this doesn't sound like something you would do."

"I give you my word that I paid Iyer one hundred pounds to use for a ticket home to India. Not giving him a way to leave this country was my prior mistake."

Perveen considered this. If Flynhall really had given Subramanian money, it could pay for silence about the Rhodes trickery and the true authorship of the mathematical proof. And there was a final advantage even greater than these. "If Subramanian vanished, and Charles' proof disappeared, it would be natural for Charles to lodge accusations against him."

"Which did happen."

"If Charles could never redo the earlier work on the proof, he would leave Oxford without a B.A. degree. And you would be quietly holding material for your dissertation, which could be presented in the next year or so, if you could figure out the last few steps on your own. Mr. Flynhall, you thought of everything."

"Almost everything." Wryly, he added, "I'm still in need of my proof. Damn you for searching this room! You've been stealthy as a snake—very Indian!"

"Actually, St. Hilda's emblem is a serpent," Perveen said.

"Oh, it's easy enough to dispatch a serpent," Flynhall said. "Not even a sword is needed when everyone's downstairs in Hall."

Trying to keep her tone pleasant, Perveen said, "You won't get away with murdering a girl in your room. Nor will it get you the papers you need."

"Then tell me, my dear."

Perveen hesitated. By now the papers were likely with Miss Burrows, but if she told him this, he might go there and trick the principal into releasing them. And there was another point to worry about. Why would Flynhall let her go, when he knew she'd report his actions? Surely he meant to kill her.

"Are the papers with your friend?"

"Yes," Perveen said. "She's just downstairs playing bridge and will be up any moment with a crowd."

"No, she won't. I understand the bridge party ended on a rather nasty note." He laughed lightly. "Don't look so surprised! Charles told me when I saw him thirty minutes ago in the Old Quad. He was in an absolute state, confessing how he'd lost his temper and nearly hit two women in front of many club members. It shall be most unsettling for me and several witnesses to enter my rooms tomorrow morning and discover Charles with your corpse."

There were many reasons Flynhall's strategy might not succeed—but justice wouldn't help if she were already deceased.

"You are very clever," Perveen said, once again aiming to feed his narcissism.

"It's true." He delivered his glorious smile. "Mathematicians can think ahead, you see. We envision the final solution; it's just the process of reaching that point that's the difficult part."

As they'd been chatting, Flynhall had slightly relaxed his pressure on Perveen's upper body. Perveen decided this was her chance.

Taking a deep breath, she yelled "Fire! Fire! Fire!" At the same time, she thrust her knees into Mr. Flynhall's tender region. He cried out like an injured dog, but just as she'd risen from the bed, he grabbed hold of her braided coronet, pulling it apart into double leashes that he held fast. Perveen screamed again as excruciating pain shot from her scalp.

Rapid footsteps came up the stairs, and there was a shaking of the bolted door.

"Damnation!" Flynhall was tight against her back as he propelled her toward one of the old arched windows.

"Open it," he said, pointing one hand toward an old latch.

She could barely breathe from the pain, and she kept her hands on the deep wooden sill.

He pulled her braids so fast and sharp that it pulled her head back. She felt and heard a cracking sound that was almost like lightning. Immediately afterward, she felt a shooting, numbing pain. She wasn't sure she could move.

"Open the window!" he whispered in her ear. "Or I'll break your neck before they come in."

She could not move her head. As if in a dream, Perveen peered through the old glass into blue-black darkness. She had gone away to a women's college in another country to be safe. And now this! How many feet was it to the hard stones below? She no longer had the power to look down, but she knew from the stairs she'd climbed that the ancient building was dreadfully tall.

"You'll try to make it look like I killed myself." She eked out each word as the pain of her neck and scalp increased.

His voice was as low and intimate as a lover's. "Miss Mistry, you came to me with a proposition based on your romantic interest. I refused, and you could not live with the humiliation."

Flynhall held steady to her, pressing her face into the glass. And then, suddenly, she felt the horror of the glass starting to break. She heard a gigantic banging sound followed by a second terrible sound that was even closer. The air was filled with a strange kind of smoke.

Flynhall was no longer pressing against her. She was able to right herself, bracing her hands against the window's deep sill.

Flynhall had collapsed on the carpet. He was gasping and holding the left side of his body. Blood flowed from under his hand and onto the expensive textile, turning a bouquet of flowers into a savage blur.

Charles McAslan stood over him. A military pistol, still lightly smoking, hung casually from the student's right hand. Behind him she saw Alice and Little and Campbell and some others from the bridge group. Two boys broke away to tend to Flynhall, attempting to staunch his wound with their handkerchiefs.

Perveen couldn't recall their names. She couldn't think of anything beyond the fact that she'd been about to be thrown out a window. And Charles McAslan had stopped it all. Putting a hand to her face, she felt blood and couldn't even think where it had come from.

"You tricked me!" McAslan sputtered, staring down at the wounded victim. "You stole my paper, and you did something to Subramanian. You're the worst kind of traitor. They hang men for betraying their fellow soldiers; you're lucky to die by the bullet."

Charles spoke as if he was back at war. This meant that anything could happen; his confusion might lead him to shoot others. Immobilized with fear, Perveen looked past him at Alice and the male students. Swiftly, the two men stepped forward, each extremely close to Charles. It was clear they were hesitant to touch him, given what had happened at the bridge party.

"Do give me the gun, Charles," Alice said, stepping around to stand in front of him. "A lady won't know how to fire such a fearsome weapon. I'll readily explain how your quick action saved my friend's life."

There was a long minute when Charles McAslan looked at Alice. Then he brought up his right hand and let Alice take the pistol. As he did so, she did something Perveen never would have expected. She moved forward and kissed McAslan's cheek.

McAslan brushed tears from his eyes. To Perveen, he asked, "Are you all right?"

"Yes. You came just in time!" Perveen's words came with a rush of air. She'd been so focused on the pain in her neck and head that she hadn't noticed that she'd been holding her breath.

"I was crossing Radcliffe Square and saw Charles with his friends and had the impulse to show him the papers. When I pulled them out, he recognized everything as his own. He was enraged and ran off toward Balliol, with the rest of us following. When he came out again, he must have had his pistol in his pocket. He didn't say anything about it but told everyone he was going to see Flynhall at Brasenose to set things straight."

"My goodness. How did you return to Brasenose without the pass I've got?"

"In disguise. I wore a rather long sealskin coat and a bowler hat borrowed from one of the fellows. Look!"

Perveen glanced at her oddly dressed friend and then at Flynhall, who was still bleeding on the floor. He'd meant to kill her. She felt light-headed with the realization. It must have shown, for Mr. Little led her by the hand to sit down on one of the chairs. His touch was warm and solid, nothing like Mr. Flynhall's had been. He reminded her, in an odd way, of her brother.

The gunshots had belatedly caused two scouts to hurry into the room.

"Sir! What on earth—" A worn-looking scout rushed to crouch near Edward Flynhall. He saw the blood and veered back.

Alice began, "I'm sorry to say, Mr. Flynhall has—"

Despite her fuzziness, Perveen knew her friend had to be halted. "Alice, it's best you keep quiet until both of us speak with proper legal counsel."

"I was merely trying to tell the scouts to call for a doctor and the police. Don't pull your hair off, my dear!" Alice snapped.

"Do I still have hair?" Perveen asked, ruefully touching her scalp.

The scout grimaced. "I reckon his lordship had a few bullets coming. But, miss, I must be requesting your name and college address, and that of the other lady, too. I'm afraid you're likely in violation of your college's rules—"

"Oh, sod the rules!" Alice said, with a laugh as rounded and glorious as the Magdalen College bells.

A LETTER FROM ABROAD

Perveen tilted her head gently to the right, and then to the left.

The surgeon from town had prescribed this practice to be done exactly three times daily. After a month wearing a ridiculously Elizabethan surgical collar, her sprained neck was feeling better. Still, she was not supposed to bend her head to read or write, and the doctor had advised against tight hairstyles. Maude put herself in charge of combing out her hair morning and evening. For the first time in her life, Perveen was letting her wavy hair remain in one loose braid—and sometimes go loose.

Perveen's free hair—and her equally relaxed academic schedule—were the envy of St. Hilda's. Many male tutors had arrived at the common room to deliver her the law lectures she was missing, but any examinations would be postponed until she could bend her head to write.

Miss Burrows was surprisingly sympathetic, even offering to read to her. The principal felt enormous guilt at having placed one of her young ladies in harm's way. She also displayed commitment to the continued well-being of Charles McAslan, whom she considered the savior of Perveen, and therefore St. Hilda's College. The principal located a modern, compassionate sanatorium specializing in young war veterans in the Devon countryside. Miss Burrows had insisted that Mr. Mason arrange a correspondence course to be given to Mr. McAslan during his treatment, so he could earn his mathematics degree after all.

But for Perveen, spending most of her days in the St. Hilda's common room or Miss Burrows' study was tedious. Alice's arrival as Perveen was finishing her neck exercise was a welcome interruption.

Holding a thick envelope aloft, Alice said, "Maude presented me with a mysterious letter from a *former enemy*."

"You don't mean Mr. McAslan?"

"Highly doubtful; the letter's from Germany."

"I don't have enemies or friends in Germany." As Perveen spoke, she remembered the words of the Italian bookseller she'd met in town. He'd said an Oxford student who appeared Asian had bought all his guidebooks on Germany. Could this be the correspondent?

Alice said, "I can't quite make out the name on the return address, but it looks as if it's from the University of Göttingen."

"Read it to me fast, before Miss Burrows comes back."

Tearing open the envelope, Alice drew out a sheet of thin paper and settled next to Perveen on Miss Burrows' chesterfield couch. "Lovely. It's typed in English!"

Dear Miss Mistry:

First, may I offer my most sincere wish for your continued recovery and well-being.

I do not yet read German fluently, so my first awareness of your courageousness came with an old edition of the International Herald-Tribune. *I read the article "The Mathematician Madman" and was horrified to learn about the continued depraved actions of my nemesis, Edward Flynhall.*

After consulting with my new solicitor, I've been advised to introduce myself to the prosecutor, Mr. Mayberry, who is pursuing Britain's case against Edward Flynhall. I am writing you to express my gratitude for your perseverance and to inform you that I am in good health here in Göttingen.

In case there is still an outstanding question to my identity, my full legal name is Vanu Subramanian Iyer. From my birth in 1882 until 1912, I was a resident of Madras, India. After receiving a magna cum laude bachelor's degree from the University of Madras, I was blessed to receive a Rhodes Scholarship for overseas study. I was accepted at Brasenose College, Oxford, beginning that Michaelmas term, and my intention was to strive for a bachelor's honour degree.

As a fellow Indian, you surely understand what it means to put nose to the grindstone. Here, Alice stopped to giggle. *I was caught up in my work and neglected to realize my classmate Flynhall's many attempts to spoil my work were the sign of pathological jealousy. I was stunned when a most important proof of mine disappeared from my room, only to be presented a week later by Mr. Flynhall, written out in his hand on his stationery, to the department head as his own work. He also submitted it to an academic contest sponsored by an international mathematics society and won fifty pounds sterling.*

I sought to amicably resolve the dispute by speaking directly to Mr. Flynhall, whom I hoped would come with me to our professor, Mr. Mason. Flynhall told me I was mistaken about the matter, that it was coincidental that we had solved the same problem, and that for me to lay claim to his work would be regarded as chicanery and an effort to grab money. I was hesitant to rush forward and present my accusation to our professor, due to his stature and my concern that he wouldn't believe a foreigner's word over that of an English gentleman. In the month that I was deliberating, I received a terrible letter from the Rhodes Committee announcing my scholarship had been terminated due to acts out of keeping with the character of scholarship students. I never learned what inspired them to sack me, but I suspected Flynhall was behind it.

With no money for tuition, room and board, there was nothing to do except leave. How I regretted leaving Oxford. I hadn't enough for a ticket back to India, so I feared a life of destitution as a common laborer awaited. But then, I was inspired to find a working position at Oxford. This would allow me the chance to use the library and continue my mathematics. Dressed in simple clothing, I presented myself using just my father's first name to the head porters of various colleges, excepting the one where I'd been. Balliol College hired me. I first served as scout to a young man studying history named Green. We were together until 1918, at which time Mr. Green graduated and a former student who'd returned from war, Mr. Charles McAslan, was assigned to the rooms.

Mr. McAslan had lost many memories of mathematical procedures due to his wartime horrors, and I did my best to assist him in review. At many times he was cross and frustrated with others, but he would calm himself in my presence. He never considered it strange I was able to help him, and this created a private joy and sense of pride for me.

Perhaps my work was too directional, but I was glad to help, especially when I learned Mr. McAslan's tutor was named Mr. Flynhall. For my student to better Flynhall became my private dream. I was also saving my meager earnings and continuing work, in the hopes that the several original proofs I'd completed would help me gain a scholarship to another European university.

Flynhall came unexpectedly to Mr. McAslan's room on a day in

November 1919, when my student was simply too weary to walk out into the cold weather to attend the tutorial Flynhall held in Brasenose. My enemy recognized me immediately but did not give it away in Mr. McAslan's presence. He came back another day, and I greeted him by name.

Flynhall said that I'd no right to be at Oxford and he could expose me. But that was of little worry to me—the porter who'd hired me was a good chap who was unlikely to fire a reliable employee just for being well educated. I also warned Flynhall that I would tell Charles McAslan exactly what he'd done with my work some years ago—and that he should be very protective of the work I'd been helping him with.

The next day, Flynhall sent me a letter—I still have it to provide as evidence if requested. He told me he would pay my passage to India if I were willing to leave without a word to Charles or anyone else. One hundred pounds was impossible to refuse; it would take several years for me to earn. So I agreed, but I insisted on taking the payment as money, not a ticket on a particular ship as he had suggested. I did this because I suspected he might cause some kind of trouble for me again.

I traveled out of Oxford in the back of a farmer's cart and then bought a ticket for Hamburg, from whence I traveled by train to Leipzig to meet with my mentor, Mr. Hilbert, who had been reviewing my work on his challenge problems during the years I worked as a scout. He was glad to see my portfolio and arranged my position as tutor at the University of Göttingen, the finest mathematics center in Europe. He also provided a statement of support encouraging the university to admit me as a graduate student, due to my existing B.A. from Madras.

I was overjoyed by the way things turned out. I only regretted what might have happened to Charles McAslan without my companionship. I was shocked to see his name in the initial article but was relieved to read in later articles that he had been cleared of all wrongdoing in the Brasenose shooting. I pray that he achieves spiritual peace at the sanatorium and is able to resume a normal life. I am writing to Mr. McAslan as well to explain this story I've just told you, but also adding in my apologies for departing without explanation.

Miss Mistry, your valiant actions may lead to justice that I never imagined possible. As a law student, this experience is surely a profound lesson. I may not be allowed to speak with you when I'm called to London to testify, but I do hope to meet with you to express my humble thanks.

Yours most truly,

Vanu Subramanian Iyer, B.A. Magna Cum Laude, Madras University; Scholar in Residence, Brasenose College, Oxford University; University of Göttingen (Ph.D. projected 1921)

• • •

"Well," Alice said, folding up the letter and giving it to Perveen. "No enemy there. Only a gentleman who's not shy about adding more letters to an already long name. "

Perveen smiled. "I hope the trial's not too soon."

"And why's that?"

"I'm keeping my fingers crossed that I'll have finished my honours law course by then. And perhaps it will be late enough that Oxford will have admitted St. Hilda's and the other women's colleges into the fold, and I'll have a proper degree and can sit for the London Bar. Just imagine if I could lay out my own charges against Mr. Flynhall."

Alice raised an eyebrow. "The prosecutor says the attempted manslaughter case against Flynhall is most sound. There's really no need for your theatrics."

"And why not? I would like to show Mr. Flynhall just

how—dazzling—a woman lawyer might be. After all, he did admire my rhetorical skills."

Alice leaned back on the pillows, studying her. "And where shall you undertake your brilliant career?"

"I've said all along that I want to practice in India. I think I've already got a job, because Father's last letter complained about the loss of his solicitor." She didn't mention that her parents had reversed course over their belief that life in England would be a quiet respite for her. They wanted her back.

"To be a Bombay solicitor!" Alice pretended to wipe a sweaty brow. "Long days of paperwork completed in a hot office with only a ceiling fan for relief. No gin and tonic until your friend from England arrives."

Perveen brightened. "Would you really visit me in India?"

"If I'm not hired as a mathematics teacher at a college, I'll ask my parents to buy me a ticket overseas. I think two St. Hilda's women could get up to quite a lot of trouble in Bombay."

"Oh, yes," Perveen said, smiling at her friend. "I'm sure that we shall."

The Ayah's Tale

PROLOGUE

Georgetown, Penang Island, Federation of Malaya
Monsoon 1952

I found Julian's book on a day that the radio presenter advised all of Penang to stay inside. By nine o'clock three inches of water covered the road from my house to the rickshaw stand. Clearly, it was going to keep on. But it had been raining for two weeks already, and I needed an escape.

New books came by sea mail to our small library in Georgetown the second week of every month. It was Wednesday, which meant the librarian, Mr. Lim, would shelve the fresh arrivals. I was aware that on a miserably rainy day, I'd have little competition for those titles.

So I went. Between the rickshaw and ferry and slogging through six-inch puddles, my journey took almost an hour longer than usual. I staggered into the library building as bedraggled as the wet crows I passed foraging in the rubbish of a nearby restaurant. I could imagine what I looked like: a water-logged Indian woman in her late forties, sloshing through puddles in Wellingtons with a drab Mackintosh covering a cotton sari clutched tightly with one hand to keep it above the rushing water.

I entered the library and blessed dryness, sliding my umbrella into the stand by the door.

"Good morning, my friend." Mr. Lim did not seem put out by my appearance, nor surprised to see me. "And how have you been keeping in our dreadful weather?"

I shook out the soaked hem of my sari while trying to think up a positive response, because I knew Mr. Lim's daily commute to and from the library was longer than mine. "Our mango trees are productive; I'm kept busy making all manner of chutneys and pickles. And no matter what the weather is like, Mrs. Abbot and I can still enjoy our reading afternoons."

"She's moved close to you, hasn't she?" he asked while taking back the eight library books I'd returned, all dry because of the waterproof satchel in which I'd carried them.

"Yes, a few months ago she shifted from the big old bungalow into a new block of flats near our place. It's easier for her. She'll be ninety this winter."

"Please bring her to visit sometime, just for old time's sake. I'm about to shelve the new shipment, but please take a look at what's on the cart." Mr. Lim ran his long-fingered, scholar's hand invitingly along the top group of books, their new colorful jackets somewhat muted by the library's protective cellophane wrappers. "We have the new Louis Bromfield, and Edna Ferber, Ellen Glasgow and a Thornton Wilder, too."

Mr. Lim recited the authors in alphabetical order, just as they'd been arranged. I'd always thought his mind must have settled that way as a mark of his profession. He and I are same age, born during the early years of the twentieth century. And although Lu-Sing Lim is Hokkien Chinese, and I am a Bengali from India, we've shared our love of English books since I applied for my first library card in 1926.

"Are there any new short story collections?" As much as I enjoyed reading novels on my own time, short stories were the perfect length for reading aloud to Mrs. Abbot. A good story usually lasts the duration of two cups of tea—the length of one of our visits, before I walked home to make supper.

"Here's a story anthology. It received quite good reviews in the *Guardian* and the *South China Morning Post*." Mr. Lim handed me a slim book with a cover design of palm trees and a grand colonial bungalow. In bold orange letters it read: *The Ayah's Tale and Other Stories of Old Bengal, By J. Winslett.*

Winslett? I hadn't seen or heard that name in decades. Turning to the back flap's author biography, I felt the hairs on my arms prickle. There was no author photograph, but a short description of the British author having spent his early childhood in Bengal before attending St. Paul's School and Cambridge. During the War, he'd flown fifty missions for the RAF. The book jacket proclaimed that he had now "turned his hand to exotic gardening, fiction and memoir writing. He resides with his wife, four children, and three dogs in Dorset."

"Why did you get this book?" Something tight and cruel wrapped itself around my chest, taking my breath. Yes. The fear was back, reaching across the ocean and all the years.

Mr. Lim's thin white brows drew together, as if he were perplexed by my question. "The head office in Kuala Lumpur ordered it from the British distributor. I'm sure they think these stories will appeal to our population. And perhaps this collection has gathered some good literary reviews."

"Yes, of course." I turned to the back of the book, where a blank borrowing card was tucked in its cardboard pocket as snugly as a baby in a cot. Mrs. Abbot would be delighted to be the first person in town to know about this book. She might tell her friends, *My Menakshi has a nose for the new; she's borrowed the new volume of stories by one J. Winslett, and it's very good.*

Mrs. Abbot liked to boast about my reading to her. It was almost as if she imagined herself in the old days, when every white lady and child in Asia had an ayah to do her bidding. In truth, I read to Mrs. Abbot because she has become blind, and I could never repay the many kindnesses she'd offered since my arrival on the island almost thirty years ago.

Back to *The Ayah's Tale.* Paging through the text, the familiar place names jumped out: Midnapore, Chinsurah, Darjeeling. Ah, the places I'd been! But wasn't sure I'd want to visit again. Sally, Polly, Nigel. These names were new to me. But two names peppered the pages that I knew well. Little Ayah and Big Ayah. And of course, Julian.

Mr. Lim's eyes blinked repeatedly behind his round, tortoise-framed glasses. It must have seemed very odd that I was handling the new book as if it might be coated in poison.

"It looks very interesting," I pronounced, trying to sound happier than I felt. "To read the British perspective from the days before independence..."

"Yes, yes." He gave a small, relieved smile. "How the world has changed, and you and I have been there for every bit of it. I can only hope there isn't another change ahead."

As I left the library a few minutes later with the checked-out book in my waterproof satchel—and a few others, in case it was unreadable—I told myself two things:

Julian Winslett had clearly survived his childhood and the second war to become a writer. But whatever fictions this British-Raj-child-grown-up-into-a-hero had woven about his ayah would be very far from the real story. I knew, because I'd been there.

CHAPTER ONE

MENAKSHI

Midnapore
Summer 1923

Right from the start, I did not trust them.

But it was a matter of money. A girl who'd had to leave school couldn't afford to walk away from possible work. So I kept standing straight, body stiff as my starched cotton sari, waiting, wishing for them to take me.

"She's very black, isn't she?" The little girl wearing a smocked lawn frock and a solar topi over golden curls circled me curiously.

"Yes, Miss Helen went Home, so now we must choose a native ayah." Mrs. Millings' tone shifted from sunny to somber, as she addressed me. "Tell me your name again."

"Menakshi." I did not add my surname. She wouldn't care

about it, nor that my late father, Promod Dutt, had been postmaster for two villages, and our family had been one of the most respectable in our small town. She knew only that I was an Indian girl who spoke English and needed work.

Mrs. Millings pursed her lips. "I could call you Mary, but it doesn't really matter, does it? If you're hired, you will be called Big Ayah by Sally and her brothers, Nigel and Julian. Your English isn't bad. Where exactly are you from?"

"My gollywog doll is black, too." Sally thrust a sticky black cotton doll into my hands. White cloth circles with black dot centers looked out blankly, and its red half-moon lips seemed to smile mockingly at me. Sally thought we looked the same? Inwardly, I shuddered.

What had Mrs. Millings asked me? It was about where I came from. I searched my memory for one of the fancy verbs I'd learned at school. "I hail from the Midnapore district, Memsaheb."

"I see. And you were at the Mission School for how many years?" the lady continued. She didn't look as old as the teachers and was far prettier. She had fair golden curls, and very pale skin without wrinkles, although covered with a faint residue that I later learned was the juice of limes, to lighten sunspots.

"From first form until this spring." I could have added, *with honors*, but that might seem like boasting.

"You were lucky they took you." Her big green eyes lingered on me.

She probably guessed I'd been admitted because of a church scholarship. My father had said that the scholarship meant I was clever. Throughout my school days, though, it made me feel different from the European students. And I knew that many nannies for colonial families came from Scotland or Ireland, especially for children receiving years of home education. Indian ayahs were considered best for wet nursing, but being an unmarried girl, I had no milk to give.

I already knew the only reason I was under consideration was that Mrs. Millings' English nanny had left the previous week, and their current ayah needed to spend all her time taking care of the new Millings baby. And the family was moving. According to Mrs. Jones, the wife of the Padre in charge of the Mission, Mr. Millings was an Indian Civil Service officer who'd just been named the Commissioner for Burdwan District. Mrs. Millings had spread word that she needed an ayah who was fluent in English to move with them from Midnapore to Chinsurah and care for their family's older three children.

When I'd arrived at their home, I could tell they were in the midst of a move. The gate to the bungalow was wide open, and a succession of lorries parked in the semi-circular drive shaded by tamarind trees. Barefoot men lurched from the bungalow steps to the lorries carrying heavy furniture on their heads and backs. They'd ignored me, just as the two little European boys did who were kicking a ball to each other in the garden. Then I'd made a big mistake by walking up to the front entrance rather than the back. The bearer who answered gave me a thorough scolding about rules for servants.

It was a difficult start, but I knew this memsaheb was the only one who'd decide my fate. Frantically, I wondered if it would be better to stay quiet or say some things that might demonstrate my skills, such as the words for addressing English family members.

Raising the pitch of my voice and smiling so hard I thought my cheeks might tear, I looked at the little girl and said, " Missy-baba, I like to read stories very much. Do you?"

She looked at me with what seemed like skepticism. "You can't read me stories until you give back Golly."

I'd been so anxious, that I'd almost forgotten the filthy doll she'd handed to me. I gave it back to her. "Thank you, he is so sweet. Do you think he'd like to hear a story?"

"She is a girl!"

"Yes indeed, Missy-baba," I said, looking at the doll with short pants stitched on.

"I don't have much time to listen, but you can try to read for Sally," Mrs. Millings tapped her slim gilt watch. "The children's books are in the boxes there. Take one."

The mixture of children's novels and histories must have belonged to her older brothers, because they were Robert Louis Stevenson, Rudyard Kipling and the like. I looked again at the small, red-faced girl. If I read aloud such long-winded stories, she might not like them, but the words were complex enough that they would demonstrate my literacy. With some misgivings I picked up *Treasure Island* and hoped for the best, but after half a minute Sally cried, "I want Pooh."

"What is Pooh?" I asked, looking from her to her mother.

"Sally, your Pooh stories are already packed in your bedtime box. The bearers have taken it to the new house."

The child took a deep breath, and I could see that she was preparing to scream. And I knew that if she started, I would not be able to calm her—she would shrink from my touch. So very quickly I said, "Missy-baba, won't you please tell me the story of this Pooh? I don't know it."

Sally's little voice rose as she narrated the story of a talking friendly bear that lived in a tree and had many animal friends living in the nearby wood, as well as a little boy called Christopher

Robin who liked to visit. I listened closely and then asked if she'd like another Pooh story—a new one, made up by me.

"Without pictures," I cautioned, but she clapped her hands and told me to speak. So, thinking it up as I went along, I told a story about a summer morning when Pooh woke up in a meadow, had a breakfast of buttercups and clover, and walked to the sea for a swim. And then a wave came—a wave so terribly large—that Pooh jumped on top of it, and decided that he would ride this wave to see the whole world for himself.

I kept talking, even though her mother walked away from us in the middle. Sally seemed interested. She had climbed into my lap by the time Pooh was on the way to Italy. I knew the names of so many countries, because my father used to mention if he'd sorted any letters that had originated in from far-away places. A post office in a small Indian town didn't get many letters from abroad, so whatever came was something to talk about. I told my father once that I would like to grow up and move to a far-away land to have adventures, and so he would have somewhere exciting to go. My father had just laughed and said that trip could only happen after his retirement.

I stopped thinking about my father as the Memsaheb came back with a tightly swaddled baby in her arms. A thin Indian woman followed behind her with an armload of clean cloths. She was smaller than me, with a nice round face and big eyes fixed anxiously on Mrs. Millings.

"Baby Ayah has brought Polly," Mrs. Millings said, inclining her head toward the servant.

I wondered what Baby Ayah's real name was. I greeted Baby Ayah in Bengali, but seeing Mrs. Millings frown, I switched to English and asked if I should tell another tale to Sally.

"You've done enough." At those three words, I felt the air go out of my throat. But then she added, "I've decided that you can start tomorrow."

"Why, thank you, Memsaheb!" I said, my breath coming back. To go home today and tell my mother I'd found a paying job would fill her with relief.

"You'll have twenty-two rupees a month, with Sunday afternoons free; Baby Ayah will cover for you then, and you will cover her break on Saturday afternoon. Your chief duty is the care of Nigel, Julian and Sally. Baby Ayah is handling Polly the first two years; after that, we will see."

I wasn't sure I'd heard correctly. According to Mrs. Jones, the advertised wages were higher. Swallowing, I mustered up my courage and said, "Memsaheb, excuse me, but didn't your notice say you were offering ayah wages of twenty-five rupees?"

Her white-blond eyebrows rose. "That would be for an older girl with a degree. In any case we are moving to Chinsurah, and wages are lower in the country. I could hire an ayah there who'll be grateful for fifteen or twenty. I'm willing to try you, but I won't tolerate insubordination. I am the one in control."

Three rupees. What could that sum mean to a woman who had so much? I glanced at Baby Ayah, who was shaking her head at me, her expression clearly showing how stupidly I'd spoken.

"I understand, Memsaheb." I forced a smile on my face because taking this job would relieve my mother's worry, make everything right for her and my little brothers. "I promise that I will do everything possible for your children."

"Everything until each one turns seven years of age," she said, raising a cautionary finger. "Nigel's only got a year left with us in India before he sails Home to join his father's old school. Julian will follow a year after that, and then it will be Sally's turn for Roedean. But Little Polly I've got for a good seven years—don't I, sweetheart?" she crooned, bending her head to the tiny bundle.

The baby burst into screams, and in an instant, Mrs. Millings had thrust her into Baby Ayah's arms, on top of the cloths she was carrying. And then both the Millings boys came running inside.

The six-year-old son, Nigel, was sturdy, with dark brown hair. He had the remains of a smashed mango on the front of his white shirt and a dirt-smudged face. Nigel was followed by a slighter boy with red curly hair, who I guessed was called Julian. The younger brother's clothing was also soiled, but in a different way: with stains from grass and red dust.

I greeted them by name and began introducing myself as their new Ayah.

"You must not let them catch your Indian accent," Mrs. Millings interrupted. "I shall be listening for it."

"I will do my best, Memsaheb!" What had I done wrong: was it the pitch or the long vowels? I had been speaking English for eight years now.

Nigel, the older boy, was laughing at me through his nose: a honking sound that reminded me of a young goose. Julian determinedly pushed a stone along the red oxide floor. It made me think of my little brother Nikhil, who played also played with little things he found outdoors. But Nikhil couldn't play much anymore. The previous week, he'd started work in a potato field.

I put away my thoughts of Nikhil and resolved that I would grow close to the Millings boys. Perhaps friendly attention could win them over. I doubted Mrs. Millings had time to offer her children the everyday hugs and kindnesses that my mother gave us. I would always have to speak to the children with the proper voice my employer wanted, but how I played with them when we were out of sight would be my own choice.

It would likely be the only situation she couldn't control.

CHAPTER TWO

JULIAN

Chinsurah
Fall 1923

Mummy said we were daft.

Daft to have gone into our baths with our clothes on getting them all wet and spoilt. And she said Ayah was terrible not have not taken off our clothing for us. Everybody knows ayahs wash clothes in a bucket and children in tubs. Nigel and I could have been killed in a bath alone! Ayah would lose ten rupees for it from her pay. We would lose pudding.

I didn't see a way that I could say anything to Mummy about what happened. But I told God what happened during the nightly prayer time. I said that we were only running through the grass all playing hares. We had to show Ayah how to do it, but it turned out she was the fastest hare of us all. But then Sally dropped Golly without noticing where he fell, and when Ayah was looking with her, Nigel slid into some cow dung on the road. We knew Mummy would be cross if she saw or smelt it so we ran back inside the children's wing of the bungalow and shouted for the bhisti to bring lots of hot water for a bath. *Yes, Saheb,* he said to me, touching his head and bowing and it made me feel tops, like I was a father even though I hadn't a cigar nor a suit.

That's why we jumped in the tub before remembering our clothes—and then we took them off and slapped them around, like the dhobi does, only there were no rocks to hit. And the water was getting browner, and suddenly Mummy was there saying, *What the Hell is going on?*

Ayah ran in then with Sally and said *I'm very sorry.* Mummy said something long and complicated that I could not understand, but Ayah, who knows all sorts of grown-up English, did. And that night, Ayah read Peter Rabbit to all of us, although it is such a baby book. But there is another reason I didn't like that book anymore. Mummy was like Mr. McGregor, always chasing after Ayah to make into a pie.

Actually, while we called her Ayah, Mummy called her Big Ayah. It was because she was taller than Baby Ayah and Mummy, and because we were the big ones, Nigel and I. We'd had Baby Ayah with us for years, but she didn't speak enough English. Miss Helen had taken care of us during the daytime, all the meals and playing, and taught us the ABCs and counting. Miss Helen was a quiet one. Mummy said the climate was especially hard for her. She overheated easily, and a lot of the time was lying on a swing or bed when we played. She called it keeping an eye on us, but usually her eyes were closed.

The day after Father heard the news about shifting to Chinsurah for a few years, Miss Helen found out that she needed to go Home to help her mother. Mummy was very cross about it, but said in the end all it taught her is that an English nanny in India is like a fish out of water. Nigel got very interested in that and brought one of the chilled fish from the icebox into the garden to see if it would start doing something surprising, but Nimu ran after us and got it back.

I was sorry for the first few days after Miss Helen had left because I'd liked her voice and she had never made us do things we didn't like.

I did not know what it would mean to have an Indian nanny. And when Big Ayah started working for us—when we had the long car ride with her—Nigel and I played as usual, not talking to her. But it turned out that Big Ayah had never been in a passenger car before. She wanted to know the names of every part of it. And then she looked out the big windows which were rolled down and told us what was growing in the fields. She knew the names of the trees, and the animals that lived in them. She saw a mongoose running fast and then Driver-ji decided to race it. We laughed and laughed, glad that Mummy was on the train with the baby. And by the time we were at Chinsurah, I was glad that she was our new ayah.

Nigel still wasn't sure, though. He tested her in different ways to see if she would get angry if he brought in garden beetles or called her names. But she did not seem to notice him doing these things. What she praised and got excited about was when one of us brought her stones, or gave something to the other one without fighting, or told a funny story.

Big Ayah was not afraid to be outside for hours every day, and she thought we were sharp enough to go beyond the alphabet to making words and stories. But all that moving and doing sometimes brought trouble.

After that time with mud in the bath, I said to Ayah that we didn't mean to get her caught out with Mummy, and Ayah just hugged me and smiled with those straight white teeth that you could see shining when she was close by in the dark nursery. And she said, *Good for you two to have tried your hand at washing clothes. And if you don't care for your fancy boarding schools, I will get you a good job with the dhobi down at the river. Nigel's head is big enough for carrying a clothing bundle and Julian's arms are strong for scrubbing. But the dhobi will insist that you never leave his area without telling him first. What do you think? Do you want such a job?*

No. This would mean I'd have to speak the dialect and wear a scrap of cloth around my waist. My chest would be bare and burnt. I knew all about native life was like from Mr. Kipling's stories. There was a big difference between being free and being native.

I thought of saying all this to Ayah, but she would be hurt to know I didn't want to join her people. She didn't know India was hard, because it was where she was brought up. She had no chance to go to Home one day, because she had no home except for ours. She would always stay at our house, working and watching the river flow by.

CHAPTER THREE

MENAKSHI

Chinsurah
Winter 1923

I'd expected the foreign buildings of Chinsurah would be just like the ones I'd seen in Midnapore, but I was quite wrong.

Because the port town was built by the Dutch starting in the 1600s, this place was much prettier than Midnapore. Government House, the Millingses' vast bungalow, was quite old, with a pitched Dutch roof painted black, and a long cobbled drive leading up to it lined with pots of foreign flowers called tulips. The tulips could only survive in the cool seasons of autumn and winter—and to my amazement they were replaced every few weeks by new bulbs that grew as tall and red as the ones before. The bulbs had been coming by sea-mail from Holland for many years, the cost absorbed without question by whoever lived in the house. My mother was very impressed by these details in the letters I sent her each week. *Please write more,* she urged. *Your little brother and sister enjoy the stories just as much as I do. They are working hard and will never see what you can. You are the eyes of not just our family, but of the village!*

"Were the Dutch any different from the English?" I once asked Nimu, the elderly bearer who had been working in the Chinsurah bungalow for many years. I was thinking my father, who had been greatly impressed by the beauty of a stamp from Dutch Indonesia.

"They were gone long before my grandfather's grandfather. But the Dutch were immoral." Nimu shook his head, which had only a few wispy gray curls. "You are lucky to only have the children pulling at your sari. So very fortunate not to be troubled by anyone but the littles—in fact, the next time you are giving them tea, won't you save a few of those nice white sugar cubes for me?"

I had suffered tongue-lashings from Mrs. Millings for every mistake, so I was nervous to commit an outright wrong. But I had to give something to Nimu because he was a kind of boss, too. Eventually six cubes of sugar made their way into the end of my sari, tied in a tiny knot, but I was careful only to do it in the morning, before Mrs. Millings woke, and I stopped taking any sugar myself. The effort was important, because the staff had accepted me and were calling me Didi, which meant Big Sister.

I did feel like a big sister. I spent my days running with the children, always wearing a white cotton sari and with my hair in plaits down the back. The children splashed wildly as I washed them in the zinc tub every morning and every afternoon; Julian and Nigel running from me as I held out their clothes, and Sally spitting out the porridge I spooned in her mouth. It was almost like being with my little brothers, except that in this household, I had books and the chance to play teacher. Sally was still too young to read, but already was becoming a whiz at adding and subtracting both English pence and Indian annas. Julian at five was enjoying learning to read with pleasure, but his brother Nigel, a year-and-a-half older, didn't like words much, and counting frustrated him. With boarding school looming, I worried for him.

These days with the children were largely my own, because Mr. and Mrs. Millings were the leaders of Chinsurah society. They gave bridge parties, cocktail hours, teas, and dinner parties every week. To their close friends, he was called Tubby, and she was Marjie.

Because my hours caring for the children had no set beginning or end, I slept on a mat in the nursery, and quickly mastered the art of reading under my quilt with the aid of a small oil lamp.

"Just one more chapter," Julian would beg, snuggling up against me on the mat after I'd murmured to him that stories were over, and it was time to sleep.

"You have a riding lesson tomorrow, dear, and you need your strength and wits for it," I replied, stroking his hair.

"Don't let's fight about it, Ayah," Julian whispered. "Read some more *Peter Pan*. Can you make the pirates' voices that funny way?"

So I read to Julian, who dreamt of being a pilot on some days and a pirate on others. Endlessly he looked through a kaleidoscope he'd gotten the Christmas previous, telling me things he saw within it. When he pushed the kaleidoscope into my hands, the little colored pieces all shifted; but of course, I said I saw the same jewels or faces that he did.

His elder brother Nigel was less interested in me, although if he wanted something, and I could not give it to him, he unleashed all manner of names on me: Ugly Ayah, Stupid, Bug Ayah. In my village, that kind of talk would have earned such punishment it wouldn't have been repeated. But I was in a difficult position. Since his parents talked badly to me, how could I argue that the children could not?

Though I was tired by nightfall, the dozens of children's books the family had brought to Chinsurah were a terrific bounty. In addition the bungalow had its own library that I roamed through with pleasure. I relied on the respite of reading after days spent listening to a hubbub of high-pitched young voices: Miss Sally's calling "Ayah, get me"—Master Nigel's, "Ayah, so stupid"—and Master Julian, who despite his rank as the second eldest, clearly showed himself as the Saheb of the nursery with comments like, "Ayah, you're quite good at reading, but other than that, you have no common sense at all!"

Nigel, Julian and Sally's voices ran together in a never-ending chorus. They were not bad children; they were just lively and always hunting for an advantage over each other—or me. The truth was that they relied on me: the cutting words they sometimes used were only imitations of the language used by their parents.

"No, no, Ayah. Are you dimwitted? If you dress Sally in cotton this afternoon, she's bound to catch cold by nightfall."

"I wasn't thinking clearly, Memsaheb. I shall change it right away." And I would try not to notice Sally's tearful face, her sorrow at having her choice of dress taken away.

"The milk wasn't boiled long enough. Ayah, you should have noticed and thrown it away."

"As you wish, Memsaheb." Even though what she saw was the

cooling leftovers, which I wanted to give to the dhobi's pregnant wife.

"That screeching of theirs is giving me a headache. I don't care what you do, Ayah, just stop the racket!"

"Oh, yes, Saheb." It would mean giving them sweets before tea, but so be it.

Although I disliked the Millingses' sharp words, I still harbored a bit of sympathy for the Memsaheb, because she had so few happy times. She fell victim to many stomach illnesses and fevers; at least once weekly, it seemed. And she was lonely. Mr. Millings did not ride with her early in the mornings, and I'd noticed during breakfast on the veranda, they didn't speak. By eight in the morning, the driver Hussain took Mr. Millings to his office. At this time the lady's work began.

First was her kitchen inspection, both for cleanliness and to check receipts that Cook had for his purchases. She gave out the separate daily menus for the children and adults because the family ate together chiefly on holidays. The last duty of kitchen inspection was the most stressful for all of us: evaluating the kitchen's stores of food. The inspection was long, and with raised voices on both sides, for her cook was an elderly local man who'd come with the house, and was disgruntled at any accusation of pilfering, or having used special foods for staff meals.

After she was finished with Cook, Mrs. Millings made rounds on the gardeners, cleaning boys, and sweepers. We were all glad when she went out to luncheons, or bridge games and tennis, for it was only then that the strong fog of L'Heure Bleu perfume and moodiness were lifted.

Mrs. Millings rested two hours in the afternoon before bathing again and dressing for the evening dinner, occasionally at home, but more often at their social club or another English couple's bungalow. Baby Ayah and I fed the children, and then I read to them and put them to bed. Baby Ayah was easy enough to get along with, but there was little she wanted to discuss outside our employer.

"She is afraid of them," Baby Ayah said to me about Mrs. Millings, one day when the mother had attempted to take the children for an outing.

"What nonsense!" I answered, shaking my head at the thought of this.

"They were only laughing and shouting in the car; and it gave her such a terror that she began breathing fast and told Driver-ji to bring them back. You know. You were there, too."

"It's not being fearful; it's just not liking noise," I suggested.

"It was because they wanted us, not her," Baby Ayah's voice was smug. "At the club, ayahs are not allowed on the chairs around the swimming pool. But they don't even want to go to that place if it means being with her!"

Almost every week, Mrs. Millings called for Sally to come and try on a fancy frock she'd had the tailor make for her; but only I could put it on the child, who shrank at her mother's touch. Mrs. Millings tended to keep the boys at a greater distance. Was it because she didn't care for them, or because she'd already learned they would not come to her?

I felt sorry that it was this way. I had never stopped wanting my mother's embrace. Of all that I'd given up by moving away from home, the hardest part was not being with her. This was why I wrote so often to her and treasured everything she sent back.

According to my mother's regular letters, protests were being mounted near our hometown against the British, and the police were looking through the mail in search of communication between local terrorists. *At least your father didn't have to bear this difficult situation,* she wrote to me, and I understood what she meant. As Christians, we were expected to be very loyal to the British. We wanted freedom as much as anyone else in that town; but he was lucky to have the post-office work, and thus could never take part in a protest or say a word that could be carried back to the Anglo-Indian who oversaw all the region's postal employees.

Because I was curious about my mother's comments, I asked the fruit-seller who came daily to give me his leftover newspaper wrappings: so the news came crumpled up, torn and stained: the pages sometimes so mixed up that I'd learn about the fifteen lashes a thief received before learning the original story of his stealing ten rupees from his master's briefcase.

These morality tales were what Nimu most wanted me to read aloud to the others as we ate our rice and dal in our courtyard each evening. And the English were talking about it, too. One Sunday evening, I was on the other side of the dining room wall, ironing napkins. The Millingses were hosting a dinner party for twenty-plus, and one man had already had to have his napkin taken away because of spilled wine, while another man had dropped his napkin and yet another lady coughed something into hers.

Nimu had gone into a panic because there weren't enough exactly matching napkins already pressed, so I'd offered to quickly iron them, because I was used to taking care of the children's clothes. So, whilst Nimu oversaw the serving of mutton and potatoes Lyonnaise, I stood in a corner of the butler's pantry, pressing an iron filled with burning charcoal over the linen napkins spread over the board. And as I ironed, I could not help overhearing the talk.

"Whoever thought, when growing up, that after training for years to come here and run a government, it would turn out we have to cater an old man in pyjamas?" Mr. Millings grumbled aloud to his guests, setting off a mixture of shouting and laughter.

"That's not a pyjama, darling, it's called a dhoti." Mrs. Millings' high-pitched voice cut through the jumble of sound. "And he's not old, he just looks old from all the hunger strikes. Good lord, if we'd just let him stay on the strike, he'd be over and done with."

"Oh, come now. Gandhi's a gentle soul, not like that rotter Subhas Chandra Bose."

"How old is Gandhi?" asked Mr. Millings. "Does anyone know the truth?"

"Sixty in June." The same man who'd spoken about Bose replied, and through the slats in the French doors separating the butler's pantry from the dining room I recognized him as a younger ICS officer who'd come up from Bombay. "But he's still full of spirit. His wife goes to prison alongside him—think of the injustice!"

"There's no end of cruelty to women and girls in this culture," Mrs. Millings said. "Can you imagine that our children's ayah's mother was forced on the funeral pyre and burnt alive after her father's death?"

I pricked up my ears at this because Baby Ayah's mother was alive and well in North Calcutta, according to her daughter.

"Really, Marjie? The short black girl?" a shocked-sounding lady's voice responded.

"No. Big Ayah's tall, and more of a tea-color. She's the one always trying to speak the King's English." Mrs. Millings' voice slurred. "Despite her education, those villagers probably would have put her on the pyre along with her mother if Tubby hadn't heard about it and sent the police to stop it!"

I smelt the scorched linen long before I realized I'd stopped ironing. Abruptly, I set the iron on its side. Why would Mrs. Millings tell such lies about me? She knew what I'd told her about my past: that my father was a postmaster who'd caught cholera and died. Had she forgot that we were Christian, and didn't cremate like the Hindus? He lay in a coffin buried in the mission cemetery where I'd brought flowers each week, before I'd come to work for her household.

"Your ayah's life story proves just how much Indians need our guidance," one of the men guests said, and there was a murmur of agreement.

You are the ones who need it! I wanted to shout through the wall. Wife burning wasn't common anymore—I hadn't ever heard of Hindus doing it in our town. I picked up the iron again and went on. The scorched one was hidden in the middle; whoever got it would think Mrs. Millings had a shabby household. This was only small way I could think of fighting back.

After that dinner, my life with the Millings family slowly shifted, just like the colored pieces in Julian's kaleidoscope. Julian and Nigel seemed just a bit ruder, and Mrs. Millings continued to tell stories that should not have bothered me, but did. To her bridge group, she described how the children had become unmanageable under my care; to her husband, she declared that the look in my eyes was mutinous, and perhaps everyone would be best off if I went. He argued back in my favor, thank goodness, that at least the children were compliant, and where else could she find someone who spoke English as well? Each morning I woke with a knot in my stomach, waiting for the moment that Mrs. Millings might lose something—a book or a jewelry or lipstick—and accuse me. She had done it twice already to the sweepers.

True to his mother's prediction, Nigel left for England at the end of spring, and along with Baby Ayah, who had known him since his birth, I cried. Nigel had annoyed me many times by pulling out my chair and slipping cockroaches under my bed sheet, but now I worried about what might happen to a boy cast adrift in England who had never dressed himself, combed his own hair, or picked up any of his possessions.

The fall term at St. Paul's School didn't begin until July. Nigel should have been able to stay until June before he sailed, but from mid-April through the beginning of July the Millings family went to the cool hills of Darjeeling. Mrs. Millings said she would lose her cottage rental if she delayed until June, and she could not possibly break the Darjeeling stay to take Nigel down to the port of Calcutta. I offered to be the one to bring Nigel to the boat, but Mr. Millings discounted my proposal, saying that I had no experience with train travel and might get lost. Therefore, Mr. Millings took his son to the port, where he met with a clergyman and his wife who would look after Julian on the voyage, and I was set to packing up the remaining children's luggage for Darjeeling.

CHAPTER FOUR

JULIAN

Chinsurah
Spring 1924

Mummy posted an order to the Army-Navy store in Calcutta for Nigel's trunk. When it came a few weeks later, it was the most smashing trunk any of us had ever seen: big, black, and it had shiny gold strapping and hinges all over. The trunk came with all the big mail deliveries on the down train. Ayah's job was to load this up with things he'd need at school, though he'd be fitted for his uniforms at a special shop in London.

I asked Ayah why England was called Home when we'd never been there. We were supposed to be excited about going Home, because there was good weather, no snakes, well-cooked food and many acceptable friends. Still, I was relieved it was Nigel going there first instead of me.

Neither of us had known what school was like. But then Mr. and Mrs. Berryman brought Linton back because there was tuberculosis at St. Paul's. He had been in the third form and told us everything.

I sat with big ears, hearing about the school where Nigel was headed and I would also go in a few years. Apparently there were no ayahs to dress you or make your baths, and it was so cold your body shook from September through July. And summer holidays were spent in a children's boarding house where the boarding-mother gave wretched meals and slapped even harder than the schoolmasters. Linton showed us a long dark red mark on his back from where his boarding-mother had hit him with a strap.

"If you've read Dickens, you've got a good idea of it," Linton said.

But Ayah had not read us Charles Dickens; when I asked she said she didn't believe in frightening stories for children. She read us Robinson Crusoe and *Treasure Island* and all of A.A. Milne. And even better than that were the stories that Ayah made up about children in an Indian village and the magical creatures that were their friends. I told Ayah what Linton had said about the boarding-mother. She said it sounded like one of Mr. Grimm's fairy tales, but that he should tell Mummy, to make sure the school and boarding house he was going to would be all right. But when he told Mummy, she did not believe it; and she said he would be staying with Grandmother and Grandfather in Bath for holidays, not Linton's summer holiday boarding house.

"The boys don't all know how to read right away, do they?" Nigel asked Linton the next time we were together for tea.

"You know your alphabet, right?" Linton asked in his pinched, sneering way.

"Bengali and English," Nigel boasted. Ayah had taught him how letters went together to make sounds that were words; but Nigel often mixed up the letters as he looked at them, and he shouted at Ayah to leave him alone. I liked reading the storybooks Ayah chose for us, but I hid my pleasure in learning to spell out the words, because I did not want to shame Nigel.

"All you need is English—don't speak Bengali or they'll tease you. At school they do lots of reading and writing and maths. It's hard. I suppose in Darjeeling it's easier." Nigel had heaps of confidence, even though he was a year younger than Linton.

Mummy and Father were determined for Nigel and me to go to St. Paul's. Everyone knew St. Paul's was the best school in England. Father treasured his schooldays and we would, too.

No mangoes in summer or grapes in winter. Cruel adults. The cold. These were my brother's fears—and mine, too.

The night before he was to leave, the two of us sat alone in the nursery, with the big Army-Navy trunk between us. Ayah had made a joke about hugging herself into a tiny ball and getting inside the case, so she could go with Nigel to St. Paul's.

At those words, Sally had begun weeping. I guessed she was remembering when Nigel tucked a stray cat in the winter clothes almirah and we all forgot about it. The smell the next month told us something bad had happened. Sally probably believed Ayah was so stupidly fond that she really would put herself in Nigel's trunk. She probably would have preferred to lose Nigel over Ayah, because Ayah played with her without hitting and did all the other kindnesses too.

But I didn't want Nigel to go away. From as early as I could remember, I played with Nigel from sunrise to sundown. If he went to England, I would be left only with my sisters and Ayah. What kind of a boy would I be, then?

"Let's run away. We can be like Tom Sawyer and Huck Finn." I said, thinking about the funny book Ayah had recently read to us.

"Down the Ganges, you mean?" Nigel said. "On whose boat?"

"There are always boats around," I said vaguely, thinking of the fishermen in light wooden vessels who drifted past our bungalow each day. "We could take one."

"But we've never rowed a boat." Nigel said. "I suppose the boatmen would do it for us, wouldn't they?"

I felt confused, because I knew adventurers did things for themselves; that was the point of our escape. But I did not want to frighten Nigel off from what seemed like our only solution. "It will be fine. But we shouldn't bring the trunk. It's too heavy to carry. We will tie bundles on our heads like the dhobi does."

Nigel paused. "But—but where would we go?"

"Up and down the river each day—who cares? We will keep ourselves busy." Mummy liked us to stay busy.

So the plot was hatched. After tea, Mummy and Daddy had Driver-ji take them to the Burnhams' party. I wanted to wait until it was dark to leave, but Nigel pointed out that if it was too dark, the mosquitoes would be thick and we would not be able to see our way. So we went at the time Ayah called dusk. We could see the dusty road well but the mosquitoes were fierce. Ayah once said that we should not complain; the fiercest mosquitoes had been drafted to the Indian Army, meaning they were carried in boxes and let free to be weapons against the enemy. *Who is the enemy?* we asked Ayah, and it seemed her face closed for an instant before she said the enemies were like the witches and warlocks from the fairy books. I believed her, but Nigel did not. But I reminded Nigel anyway, as we slapped at our faces, arms and legs, that the worst ones were in Army boxes. But I was thinking that I would rather have been home, in the quiet nursery with the mosquito coil burning its limey smells. And then to have Ayah tuck the net around me and spend five minutes checking that no mosquitoes got inside. It was because Ayah was putting Sally and Polly to bed that she missed seeing us leaving. She'd thought we were putting *Huckleberry Finn* in Nigel's trunk.

We did not run away with that book or any other, because we both knew that Nigel would never be able to read it; for he would never go to school. We would sail the river catching fish and sell them to the Indians fishmongers who would then sell them to the cook at Government House. In this way, we would still be close to everyone. Thinking about Ayah and Sally and Polly having fish curry for lunch without me made my eyes dampen, but I remembered that this was the kindest thing to do for Nigel: to keep him from school. And if we stayed together, I could not be sent Home either.

I did not feel the mosquitoes biting anymore as Nigel and I approached the area in the village where the boats were brought in for evening; it was too small of a place and too ramshackle to call a dock. But as we drew close, we saw that each of the boats had men on them still; sleeping, lounging, smoking their funny cigarettes that smelled like spice. Some were even cooking supper over small braziers, with a few mangy red dogs. As we approached, one dog lifted his head toward us and barked; his friends joined the chorus and then half a dozen men were looking at us, standing up, coming forward.

"They'll get us," Nigel said, his voice uncertain, for we had not ever been alone in the village without Ayah to talk for us. In Bengali one of the men was saying something I could not understand except for the occasional word that sounded almost like "Ayah." Nigel started talking then, saying he wanted to get on the first boat, and that we would allow them to keep the others. It was the way he talked to everyone: he would do the thing Mummy or Ayah wanted only if he got something for himself. I did not think this was the proper way to speak to these men with their smears of red on their foreheads and their mad eyes. But he was my leader.

"I don't think they will do anything if we go away. They don't know what we were planning," I said in a low voice. "We should walk back."

"We have come too far. My feet hurt. I want to ride on that boat!" So to my amazement Nigel strode forward right past the men and put his hands on the edge of the boat.

A great cry went up as the boat swayed and the people on it did, too. The brazier skidded to the edge and turned over; the flames leaped, but quickly men threw river water on it. Now one circle of men had formed around Nigel and another round me. One man was unwrapping my bundle of necessities and examining them: a tin car, an extra shirt and short pants, a toothbrush and paste.

"I will have you punished!" Nigel shouted with tears in his voice.

I was so frightened that I did not have the words to say anything; just kept my eyes on the brown, bare feet that ringed me. There was talking all around, some excited yells, and then I heard a voice I knew. It was Nimu, our butler; but he was not dressed in his white livery but a rough cloth tied around his waist and vest, which was his off-duty clothing. His eyes were popping with fury.

"What is this nonsense, Chota-saheb? Why are you so far? Ayah and everyone are searching."

"We wanted to see the boats," I said.

"Why boats?" Nimu's gaze went to the lumpy bundle I still held tightly. "Boats you can see from the verandah. It is not safe to be outside by yourselves. Memsaheb and Burra-saheb will be angry when they hear." Then he shouted in Bengali to the fishermen who'd caught Nigel. They stepped away and let Nigel run to Nimu. He caught him by the waist.

"Take me away from them, Nimu. But don't take me home."

"Yes we are going home. Certainly!" Nimu shook Nigel, but in a gentle way.

"Don't you know? If I go home tonight, I'll go to Calcutta tomorrow and then England."

"He doesn't want to go to school in England," I said to Nimu. I did not explain that we'd been trying to get a boat, because it seemed clear that he was friendly with the fishermen and wouldn't think it was our right.

"Not want to go?" Nimu said with a laugh. "But everyone must do what their parents want. Look at your ayah! She was going to school when her parents wanted and leaving school when her mother said she must. And I had no school at all but had to leave home to work very young—as young as Nigel-saheb."

I hadn't known Ayah had been to school. I had never given thought to why she could read and the others could not. Now I wanted to ask her about it, and I did, after we'd returned to the bungalow and gone in for our baths.

"School? Yes, I was there." Ayah rubbed the soap between her hands and began lathering me.

"Did they beat you?"

"Certainly not. Children who behave are not beaten; don't worry!"

"And did you like school? Nimu said you did not want to leave."

A strange expression came across her face. "Yes, I liked being there."

"But now you have us."

"Oh, yes, best of all." But she said it without smiling, and suddenly there was a doubt planted in my mind about whether we really were the best people she knew.

"Ayah, don't let them send me to Calcutta tomorrow," Nigel begged. "I will run away again there, you know; stow away on a ship going to Hong Kong or something."

"Hong Kong?" She winked at him. "I would like to see it also, Chota-saheb. But Sally and Polly need to be dressed and fed."

"You will have to choose going away with me—or staying in this old place," Nigel said. And here I quivered because I did not want to lose Ayah for my brother's sake.

"I choose? No, Master Nigel, you are the one with the world in his hands."

"What?" I looked with confusion at Nigel, who was rolling a dusty ball from one palm to another. It did not look anything like the handsome globe that sat on the library desk. "How does Nigel have the world?"

"Because Nigel goes to that school in England, he will grow tall. Englishmen only grow tall and strong in cold weather, everyone knows. And he will be clever with words and numbers. He will be able to count the thousands of rupees he will earn when he comes back to work in India."

"I don't want to do what Daddy does; it's deadly dull," Nigel said. "I want to have my own boat and sail the seven seas."

"Here you were looking to travel the Ganges; the water is stagnant, full of snakes and mosquitoes. To sail the seas is a much greater goal, but you must be able to properly read a map and understand the compass. Look what happened to poor Gulliver."

And then she was off, telling the Gulliver story but without the book, so that we became the stars of it and the local fishermen the Lilliputians. That was Ayah's game: taking other people's stories and making them our own. But she could not make Nigel feel any better about leaving the next morning. He cried all the way out to the tonga with Father dragging him by the hand. Watching him go from the verandah, Ayah and Sally were crying, while Little Polly wandered about, falling down without anyone even noticing.

That evening Father came back alone. While he and Mummy were having drinks, I sat under their table draped with the long cloth, listening.

"One down. Only three to go." Father said. It took me a moment to understand he was talking about us.

"I sometimes wonder why we have children, if only to send them away."

I could hear the sound of someone pouring more drink, without waiting for the bearer.

"If they stay here, they die." Father sounded impatient. "You've seen it around you. The dysentery, cholera—"

"But we could catch that. And we stay." I heard Mummy take a long sip, then set the glass down hard.

"Are you saying that you want to leave? You don't have to stay." Father again.

"I only wish more people were around. It's quite lonely. And with so many ayahs and other servants about, the children hardly know us—"

"You could take care of them," Father said. "Just an idea."

"And you?" Mummy drew in her breath. "What are you willing to do, Tubby?"

"I rule the district." Father's voice was like Cook's knife flashing down on a chicken's head. "Exactly what do you expect me to do, when you are home all day and can't do as much as dress a child or read a story or—"

"Do shut up," Mummy said.

And after that, there was only the turning of newspaper pages.

CHAPTER FIVE

MENAKSHI

Darjeeling
Summer 1924

Mrs. Millings had been to Darjeeling many times before, and from the way she spoke about the place, I expected the trip would lift her spirits. But from the moment we left Chinsurah together, she was glum.

The long, rough, switchback train ride up the mountain disturbed her constitution. When we arrived, she already had a nasty, sneezing cold. As the other servants and I unpacked the suitcases inside the vast resort cottage, she huddled close to the fire burning in large stone fireplace. The whole two months we stayed, the fire had to remain lit. The first week she sat with a shawl around her in the morning, with rum-splashed tea, and her bottomless glass of sherry in the afternoon. Occasionally she had ladies in for tea and bridge, while Baby Ayah and I played just beyond the veranda with Julian, Sally, and Baby Polly, who could totter a few steps now, if her hands were held.

Our cottage was like many others filled with English mothers and children at the Windemere Resort on Observatory Hill. There was a master bedroom, a guest room and the nursery. Baby Ayah and I laid the sleeping mats we'd brought from Chinsurah on the nursery floor. I didn't like it because there were rumors of rats, one of whom was said to have chewed off part of a sleeping child's nose.

Despite the worries about rats and catching cold from the damp, chilly morning and evening air, Darjeeling was much like the Europe I'd seen in the children's picture-books. The air was rich with the scent of a tree I'd never seen before—pine—that instead of leaves, had needles. There were many novel flowers to pick, and Mount Kanchenjunga in the distance, with snow on the top just like the sweet white icing on fairy cakes at Kevlar's Bakery in the shopping district. You could not see the mountains every day because of the cool mists. But if they suddenly became visible, Julian would notice and yell for me to look at them, too.

After my father's death, I'd given up praying to God. Looking at the grand mountain, though, I thought of the Millings child who was missing: Nigel. I sent a wish into the universe that he would not suffer at his school, but find friends and comfort. I couldn't share my fears with Julian and Sally and Polly, but I confided in Baby Ayah.

"No need to cry for him; his childhood is over." Baby Ayah spoke while she ironed Polly's nappies. There were a stack of them she'd washed the day before, but the cool air made it hard for them to dry properly.

"He's too young to be away from home. My own brother, who is the same age, is not living apart." I thought of Nikhil so far away from me, but at least still in the embrace of our Ma's arms.

"They go to England, and they change." The hot iron hissed as Baby Ayah made quick, angry strokes on the thick cotton. "He will come back even ruder. He will not want to speak the Bengali we taught him."

"We don't know that Nigel will do that. He may miss India; remember how he cried when he left," I said, taking the clean, warm nappy she'd handed me to fold.

"My mother was an ayah, and my sisters are too. From them I know it is always this way. Don't trouble yourself. Be glad it's one less child to wash and feed."

"But you cried for him when he left!" I was stunned by Baby Ayah's words.

"I was sad then, for the child who was leaving." Baby Ayah's dark brown eyes were as hard as her voice. "But when we see him next time—if we are still here—he will be just like his father. So will Julian, some day: and the girls will take after their mother. Just wait!"

Baby Ayah may have known more about the English than I did; but I still felt sorry for Nigel. He had never dressed or bathed himself, nor did he know his letters. The Berryman boy had spoken of terrible things happening to the children at schools, although he hadn't been at St. Paul's, so I tried to convince myself it might be different for Nigel. Still, I imagined Nigel's likely difficulties.

Mrs. Millings did not speak of Nigel except to tell her friends that he was at St. Paul's, where his father had gone. She would be happy to visit him if only the sail wasn't so long. Maybe she'd go over, when it was time to take Julian or Sally.

"India's been nothing like I thought," Mrs. Millings complained to Mrs. Berryman as the two of them drank gin and tonics on the veranda, and I played cricket with the children in the garden just below. "We are wasting our lives, following our husbands and trying in vain to set down roots, only to have to pack up again? Five moves in less than ten years."

"But Tubby's got a top job now. You couldn't live like this in England on the same money."

"I suppose." Mrs. Millings sighed the way she did when her husband told her something she didn't like hearing.

"Think how hot it is on the plains, and how Tubby is suffering without you! Buck up, my dear, is all I can say. Once you try acting in a theatrical—or come to a dance—you'll be distracted. And there's no lack of male attention here."

I didn't understand what that meant. Not until the young gentlemen began stopping in at the cottage to bring Mrs. Millings out to dinner and dances. Less than thirty years old, these were bachelor officers from the Army or Indian Civil Service on leave. They joked and played charades and cards, and Mrs. Millings' gloom eventually slipped off to reveal her as a laughing, lively lady. I had rarely seen her like this—only after many drinks at a Chinsurah dinner party. But this was becoming her daily condition. It was quite easy for the young men to spend an hour chatting with her beside the fire, having the first drink of the evening.

Mrs. Berryman's advice was just the tonic for Mrs. Millings. Within a few weeks of being in Darjeeling, my Memsaheb was only at home to sleep, change clothes or receive visitors for drinks by the fire. She went out every afternoon, and after dressing for dinner, she stayed away until dawn.

This gave me more freedom with the children than I'd ever had. We explored the fields and paths, and enjoyed the strange sensation of playing outside, without ever a threat of sunburn or sweat. The Gurkha people were so different from Bengalis, with their quilted clothing, broad, flat faces, and short, strong frames. I wrote letters about Darjeeling to my mother and sisters, telling them everything except what happened after the trip to Ghoom.

It all started with a marvelous surprise. Mrs. Millings called me to speak with her by the fire one morning. As she sipped her rum tea, she said that she and Mrs. Berryman and some others would make a trip the next day to a neighboring mountain town. Ghoom was famous for its beautiful views and Buddhist monasteries. I'd read all about it in a book I found in the rented cottage and had been thinking of a way to beg her to let me take the children to see it. So I was delighted when she said that she wanted photographs taken there with the children. She said Baby Ayah and I should bring them by train, because the walking would be too difficult for them.

"Of course," I said, thinking with wonder that she had finally come up with a family activity. I listened closely as she described how she and Mrs. Berryman would leave the Windemere before dawn in order to trek the beautiful hills, stopping to see the sunrise at Tiger Hill. They would breakfast there and continue to Ghoom, arriving around noon. After we'd met, we would share a picnic lunch with us then and tour the famous monastery.

After a half-year with the family, I wasn't sure there was a way for Mrs. Millings to find the happiness I sensed she wanted with her children. Being away from her Chinsurah responsibilities must have freed her to try new things. Here, the lifestyle was much more relaxed. The memsaheb had not been as cross with Baby Ayah and me. Every evening before going out, she hugged and kissed the children. I only wondered that the walking might be difficult for her, because I rarely saw her take exercise. Or that she'd get lost. Although Mrs. Berryman knew the area, because of her children.

Linton Berryman and his younger sister Beverly attended boarding school in Darjeeling, so they had plenty to tell about the locality as we rode the train together.

"That is where the snakes live." Linton pointed to a stream rushing by our train window. "Watch yourself when we get out, because they slither throughout the old buildings and will curl around and suffocate you if you don't believe."

"Believe in what?" Julian asked while Sally whimpered and clutched her Golliwog tighter. I reminded her that we saw snakes every few days in Chinsurah and nothing came of it.

"Believe in the Hindu gods," Linton said. "You've got to pray aloud in Hindi to the eight-armed devil if you are caught and hope to survive."

Now I could not keep myself from correcting him. "This is a Buddhist area, Master Linton. When they pray, they speak an ancient language, and those prayers are peaceful. We will all hear more about it at the temple where we're going."

"But if you are going, Hindus must be allowed in."

"Yes, I'm taking you," I said, ignoring his comment about my religion. "But you won't see the figures of Hindu gods there, you will see a smiling Buddha. It's supposed to be a marvelous statue."

"Linton, don't you know that Ayah's Christian," Sally interjected. "She's going to heaven, just like us."

"Really?" Beverly looked at me in surprise.

"She's only bread and butter Christian," Linton sneered.

"What's that?" Beverly asked.

"They say they're Christian to get food. That's pretty much the case for all Indian Christians."

I didn't know why my parents had converted. But my father had landed his good job sometime soon after, and I'd qualified for a scholarship to school. I looked away from Linton, trying to keep my irritation with him to myself. I'd been planning to tell Mr. Millings that I though Julian might be better off at Linton's boarding school, but now I realized this boy could be a nasty influence.

"Well, you don't even have an ayah, so don't talk nonsense," Julian shot back, as if he was defending me.

"And I really like bread and butter," Sally said. "I'm a bread and butter Christian, too. Ayah, can't we have a little something to eat now? This train is so very slow."

"I've got some biscuits with me," I said, smiling at both of them.

The ride was short—only three miles. It was uphill, though, so I wondered how tiny, slim Mrs. Millings was faring. She had bought her first stout walking shoes the day before in a town shop, and a pair of knickerbockers to match. Still, I had never seen her walk farther than the Chowrasta to the Windemere on Observatory Hill, and always it put her out of breath.

At Ghoom Station, it took a good ten minutes to disembark. First, I found porters to carry our picnic baskets and rugs, and then I helped each child climb down from the train to the platform. I paused to let Julian read aloud for everyone a sign saying that we'd arrived at the highest railway station in the world, and the last stop in British India. I joked that we could walk to Nepal or Tibet—if we were strong enough.

Baby Ayah cradled Polly, and the rest of us held hands, as we made our way through the cobbled streets to the red gate guarding a grand white building with the special towers and scalloped roofline. This was the famous monastery. I walked around the building with the boys, hunting for their mothers, but they hadn't arrived.

Since everyone was at loose ends, I decided on a comfortable shaded place close to the entrance for the bearers to set up the picnic for when the mothers and their companions arrived. Mrs. Millings had departed the cottage six hours earlier for a two-and-a-half mile journey. It surely should not take so much time to reach Ghoom.

"We could look inside the temple, to see if they are waiting for us there," I said to Baby Ayah, and she reluctantly agreed. So I gathered up the boys again and went inside the high-ceilinged gilded chambers where I found plenty of Buddhists and several Britishers, but not our Memsaheb.

We returned outside; the boys were laughing about something, but I felt worry creeping down my back like a little spider. The bearers grumbled because they wanted to eat their own food and couldn't before the young masters and mistresses ate.

"We must feed the children," urged Baby Ayah, and I assented. Under the shade of an ash tree the big ones tucked into their cheese-and-chutney sandwiches and drank down bottles of lemonade, and fought for the extra cakes. Baby Ayah called for the bearers to give us our own food, and I ate that just as hungrily with her, for the Tibetan food was delicious—round dumplings stuffed with spicy greens, and thick breads used to scoop up dal and potato curry.

The bearers chatted about what might have happened to the adults who had been foolish enough to take a walk without the aid of Sherpa guides. Perhaps one or more of them had fallen on the rocks. Or they could have been robbed and killed by the Khancha tribesmen who carried thick curved knives.

Their stories were no likelier than Linton's tale of the snake, but I was even more unsettled. An hour had passed, and while I could take the children into the monastery once more, they would become irritable if they lingered through the afternoon with no new activities. And the last train—when did it run? What did it matter, I thought to myself. Mrs. Millings had not given money for tickets for the homeward journey. She'd said she would ride back with us, which meant we'd use the special railway pass from Mr. Millings' job that allowed his family and essential servants transportation. So we went back into the monastery again—because Sally, Polly, and Baby Ayah had not yet seen it—and this time, I made the boys read all the posted English signs about the antiquities to pass the time. And while we were standing—reading about the making of the 15-foot tall golden Buddha called Maitreya—Julian finally called out that his Mummy had come.

I turned with relief to see that Mrs. Millings and her companions were making a loud entry into the grand temple. From her staggering gait, she might have been injured during the walk or had done some drinking. Her hair was mussed, and broken leaves and twigs clung to her tweed walking-suit. Something else was different from when I'd said goodbye in the early morning hours, but I couldn't put a finger on it.

She was laughing up into the face of a man who held her arm, as she came into the temple. It was not until Sally had run up and hugged her that she realized we were all there before her.

"Take her; she's messing my clothes!" Mrs. Millings said, and I caught the strong scent of alcohol on her breath. "Sally, look at what you've done."

"They were already all leafy," Sally said, her face falling. "Mummy, you must change into something clean."

"The trekking—" Mrs. Millings ran a hand through her disheveled hairstyle.

"Did you lose your pith helmet?" I blurted, realizing what was missing.

'Did I?" she said vaguely, touching her head.

"We set off before the sun, remember, so we didn't bring them." Mrs. Berryman looked at me in a way that said I shouldn't have been so forward.

But I'd watched Mrs. Millings from the crack in the nursery door when she'd left. She'd had her helmet then. I imagined those helmets, rolling to the side as the ladies laid themselves down on a pillow of sweet mountain brush. I imagined—then I blushed, and stopped thinking.

• • •

We left Darjeeling a month later, when Mr. Millings sent a series of telegrams saying that the monsoon had arrived, and it was cool again in the plains. I knew because I saw the succession of envelopes brought by bearers from the resort and overheard Mrs. Millings telling her friends that regretfully she was leaving. I heard her crying some afternoons, but she kept on dressing and going out at night, as if she'd resolved to enjoy a few last events before returning to Chinsurah.

But I didn't mind leaving Darjeeling. From the moment we packed up, all the way through the difficult train ride down to the plains and the smooth connection to Sealdah Station in Calcutta, I felt only relief. Going back to the big bungalow in Chinsurah meant life would once again be predictable. No more nighttime knocking and shouting at the front door when Mrs. Millings forgot her key to come in. The telephone wouldn't shrill at all hours, and I wouldn't feel the damp cold. For despite the fabled lovely climate, I'd found myself beset with such shivering as the sun dropped that I became willing, at last, to submit to Sally's plea I join her in bed. Then I had to let Julian pile in, too, so we could fall asleep warm.

Baby Ayah went to sleep with Polly, too. It was a secret among all five of us; but we knew there was no chance of Mrs. Millings ever entering the children's room between seven at night and noon the next morning.

• • •

"Are you back in the plains for the rest of the summer?" The ticket inspector, a swarthy young Anglo-Indian, surprised me out of my thoughts. He'd guarded the entry to the first-class carriage when we'd boarded in Calcutta, after a long seven hours on another train coming down from Darjeeling. This was the final, easiest stage of our journey; a two-hour ride in a regular steam locomotive train west to Chinsurah. The young man didn't ask Mrs. Millings for the rail pass, which wasn't surprising. She was known to many railway employees as the wife of the commissioner of Burdwan.

It seemed that I was the only one who heard the inspector's question. Baby Ayah was playing pattycake with Polly, not noticing him at all. Nervously, I looked to Mrs. Millings for a response, but she was keeping a stony gaze on her fashion magazine.

"Yes, Sir. We are returning from Darjeeling." Then I added a question, because I felt embarrassed my employer was ignoring him. "How is the weather these days?"

"Still hot enough to fry eggs on the street." He grinned. "I'm based in Kharagpur which, as you may know, has the longest railway platform in the world."

"And Ayah told us that Ghoom Station has the world's highest train platform!" Julian said happily. "So two of the world's most important railway stations are in Bengal."

"That's right, young sir," the railway man said, grinning at him. "And you've been to them both! I like your home station, too. I've got some family living in Chinsurah. It's lovely."

"It's a nice town for children." I stroked Sally and Polly's heads: both were on my lap, while I remembered something. Hadn't Mr. Millings telegraphed his wife that the rains had already arrived? Why had he called her to come back, if the weather was still sweltering hot?

"Please let me see your hat!" Julian said, bringing my thoughts back to my charges.

At least the boy said *please*—although it was still rude for a child to ask a stranger for such a favor. But the inspector grinned even more widely. He pulled off the stiff Bengal-Nagpur Railway cap, revealing thick black wavy hair left long in front, which was the English manner. He tossed the cap so it somersaulted in the air, caught it, and pushed it down over Julian's red curls.

The hat was much too large, coming down almost over Julian's eyes, but he beamed. "It's just right."

"They say if the shoe fits, wear it. Same goes for caps, I expect," the man said. His voice was casual; I tried to guess his age. More than twenty, but less than thirty. It was hard for me to know, as I hadn't been around men very much since becoming an ayah.

Mrs. Millings looked up sharply and saw her son. "Julian! You mustn't wear another person's hat. You could catch—"

"Here you are," I interrupted, whipping the cap off Julian's head and handing it to the inspector. What would Mrs. Millings have said if I'd let her finish?

"Young ones keep you busy." The inspector's voice was wistful as he settled his uniform cap back on his head. "I don't have any of my own, of course, being a bachelor—Ram Hollander's the name."

"That's an interesting name," I said in a low voice, because Mrs. Millings had closed her eyes as if she was trying to sleep.

"Hollander is what it sounds, a Dutch name. And my first name is actually Ramsey, after my grandfather. But Ram's easier in India, isn't it?"

How odd that he was speaking to me so informally. Because he had his hand outstretched, I took it, and belatedly remembered this meant that he expected my name; and I should not say anything as silly as "Ayah." In a low voice, I said something I had not in a very long time.

"I'm Menakshi Dutt."

"I work this route most days; I'm surprised I haven't seen you before, Miss Menakshi. How long has it been that you've worked for the Commissioner's family?"

Mrs. Millings's eyes suddenly opened. "Ayah, don't gossip!" At the same time, I felt a sharp pain in my shin. One of the children had bumped into me; I had not given them enough room. I had not been paying proper attention.

The ticket inspector called Ram mouthed an apology to me, but then said aloud in a properly remote voice, "Good travels to all of you! Just two stops to Chinsurah."

CHAPTER SIX

JULIAN

Chinsurah
Monsoon 1924

I was chuffed to find seven letters from Nigel when we returned to our bungalow. I brought the letters straightaway to Ayah, who enjoyed looking at other-country stamps. But then I saw the envelopes had already been torn open. *Your father must have wanted to read them,* Ayah said.

But the letters were all addressed to me, not Father. And Nigel's mixed-up writing was something he couldn't possibly understand.

"*I ahte my perfect,*" Nigel had written. Ayah guessed that it meant he hated his prefect, because Linton had told us about what older boys at St. Paul's did to the new ones. "*Hed in WC*" was another comment that made no sense until Ayah puzzled it out a few days earlier. "Poor, poor boy! And what a risk for disease!" She had thrown down the letter and put her face in her hands before going on. "He must tell a teacher that boys are bullying others in the toilets."

Father seemed pleased enough with Nigel's letters, but not to have understood anything he'd written about. The day after we'd returned from Darjeeling, Father had tea with Mummy on the verandah. I was underneath the round table with the long linen cover, hunting a garden snake that slithered in from the rain.

"Did you see Nigel's letters, Marjorie?"

"I glanced at them, but couldn't make heads or tails of his writing," Mummy answered, and her spoon stirred the sugar clink-clink.

"He has dire need of help with writing; it's a good thing he's placed where he is." Father took a long, loud sip of tea, then said, "Why don't you see if we can send Julian to join him this fall, if there's an opening. It would be nice for the boys to be together."

"But Julian will still be six." Mummy said. "And he is such a good playmate to Sally. These are magic years, when the children are small and still with us. Why cut them short? And I've been thinking about school in Darjeeling, too!"

At first I wanted to run up and kiss Mummy for saying this. But then I got it. If I was away in England, she wouldn't have as many reasons to see Mrs. Berryman and the other Darjeeling friends.

"Marjie, you've pointed out that Ayah is not a great intellectual influence on the children. If we want the boys to succeed, we have to cut the apron strings sooner."

"Ayah doesn't wear an apron!" I'd got so anxious about their talking that I revealed myself. "She's the only one who can read

Nigel's letters. The boys are hurting him. He hates everything about St Paul's except for games and pudding on Sunday."

"What? Julian, why are you under there?" Father slid his foot under the table until it hit me.

"Ow! And I can read. I understood most of the letter, except for what he misspelled," I said crawling out.

"Of course you're reading." Mummy said the last word in a patient way that told me she didn't believe it. "You've got a good memory and a penchant for storytelling, don't you, darling?"

"You're not listening. Nigel doesn't like school. He wrote they put his head in the water closet."

"Nobody likes school at first," Daddy said. "But fagging is part of growing up; Nigel will be on top of he world before he knows it. Now, run along. Mummy and I must sort through the rest of the post that came when she was away."

• • •

I hated them dismissing Nigel, and me, too. I could read and write, although my penciled words were big and wobbly. Unlike my brother, I didn't miss or mix up letters. Once I knew how something was spelled, I remembered.

TICKET INSPECTOR, I wrote that evening on the little blackboard I kept by my bed. I would grow up and become one. Mr. Ramsey Hollander wore a sharp uniform much nicer than Daddy's rumpled suits. He carried a whistle that was chained to his belt that he could blow whenever he wanted. His laugh was really funny, and he had spoken nicely to Ayah. Ayah told him something she'd never said to anyone else: her name, Menakshi Dutt. I had always thought Ayah was her real and only name.

I wished I had my own whistle. I would blow it hard to let Ayah know that whatever she was doing around the bungalow, it was time for her to run to me and tell another one of her tales about Buddhist monks, Kancha warriors and snakes. I could also blow the whistle to make Sally and Polly wince and clutch their ears, or to get Nimu to bring me tea and cakes. I didn't know what I wanted more for Christmas: a trainman's whistle or a cap. So I wrote down both in the letter to Father Christmas.

Ayah promised to mail it straight away, because who knew how long sea mail took to the North Pole. Nobody did. We were far away in India, which was grand most of the time, but difficult when it came to times like Christmas.

CHAPTER SEVEN

MENAKSHI

Chinsurah and Calcutta
Winter 1924

After coming down from the hills, I fell back into the old routines with the children, who were sulkier than before. All they could think about was Darjeeling, where there had been so many other children nearby. In Chinsurah, I was the primary playmate, and that bored them after a bit. The only things that diverted the housebound children were drawing pictures to go along with stories—and now they didn't want them just at bedtime, but in the morning and afternoon as well. We finished the whole library of books in the nursery, and while old favorite books always held interest, I began to tell them more of my own tales, made up as I went along.

In the beginning, I made new adventures for Winnie-the-Pooh, Hansel and Gretel, and Robin Hood. But the stories they requested most were about a character I invented: a little Indian girl called Zara who was touched by magic. Zara was clever enough to catch a fish in her hands, but then the fish would talk to her, and convince her to let him go. Zara made a broom from wild grasses, and it swept her hut by itself. And when she undertook the villager child's task that Sally and Julian thought most loathsome—patting fresh dung into patties that would be dried to serve as fuel—fairies jumped out of the patties, each offering to make her wish come true.

"What should Zara wish for?" I asked Julian as I prepared to create a story for him one morning.

"A round-about carousel," he answered. "Then the others could play with her on it, all day long."

"That's very nice. And you, Sally, what do you think Zara's wish would be?"

"I don't know—to have her parents? Does she have a Ma and Baba, and are they magic?"

I'd never spoken about parents in any of the Zara stories. I hadn't realized it, though, until Sally had spoken. Before I could come up with something, Julian cut in.

"No reason to include them; parents are always around. And they're not interested in fun."

Julian's statement was not quite right. Mr. and Mrs. Millings often went to parties in Calcutta. As the rains slowed, their city friends visited Chinsurah for overnight parties, during which time all the spare bedrooms were thrown into use, and if the skies looked clear, a few tents set up in the garden for outdoor dining and dancing. Then the house was filled with laughter. Mr.

Millings sipped gin and watched Mrs. Millings chatter and joke with their friends.

The fall season in Chinsurah was very pleasant, with the air so cool at night I needed to wear the soft wool cardigan I'd bought in Darjeeling. By day, it was sunny and pleasant; we studied the lessons I'd created for the children outside in the garden. After the Hindu holiday of Durga Puja, Christmas was coming. Mrs. Millings told me I would go with her and the children in late November to stay at the Grand Hotel in Calcutta. This would allow her a chance at shopping and give the children some city excitement. Baby Ayah would stay back with Polly, whom Mrs. Millings thought was too young to appreciate big city excitement.

I was surprised Mrs. Millings would include Julian and Sally on such an excursion, and that she was so enthusiastic about Christmas. But as she went about, talking with Mr. Millings about the need for this sudden trip, she explained she needed to beat the rush of shoppers interested in toys shipped from England.

"It used to be that only we were the buyers, so we could shop with leisure—but now any Ranjit with rupees is coming in too!"

He'd snorted and said, "I'm glad you're not expecting me to go with you for this shopping madness."

At first I was puzzled by Mrs. Millings' comment, thinking she was referring to one of his clerks. But as I thought about it, I understood that she used the name Ranjit to talk about Indians in general. It amazed me that Bengali parents existed who were prosperous enough to shop in these famous stores. I composed a short letter in my mind to my late father, telling him about this. I could just imagine his laugh.

For him, Christmas meant one day without work. For me and the other Christian Indian children, it meant a one-day celebration at the Mission. An unfamiliar tree with a lovely scent was set up on a stand, and we children in the Christian Education Program draped it with shiny tinsel and jasmine garlands. The English ladies were the ones to set candles in special holders on trees and light them, so the ordinary tree was transformed into a glowing marvel. I would take my eyes reluctantly from this sight and toward the hymnal that contained the verses to the *Jesu, Joy of Man's Desiring* and *O Come All Ye Faithful*. Afterwards everyone had tea and tried to resist snatching too many sandesh and rosogolla and barfi sweets from the big silver trays. Two mottled black puddings were also offered, but never completely eaten. These so-called Christmas Puddings had a smelly, bitter taste, and there were whispered rumors about meat of unknown origin chopped up with the dried fruits. I always bobbed my head when I took a piece from Mrs. Wilson, the minister's wife. I'd find a way to go unnoticed into the garden, where that strange sliver of English food would drop into some flowers and be consumed by an appreciative snake, mongoose, or mouse.

In the days that we prepared to go to Calcutta, I told the children funny stories about Christmas at the Mission in Midnapore. Sally wanted to know the best thing that Father Christmas ever brought.

"The sweets were our gifts," I said. "And the sight of the tree!"

"Does he not bring toys to Indians, then?" Sally paused. "Is it because of that bread-and-butter thing Linton was talking about?"

I was confused for a moment, then remembered the Berryman's boy comments about religion on the way to Ghoom. "Father Christmas brings all children who believe in him what they want. And in our case, we really wanted those delicious sweets."

Sally nodded, satisfied with the answer.

"So anything I'll ask for—I'll get?" Julian was staring at me hard, and for a moment he reminded me of his mother.

"Father Christmas is a European, not an Indian—so you naturally would know more about him than I do," I answered quickly. "But it's my understanding that he brings what he can manage for you, yet still share with others. For example, you like pistachio barfi very much—but did you have any last Christmas?"

"I don't remember!" Sally said.

Julian shook his head. "We always have iced gingerbread at Christmas. Not Indian sweets."

"Just my point! Although you certainly like all kinds of Indian sweets, the elves only make a few thousand pounds of it. Father Christmas delivers those sweets to the children who really want them most: to children who don't care so much for gingerbread and plum pudding and toy trains."

"Are you sure?" Julian said. "Don't you think all boys like trains?"

I pictured my little brother Nikhil, just his age, but working in a potato field. If he saw a toy train, he would be afraid to touch it, lest it break. He would know—just as I'd grown up knowing—that these things weren't meant for us.

• • •

On the Thursday morning that we were dropped at Chinsurah station, we were on the first class platform only a few minutes before the Calcutta local arrived. In the doorway, Ram Hollander stood, looking—before the train had stopped, his eyes had locked with mine. I was suddenly glad that I was not wearing my usual white cotton sari but a flowered silk one lent to me by Nimu's wife, who thought I should look smart for the city. Over my shoulders I'd thrown an embroidered red cashmere shawl I'd bought on sale during our time in Darjeeling.

"Chinsurah Station! Disembarking first...kindly allow them room...now all aboard!" Ram called out merrily, first in English and then Bengali. He hopped gracefully from the door to the platform, and in an instant was helping Mrs. Millings and the children ascend the short flight of steps. To my surprise, he offered to give me a hand up, standing so close that I smelled his shaving cream and tobacco. The warmth of this unexpected touch, and the courtesy he'd extended to me, flustered me as I found our compartment and settled the children.

After the train had started, Mrs. Millings left for the dining car. I unpacked toys. Within a minute of her absence, Ram slid open the door of the compartment and said hello.

"Mrs. Millings has the ICS rail pass with her, I'm sorry—" I began.

"Yes, I've already marked it down in my record—just tell me your destination?"

"Calcutta!" Julian shouted.

"Well, we'd better get a journey like that off to a sweet start." He lobbed a small package of glucose biscuits at Julian, who caught them. Sally missed hers, but I caught it.

"This is kind of you," I said.

"The littlest girl is missing. Is everything all right?"

Before I could explain, Julian said that Polly was too young to go shopping all day in Calcutta, and Sally added that such a small girl might fall off the carousel.

"So, Miss Menakshi, I see you're on easy street with these two," Ram said. "But I suppose you've got Madam to contend with."

"Sshh!" I said, hoping the younger two wouldn't understand.

He glanced down at the papers in my lap. "What's that you're reading?"

"My school newsletter—I left early," I said, because I didn't want to pass myself off as a graduate. "My sister forwarded it from home for me to read."

"I've heard of that school." Ram surprised me by saying he hadn't finished at the Anglo-Indian school in Kharagpur. "I was never one for reading and remembering. I only wanted to get on to work the trains like my father—he's an engine driver. But they say I'm not on track to drive the train or run a station."

"Oh," I said, not wanting to say "Sorry," because I didn't want him to feel badly about it. To my eye, his job looked about as hard as mine—but at least he was able to travel all sorts of places and see new people every day.

"It doesn't really matter, I suppose. When Britain frees India, all those set-aside jobs for Anglo-Indians on the railways will be gone."

"Nobody knows if that will happen," I objected.

"Surely independence is coming—but whether it's two years or twenty is what we don't know," Ram said. "I don't mind going abroad. There are train lines expanding in Malaya, Singapore, all those sorts of places. I may get a better chance at rising there."

I remembered what I'd said to my father years ago about wishing to travel to foreign countries. This could be Ramsey's fate.

Julian interrupted my slightly envious thoughts. "But if all the railway men leave, who will be here to take our tickets? Or to even drive the train?" Julian said.

"Young Master, your clever ayah may be driving the train then," the man said mischievously to Julian. "Indian ladies are the world's strongest; don't you know?"

• • •

I hadn't expected that Ram Hollander would be so admiring of Indian women. Weren't Anglo-Indians supposed to only be interested in each other? They were a closed society, just like English, and Hindus and Muslims. After he'd moved on to the next compartment, I wiped up the crumbs from the children's biscuit feast and decided that Ramsey Hollander was most likely a flirtatious young man who felt it a duty to chatter with any unattached female who could speak English. Although he couldn't flirt with an English girl; he'd have his face slapped, or lose his job.

My pique about the conversation faded upon arrival in Calcutta. My first vision of the famous city was overwhelming. As we stepped out of the bustling Sealdah Station, Mrs. Millings told me to locate the hired car that somebody from Government House had sent for us. I was confused and didn't know where to begin, but a driver in smart livery came running up, called for coolies, and escorted us and the luggage to a large Buick. The children and I could not stop gawking at the buildings and hordes of people along the way to our hotel in the middle of a busy shopping street called Chowringhee.

"Why so many children running alongside the car? Who are they?" Julian asked.

I could have just said beggars, but I didn't want to dismiss them as a group. "I don't know their names. There are a lot of children in the city—more even than in Darjeeling. You'll see!"

Mrs. Millings had booked us into a place that filled most of a city block and was appropriately called the Grand Hotel. I had brought a mat set out to sleep in the children's room, but Sally had already whispered that she wanted me to sleep with her in the large, high bed next to Julian's. I decided I'd risk it, because Mrs. Millings' room was all the way on the other side of a vast sitting room. She'd already informed me that it would be best to order up food from room service, because servants of course could not sit at the table with children in the hotel's dining room. I'd seen a few Indian guests in the lobby: gentlemen in English suits and ladies in fine saris and jewelry with their offspring dressed in short pants and jackets and ruffled frocks just like English children. These were the ones whom Mrs. Millings thought might snatch up the toys she wanted for her children.

And when we finally did enter the fashionable shopping emporium, which was just a short walk down the street, my hopes were fulfilled. There were rich Indian women trailed by servants holding shopping bags who were slowly looking at goods with a critical eye. But I was unable to see which pieces of jewelry or toys they were choosing because Julian and Sally had caught sight of a real round-about carousel, and were pulling me toward it.

"With magic horses going up and down! It's just like Zara wished for!" Sally squealed.

Mrs. Millings folded twenty rupees into my hand, to use for riding the carousel and having lunch afterward. She glanced at the watch on her wrist and said, "Goodness, I've got to start, or the shopping will never be done!"

So quickly she moved off not even the children looked after her. But as she sailed up the moving staircase, I saw a young man with light brown hair in a grey city suit and bowler step on behind her and put his hands on her waist.

I was shocked at the intimacy of this—even more that she turned around to smile at him. I hadn't seen his face but thought something about him was familiar—perhaps the long-lost hiking companion—or was it the Scottish officer she'd seen for a week? Now I was beginning to reconsider the reason behind this family trip to Calcutta.

I followed Mrs. Millings's instructions to let the children play as long as they liked on the carousel. I imagined I might not be able to sit with the children in the restaurant, so I braved the moving staircase with the children to look for my employer. I didn't see her—but perhaps that was for the best, because it would be awful to catch her buying something the children were supposed to believe came from Father Christmas.

I took the children out on the street and went around the corner to find a real Indian restaurant. The friendly waiter told us about pony rides just a few blocks away in a grand park called the Maidan, so we filled the rest of the afternoon with horses followed by balloons made into the shapes of the children's favorite animals by a balloon-wallah on the street.

How I hoped Mrs. Millings wouldn't be upset we left the store, I thought as we arrived back at the hotel by teatime. I used the extra key she'd given me to enter our suite, but it was empty. The children didn't seem to notice, so I bathed them and then we read the room service menu together before ordering a lavish tea complete with sandwiches, scones, and cakes.

The next morning, the door to her suite was cracked, and she was snugly in bed, snoring. After the children had finished breakfast in the sitting room and were eager to go out, I looked again through the crack in the door to check if Mrs. Millings had awakened. She hadn't. Strewn across the floor was clothing: but not the smart jacket and dress she'd worn out to the shop. There was a black evening dress with gilt embroidery, and shoes to match.

She must have gone out wearing new clothes she'd bought at Whiteaway-Laidlaw. But why wasn't her smart day suit that she'd worn shopping also in her room? I lingered in the doorway, not daring to wake her. I must have made a sound, because Mrs. Millings finally raised her head.

"So tired..." she sighed gently, shifting position. As she caught sight of me, she mumbled, "Who is it? Ayah—why are you here?"

"Memsaheb, please excuse me, but I'm wondering about the children's program today?" I whispered. "Should I take them somewhere in particular?"

"I gave you money yesterday. Is some left?"

"Just a bit—"

"Take them out, then. There should be a Punch-and-Judy show somewhere."

I asked about it at the front desk and learned there was a noon performance at a big theatre not too far away. "Punch-and-Judy's Christmas" was a comical puppet show set up on a special small stage. The audience laughed and called out loud warnings to Mr. Punch, a puppet with a hat like a clown, about various other characters who were entering the drama. Mr. Punch clenched a big stick which he swung at almost everyone who upset him including his wife, Judy. Some of the children laughed along with the adults, but quite a few cringed or sobbed. Julian sat ramrod straight, looking uncomfortable during all of it; whenever the hitting happened, Sally buried her face in my arm.

"We all need something sweet," I said to console them afterward, because I'd heard Flury's Confectionary was a nice walk over to Park Street. After big cups of tea and whipped cream tortes for all of us, I decided the next stop would be the Zoological Gardens in Alipore.

I had not been inside a taxi before, so I had no idea if the fare that the driver charged for the ride was fair. But the sight on the children's faces as they entered the beautiful gardens full of lush trees and strolling peacocks was worth any price. Here were the animals we'd read about in storybooks. Sally was surprised to see that bears were big and black, not small yellow creatures like Pooh. Julian was fascinated to see white tigers, which he informed me were the same species as the Bengal tiger, just a different color.

"It's like you and Ram. You are the same species as our family, but you look different," he said.

I remembered, a year earlier, Nigel and Julian using the word "native" for any Indian—although the fact was, the boys themselves were born and raised in India. That had made me feel angry. Now, as I studied the white tiger pacing its cage, and the yellow one in the very next enclosure, I wondered why the zookeepers hadn't housed them together. They were both just Bengal tigers, weren't they? They would know how to communicate and play.

Then I realized that the white one, who was female, was probably being kept alone so she would breed, when the time came, with a great cat of the same color. The likelihood of the baby tiger being white would increase—just as it did for the Anglo-Indians who only married each other.

I'd never been to a zoo before and expected that I'd be thrilled—but pacing, dull-eyed tigers made me regret the idea. They couldn't escape their world any more easily than I could escape mine.

I didn't see Mrs. Millings that evening—nor even the following morning. Julian had spent some time in the hall looking out for her, until I'd made him come in for bedtime stories. Now I looked in disbelief at her smoothly made bed. This meant she'd been bold indeed and slept somewhere else during the night. She could do it, because there was nobody who'd question her. A servant like me was supposed to only think of the children.

The Monday that we left, all the boxes I expected Mrs. Millings to have accumulated were waiting in a tall stack in the doorman's office. And when I packed up Mrs. Millings' things, in addition to the evening dress and shoes, there were two new silk nightgowns. But despite these successful purchases, Mrs. Millings seemed sad as she turned in the keys at the front desk. It reminded me of how deflated she'd been when she'd left Darjeeling. She did not want to return home to Mr. Millings; but that was her lot.

"Penny for your thoughts," Ram Hollander said when he came through with chocolate bars for everyone, a few stops before the final one. "I've been waiting to hear what you think about Calcutta!"

Mrs. Millings had seen a lady friend when we were boarding, and had gone to join her in that compartment, so I did not have any worries about his presence bothering her. But I could hardly tell him all that had happened. Smiling, I said, "It's a wonderful place, but the pennies disappear quickly as one goes around."

"Pennies are in England. Paise are here," Sally said cheerfully.

"Would you like to see Sally add up paise?" I asked. "Give her any amount, and she can do it."

"Me, too—"

"Julian, of course you can count. You're a big six-year-old. But Sally's just learned—let's see her do it," I said.

"Sally, can you really count coins?" Ram asked.

"I can!" Sally answered proudly. "Please give me anna coins too. I know that sixteen annas make a rupee."

"You're right about that, Madam. Total this for me, please." Ram fished into the satchel he wore and brought forth a dozen or so coins; he placed them on the little table that sat under the window.

"Sir, isn't that passenger money?" Julian said.

"Yes, indeed. It's money I take from people who neglected to buy tickets at the station office. I'll put it all back when Sally's done."

"Eighty two paise," Sally said, pointing at the pile she'd made. "If there were twenty more, it would be a whole rupee."

"No, it's eighteen more," Julian corrected.

"You're a sharp one," Ram said, looking at him appraisingly. "You could do this job."

"How much total is in your bag?" Julian asked.

"By day's end, usually two hundred rupees or more. Quite heavy, all those coins," Ram said, patting the satchel.

Julian attempted a whistle and said, "What if I robbed you?"

"Julian!" I said reprovingly and then to Ram, "He has been enjoying Robin Hood stories far too much for his own good."

"I like Robin Hood stories too," Ram said. "Tell me, which one's your favorite?"

"The one about Robin Hood freeing the zoo animals and giving them kitchuri and ice cream."

I flushed, because this was a silly, made-up story I'd told them the last night in the hotel, after we'd come back from the zoo. But Ram was nodding his head, looking quite serious. "Yes, I know that story quite well."

Was Ram having Julian on—or did he just not know *Robin Hood?* I pondered this after he'd gone, and Mrs. Millings had come back from the dining car with the remnants of a cocktail which she slowly sipped as she read *Vogue*. It was lucky she'd taken her time, because Ram had spent a good ten minutes in our compartment chatting, and on the way out, he'd pressed a note into my hand.

In neat block letters, he was inviting me to a dance at the Railway Society the next weekend and had included his address in Kharagpur and a telephone number. I knew from stories I'd heard at school that English and Anglo-Indian girls participated in dances where they allowed boys to touch their arms or waists as they moved in unison, just inches apart to popular English or American music.

Of course I couldn't go. Between my traditional Indian upbringing—and being a servant in the Commissioner's home—there was no chance I could participate in a dance. Ram must have had an absurd idea about my character to think this was any kind of possibility. Or I'd been too free with him—it was my fault.

When Mrs. Millings, the children and I came down the train's short stairs, he was on the platform, with a hand upraised to assist people disembarking. I took my time getting off, wishing he hadn't perched himself at the doorway closest to our carriage. This time, I did not let him take my hand.

"Menakshi?" He looked up only at me, ignoring Mrs. Millings' sharp, surprised glare.

Without missing a step, I shook my head no.

CHAPTER EIGHT

JULIAN

Chinsurah
Winter 1924

Father asked what I thought of Calcutta, just as he'd asked about Darjeeling. I huffed out all my breath and said, "I miss it."

I was done with my bath, and was on the veranda spinning a little wooden top Ayah had given me for my last birthday. She was giving the girls their bath and had told me to speak to my father, because he hadn't seen much of me since our return.

Father was in his favorite lounge chair and on its arm had balanced next to his gin a plate of sardines on toast, the teatime meal he requested when Mummy wasn't around. He chewed up a sandwich and then said, "What can you possibly miss about it? Even though I go up for meetings and parties, it's such a noisy crowded place. I prefer the quiet we have here, watching the Hooghly River flow by."

"But in Calcutta there are big cinema houses. We saw a film with the actress Veruka. She beat up six men and jumped off a building and onto an elephant's back. Truly, she did it!"

Two tight lines appeared in the space between Father's eyes and above his beaky nose. "So you saw your first film?"

"Yes, and we had seats in the middle of everything!" In a rush I described the delicious smells of sandalwood and samosas and coconut coming from the Calcutta people sitting around us, and their laughing and calling out to the screen.

"What did Mummy think?"

"Oh, Mummy wasn't there. She was Christmas shopping." With a twist of my fingers, the top went around. And around again, reminding me of the electric round-about in Whiteaway's, but much faster.

"So Ayah took you."

"Mmm," I answered, keeping my eyes on the top.

"She was shopping with Mrs. Marshall?" Father asked. "Did the Marshall children see the film with you and Ayah?"

"Not Mrs. Marshall! She was with that man, I think—"

"What man?" Father carefully set down his glass.

"The brown-haired one from Darjeeling," I answered, keeping my eyes on the top. "They were happy to meet again. He was following her at Whiteaway's."

"Ah, Whiteaway-Laidlaw!" Father said with a chuckle. "He was a floor-walker, I imagine. All the best shops have them."

"Really?" I clapped as my top teetered to a stop and finally hit the stone floor.

"What else did you do in the city?" Father asked.

"We had fabulous meals—much better than cook makes here. Ayah ordered us the most enormous plates of biryani and bowls of chicken curry and fizzy drinks with drinking straws. And so many ice-creams! Tutti-frutti ice cream is my favorite. What's yours?"

Ignoring my question, Father said, "Many of the restaurants in Calcutta serve excellent Continental food. Did you try fillet meuniere?"

"Well, for supper we usually had the hotel room service. Another time we went out to eat cakes—"

"You stayed in a hotel? I thought you were at the Marshalls'."

"No. It was the Grand Hotel. A room for us and Ayah, and just down the hall was Mummy's friend's room." I looked up from my game, because he sounded so strange.

"What friend?"

"That brown-haired man from Darjeeling and the shop. You call him Mr. Floorwalker, but he never told me his name. He doesn't ever talk to us. Just Mummy."

"Ah." Father was not even looking at me anymore. "Well, then, run along. I've got some reports to finish."

I picked up my top and went down to the garden, trying to think of what I'd said that had made Father want me to go away. Was it because of the brown-haired man? I hoped he wasn't angry with Ayah for taking us to eat Indian food or sit with Indians at the film. He and Mummy were always quick to blame her. But lately it seemed they didn't think well of me either. Mummy didn't like my cowlick and that I talked so much. Father didn't like that I wasn't interested in his precious St. Paul's School. Now it was clear that he didn't approve of what I'd done in Calcutta.

Sally and Polly, who looked so much like tiny versions of

Mummy, never made Father frown. He would pat them on the head and call him his golden girls. I wondered what they would say if he asked Sally about Calcutta; for she had liked all the same things that I had. But she hadn't liked Calcutta quite as well without Polly. Although at home, the two fought like street dogs over each other's toys. Ayah begged them to be kind to each other for the life that sisters spent together was too short to waste. She had not seen her own sister in a very long time.

"Why doesn't your sister ever come to visit you?" I asked Ayah one afternoon. She was in the garden watching us, but at the same time writing a letter set on the corner of the tea tray. "Or your Mummy and brother?"

"They'd like to, but it's not possible." She folded the letter in two and slipped it into an envelope.

"People are visiting here always—"

"People are *always* visiting here," she corrected. "Master Julian, your parents won't like it if you pick up Anglo-Indian grammar. But I can't have my sister stay because this is not my home. I am only living here because your parents allow it. "

Her words made me uneasy. I asked, "Won't you *always* live here?"

"As long as there's someone young who needs care—I hope so." Ayah's smile didn't go through to her eyes—and this made me not want to look at her anymore.

Picking up a good-shaped, smooth stone, I clenched it. "They'll send me away to England next year."

"We don't know that is true." Ayah unfolded my fingers from around the stone and examined it. "What a fine stone—a strong, smooth shape. And don't worry so much. Your mother might convince your father to send you to school in Darjeeling."

"Why?" I kept my eyes on the ground. Mummy had said something to Father, but I thought he'd ignored it.

"Mrs. Berryman suggested it. It would be nice for us to have you only a day's train ride away, wouldn't it? To spend every holiday and summer season together?"

Ayah meant to cheer me up, but I hated the thought of going to school in Darjeeling almost as much as England. Linton was mean. He would probably not even want to be my friend there. And if I were at boarding school, I'd be away most of the time. Ayah would stop thinking about me, just as everyone had stopped thinking about Nigel. And before you could say Jack Robinson, my sisters would be off to a girls' school and Ayah would choose to work for another British family with younger children. How much I longed to tell Ayah that I knew she was the only one who loved me; and that I loved her, too. But a woman her age could not wait for me to grow up to marry her.

"What is it, Julian dear?" Ayah put the stone back into my palm and ran her own hand over mine, closing it in.

"They can't make me go to school in Darjeeling."

"Let's not think about that anymore." She hugged me close to her and said, "But education is good. Without one, there are few choices. Look at what happened to me. I lost my chance at school. It is not an easy life, Master Julian."

Was it hard taking care of us? I thought she did it with joy, except for the times Mummy shouted at her. Mummy had gone to some kind of school and it hadn't made her happy. Father had even more education and that he was the saddest in the whole family. I squeezed my eyes shut, concentrating, trying to think of somebody who laughed while he worked, and thought of the trainman.

"What about being a trainman? Can't I do that without going to boarding school?" I said, remembering the way she had spoken admiringly to Ramsey Hollander. And railways were exciting, because Chinsurah and Calcutta were only two stops on very long routes that traveled hundreds of miles to strange cities I could only imagine.

"I'm not sure." Ayah paused, then said, "Of course, if you chose an education in England you might become head of the Bengal-Nagpur line one day. But first you must study business or engineering."

"Engineering? Isn't that what the engine driver does?" I thought of the big man who liked to wave at me when I stood on tiptoe to see him in the car.

"No. I mean a person who designs bigger and faster trains and maps where the new tracks should run. Just think, you could plan out paths to wild places that nobody knows yet. Places like Pooh's forest!"

"But in India, native people are already living in the forests."

"There are always people living in such places. You would meet them, and perhaps persuade them to help you build the railway line."

"That's what the English have done in India, isn't it? Built roads and tracks into places that were already some other peoples' home?"

"That is true." Ayah was looking at me with a strange expression.

And it wasn't fair; suddenly, I knew it, with a force as sharp as Father's hand, the last time he'd spanked me. "Ayah, what do you think? Is it fair to just build your houses and tracks somewhere without asking the people first?"

"Julian, in the very beginning some wealthy Indian rajahs gave some Englishmen permission, and—I don't know much more." She shook her head, and I saw the braids that she wore coiled around the top were coming undone. "This is the way that a colony is made."

"Father's a colonial man, isn't he?" I asked.

"Yes. He's the most powerful man in Burdwan District."

"I'm tired of Burdwan," I said. "I want to take a train ride somewhere else. But Mummy keeps that train pass to herself—I can't use it alone. Please, Ayah, you've got a little money. Can you help me get away?"

There were tears in Ayah's eyes as she regarded me. After a long moment, she said, "I can't take you anywhere, Julian. But if you keep your heart open to the people around you, and you undertake your studies with that same kind of heart, you will get a ticket to happiness."

I wasn't sure I'd understood the name of the station she was talking about. I asked, "Is there really a town in India called Happiness? Is it in Bengal or farther away?"

Her eyes had a faraway look. Loosening her hold on me she said, "Right now, your happiness is a point unknown. But nobody can take the ticket away from you. Always remember."

CHAPTER NINE

MENAKSHI

Chinsurah
Winter 1924

Julian's inquiry about seeing my family stayed with me for days. I was supposed to be allowed two weeks leave per year to see my family; Mrs. Millings had agreed to it in the job interview one-and-a-half years earlier. But so far, there had been too many complications for her to allow me to leave.

Now it was well past the end of my first year anniversary of working. The letters from home were not coming as often as they had—which worried me. We were a postman's family—letters were like food to us, always had been. Maybe there was no family news because they were struggling; had they no more funds for paper and stamps?

A week after Julian's question, I went to her while she was doing her morning accounts and asked if I could take leave.

"The week before Christmas—and coming back by New Year's Eve. I know that you'll need me most after the New Year, when you all have the camping trip to the jungle." It was not a holiday, but a time Mr. Millings listened to petitions from the local people, and Mrs. Millings visited with Englishwomen whose husbands had remote postings. The children enjoyed looking for animals, although I'd had to keep a very tight rein on them the previous year we'd gone, in order that they didn't step on snakes or get lost.

"Christmas is a Christian holiday. I can't understand why you want to go just then—"

"I am Christian. That's the chief reason you hired me," I reminded her.

"Don't tell me why I hired you—you can't possibly know, and sometimes, I wonder myself," Mrs. Millings grumbled. "Very well, then, go if you must but certainly return before December 31st. You may pack a small bag—not all your things."

"What do you mean by that, Memsaheb?" I asked, trying to hide my elation at finally being allowed leave.

"Don't run away. So many of the servants go back to their villages for holidays and never return because somebody's sick or they want to get married or help with a sister's baby. I've heard it all before, and I don't want to hear it from you."

I supposed that if Memsaheb wanted me back, this meant she was satisfied with the work I'd been doing. So I bobbed my head and said of course I would return, and it would be with Christmas gifts for all. I was remembering my mother's needlework, of course.

• • •

The train toward my home wasn't one that used the platform I'd always been on before; it was entirely another direction from Calcutta. I checked and re-checked with the ticket agent and other passengers standing, to make sure I wasn't mistaken about this being the Midnapore line. I knew I couldn't afford to lose half a day of my precious break by getting on the wrong train.

As I waited, I recalled how anxious I'd felt that morning as I kissed the children goodbye, worrying they would make trouble for Baby Ayah during the day and wouldn't go to sleep without my stories. Julian had cried along with Sally and Polly, surprising me with the depth of his affection. But as I stood on the strange platform in the crisp December morning, those particular worries ceased. As much as I loved the three of them, I was glad not to be anyone's ayah for two weeks. I would be a daughter in the cozy cottage I'd grown up in. Ma would cook for me, brush my hair, and maybe even massage my tired, rough hands and feet with mustard oil.

I spotted Ram Hollander threading through the crowd on the platform across the rails in his smart black winter uniform. No doubt he was getting ready to ride his train.

I waved and called out, "Mr. Hollander!"

He caught sight of me, grinned, and waved his fingers frantically in a gesture that seemed to say he was coming over. And to my surprise, he ran lightly as a cat across the tracks to meet me.

"You're on the wrong platform if you're headed to Calcutta! And where are the children and the Monstrous Memsaheb?"

Smiling back at him, I explained that I had leave to visit my family for the Christmas holidays.

"And where is home?" Ram Hollander inquired at the end of my explanation. "Perhaps I could hop a local on my day off and come give my regards to your family—"

"No, you can't!" I was so horrified that the words burst forth impolitely.

"Why not?" Ram Hollander looked as puzzled as Julian did when we had to hurry quickly away from the nest of snake eggs he'd discovered in the hollow of a banyan tree.

"My family would be very upset." I didn't want to say that my family could not imagine me socializing with a man outside our community. Nor that I thought that Ram would be horrified by the modesty of our home life. He would not know how to comport himself—and he would feel just as uncomfortable as my mother and sister would.

"But they're Christian. Do unto others and all that—"

"How do you know that's my religion?" I asked defensively, remembering how Linton had mocked me.

"You just said that you were celebrating Christmas with them. And I've seen the cross that you wear."

Reflexively, I touched the silver chain and crucifix that I'd worn continuously since my interview for the ayah position. "Yes, I wear this, but it doesn't mean that we're the same. My family and I are Indian. We don't step out with anyone before marriage. Not to go dancing or to films. It's not our way, Mr. Hollander."

"It's Ram, remember?" His face was flushed, and his eyes shining. For the first time, he was speaking in Bengali. "And I'm Indian, too. I was born here and just like you, can't go into the schools and clubs and parties where the Millingses and their kind go."

Except for school, he was talking about an entire category of event that was foreign to me. He didn't understand I didn't fit into it—didn't want it either. I countered, "But you're still different than I—"

"Actually, it's like each of our groups is assigned to a different train compartment." As I looked at him uncomprehendingly, he said, "The British are first class, Indians are third, and we Anglo-Indians are inter-class. Tied to both, but welcomed by neither."

He was right. Nobody had put it so clearly before; But I had to admit that I'd never had an Anglo-Indian friend before him. It had seemed to me that the Anglo-Indian girls at school had been adamant about calling themselves Domiciled Europeans and not mixing with the Indians. But I had not ever smiled hello or made an invitation to them. Could this be the second half of the problem?

This was much too big a thing to be talking about, especially at the station I was trying to leave—and where he was employed. In a low voice I said, "I'm worried you will get in trouble talking to me over here. Isn't that your Calcutta train there? Couldn't it leave without you?"

"Not until I blow the whistle." He was looking at me intently. "When will you return?"

I hesitated. But somewhere inside me, I knew it was a gift to be able to talk like this. "On New Year's Eve. It will be the early afternoon, I believe, when I pass through here."

"Now I'm glad I was scheduled to work that day. My train passes through at 15:20. Maybe I'll catch a glimpse of you," he said in

English, his old cheerfulness back. "Would you stay a few minutes? Just so I can give some gifts to you for the children?"

"Yes." I wanted to say more but Ramsey Hollander had dashed back across the platform, his lean figure in the khaki uniform vanishing in the third class sea of beige and brown homespun. Ram wasn't tall, so I could no longer see him, although I heard the sound of his sharp, shrill whistle.

• • •

Everything seemed dustier in Midnapore: the buildings, the red-dirt streets, the tonga carts pulled by horses. It was five miles to our house in the nearby small town of Bhattnagar. Though I tried to buy a ride on the back of a lorry headed that way, the only one willing charged too high a price. So I walked, not minding very much because I was glad to be nearing home. As I walked, I thought it was a good thing indeed Mrs. Millings had insisted I take a small bag, because I could easily handle it myself.

In the air were the sharp smells of cow dung and overripe fruit, aromas that you could smell in any Indian marketplace, but that were somehow exactly right here.

As each mile passed, I felt happier, and kept my eye out for interesting things to write about to the Millings children. Julian and Polly and Sally had wanted to know about my home; they were interested in whether it was a hut or a bungalow, or even if I had my own Ayah waiting to greet me. At the last question I had burst into gales of laughter, and I told them I had begun taking care of my brothers and sisters when I was Polly's age. And my family house was like a storybook cottage to me. It had a strong tin roof and scrubbed red oxide floors that felt cool and clean underfoot. Until my father's passing, we'd had a daily lady come in to help my mother with the cooking and dishwashing. I loved this place where I'd been born and spent my first sixteen years.

As I walked into our village, almost two hours since leaving the station, I nodded to people who looked familiar and was happy to tread the familiar lane toward our home. But a few feet short of the place, I stopped in wonder.

The house was the same—but looked so different! The chicken coop was gone, and the cottage had been freshly whitewashed and had a new, green door. Had the money I'd sent Ma over the last 18 months really been enough to pay for her necessities and a door that would hold fast? As I drew closer, I saw a lacy white pattern of rice powder in the step before the door. Renuka must have made the beautiful designs of flowers and stars to welcome me. It was a Hindu tradition—not a Christian one—so I was a bit surprised. But the alpana patterns surely meant that my letter telling about my holiday leave had reached them.

"I'm home!" I called out and pushed on the new door. But it was locked. I heard a man's voice shout inside; who could that be? I stood uncertainly on the step.

And then the door opened. It was a man I didn't recognize at first, with a full face and wispy black-gray hair. Then I realized the stranger was someone I knew very slightly: Janak, a Hindu farmer who had a potato farming business on the outskirts of town. Had Ma married him? I went rigid with shock, but then remembered my manners.

"Good day to you, Janak-babu," I said in Bengali. What I couldn't say was, *what are you doing in my home? Why did you answer the door, and not my Ma?*

Janak glared at me. "What is it? The doorway area should not be touched. We have important people coming."

So he didn't recognize me. "I'm Menakshi Dutt, come back from working in Chinsurah. I am looking for my mother."

"Oh, Lata Dutt's Menakshi!" His expression relaxed. "Don't you know that your mother has moved from here two months ago?"

So Janak wasn't my new stepfather. This was very good news, but why had my mother moved? "I didn't get any letters about it. What has happened?"

"She could no longer pay the money-lender. The house became available, and I had needed a place in town."

"So you came here... where did she go?" My words came slowly, like Sally's when she was trying to puzzle out alphabet letters.

"I hear she is staying in a bustee near the station these days. I've not seen her, but have kept some letters that came for her."

A bustee was not an ordinary neighborhood; it was a slum. My head swam with the unreality of this. "Is she with my sister and brother?"

He shook his head. "Renuka stays where she works, in the house of one of the judge-sahebs. Little Nikhil stays with some of my workers near the fields."

I'd known that Nikhil was working in the fields, but not that he was in the employ of Janak-babu, who had a reputation for being a hard taskmaster.

"Too bad that he couldn't go to school like you and your sister." But Janak-babu's round face was smug. He was illiterate and had complained years ago about the unfair advantages given to the Christian postman's daughters. "I took your brother out of kindness because he's not very strong and still a slow worker.

Now, I am preparing for a visit. A family is coming to see my daughter."

Janak gestured toward the alpana designs I'd stepped around with care. I remembered that his daughter Nandita was a year younger than I, the perfect age to be marrying. It didn't matter that she couldn't read; she had a father with a good business, and now a respectable-looking home place.

"It is lucky you came, because some letters arrived for your mother that I've been holding. I did not trust your little brother to be able to keep them safely."

He disappeared into the darkness of the house that was once mine, and I thought immediately that he might not have ever given them my letters if I hadn't arrived. But now I was here, I would surely speak to them of the letters; and then he'd be in an embarrassing position, if he still had them.

Unaware of my distressed thoughts, he came back with a satisfied smile and some letters: one from a bank addressed to my mother, the others from me. Two whole months' worth of correspondence, I could tell by the dates. I grunted out a short thank you, wondering if they'd been steamed open and had the cash inside removed.

"My driver will carry you on my cart to the bustee." He spoke as if he was a lord, granting a favor to a peon. "You are looking much older, Menakshi. Even more than your years. I'd thought you were growing spoilt living with the rich, but you must be working as hard as your sister and brother."

I said nothing, because anger blazed inside me. After all, he had taken our house.

CHAPTER TEN

JULIAN

Chinsurah
Winter 1924

Christmas was coming, and I felt like I was humming inside. My letter to Father Christmas had been posted so long ago that his elves had time to make everything I'd asked for. I wanted a Meccano clockwork motor model train with a locomotive engine and at least six carriages. I also wanted a spyglass for looking at things, and a cap just like Mr. Hollander's.

I knew from all the Christmases past that not only did Father Christmas bring things, but English relatives sent boxes, and Mummy and Daddy's friends and all the servants gave presents, too. The English gifts were sometimes useless: clothes that were too small or toys too babyish because nobody had ever seen us.

For my last Christmas, Aunt Cecily sent an English history book to Polly, who was such a tiny baby she didn't care about history. She also sent a stuffed teddy to Nigel, who didn't sleep with any animals anymore. Sally took the teddy—and I got the history book—because Nigel liked the largish swimming costume I'd received and Polly was best suited for the silver baby cup meant for Sally.

It was fun that way—all the swapping around. But someone had to be the leader and tell everyone who should get what. It used to be Nigel who did that—but this year, since he was away, it would be me.

The gardener, Firzad, had cut down a small tree from near the river and brought it to the veranda where he stood it up in a pot with lots of earth and moss all around. Baby Ayah helped us hang the tree with tinsel and colored balls from Mummy's special box, the one that came out from deep in the storage room just for Christmas. It was funny having Baby Ayah run after us and get out of breath when Big Ayah would have won the race. Mummy said that Baby Ayah was not able to look after all of us very well and we must not give her trouble at such a busy time of year.

"Why did Big Ayah go away? She was here last year for Christmas," Sally asked me for about the hundredth time.

"Mummy said she'd not taken leave for a very long time so the days added up, just like money in my jar. And if the jar isn't cleaned out now, she might want to leave for a whole month altogether when it's very inconvenient." I knew that Sally envied my jar. Father gave us paisa and sometimes even a rupee if we behaved nicely when we met guests. Sally always spent her reward money straightaway on sweets or small toys at the Chinsurah bazaar, but I was saving mine, because I knew Ayah approved of this. She hesitated to spend even a paisa of her earnings; she only bought things she needed, like sandals and hair oil. I'd seen her looking at books with bright covers written in Bengali, but she always passed them by, saying she hadn't enough money to spend on something that would be used up after just one reading. The Club had a big library inside it where people could borrow books; but she shook her head and reminded me she couldn't, because she was not a member.

"How many days are left till Christmas?" Sally asked.

"Nine," I said. "Can you remember nine?"

"How will Big Ayah give us our Christmas presents when she's far away?"

"I'm sure she'll give them when she comes back." It was getting tiresome, having to answer the questions for Sally that Baby Ayah could not.

Big Ayah's presents the year before had been absolutely smashing. She'd made slingshots for Nigel and me, given with the promise we could only use them outside, facing toward the river and not people. She made an Indian blouse and long skirt for Sally out of one of Mummy's old dresses that Sally wore very happily for dress-up time. Mummy didn't even recognize the material which made all of us laugh. She'd covered a small box with colored paper for Polly. When Polly ripped it off, she found an old biscuit tin with a picture of a baby on it. Nothing inside, but Big Ayah said it didn't matter. Babies liked tearing up paper and seeing other baby faces. That tin became one of Polly's favorite things for banging.

"Your ayah is gone—now is the time to make her Christmas present!" said Baby Ayah, who was sitting nearby rocking Polly into her afternoon nap. "She watches you so many-many hours.

You did not have time to make a Christmas present without her seeing. Now you do."

Ayah had told us that Father Christmas hadn't brought her toys when she was little—that all she'd had were sweets at the Mission. We could do better than that. Polly was too little to do anything, but Sally could give her a gift, and so could I.

"Yes, let's!" I said, my thoughts beginning to stir.

"But we're not good at making things!" Sally protested. "I can't sew and Julian can't build things. We can't make things like Big Ayah does."

"You play so much," Baby Ayah said crossly. "Too much playing and not enough working. Indian children are different."

I stared down the driveway, knowing that Sally was right. We couldn't make something good enough. Even if we drew pictures, or wrote down a story, it would be childish; not something she really wanted. But then, there was my money.

"We could buy her something." In my head I had a vision of the two of us shopping the bazaar just like grownups, with Baby Ayah following behind us.

"No we can't. You're rich, but I've got nothing!" Sally cried.

"I'll lend you a rupee from my jar, but you'll need to return it later," I offered. It was in my own interest. When Ayah thanked Sally for that gift, I'd whisper to her that the money had come from me—and then she'd be even more pleased. Ayah might say that I was very mature or good-hearted. I'd missed her praise. I needed lots of it, when she came back.

• • •

Cook said there was room for Baby Ayah and the three of us to ride in the back of the Packard when he traveled into town two days before Christmas Eve. Mummy and Father were hosting a big party for the local Civil Service office families on Boxing Day, so Cook was hunting for special sugars and wine and port. Normally the wines and other grown-up drinks were delivered to the house, but for this big party he needed to meet a liquor-seller to see what merchandise was in stock to make the order.

Cook was very nervous because he did not drink alcohol and would not know what tasted good. If he were cheated by the liquor-seller, the Memsaheb would have his head. But Mummy couldn't go in the shop, because it wasn't proper for ladies. I said that I'd like to go into the liquor-seller's. But Cook was worried that would also be improper, make even more trouble, so Mummy agreed that he would telephone her from the place to tell the names of the wines for sale. And during this time, Baby Ayah could take us around the bazaar.

We had been to the bazaar many times before, but with Christmas on, it was even better. Garlands of flowers tied with gold ribbon decorated shop entrances. The confectionary had Christmas cakes and special biscuits molded in the shape of windmills.

"I want to get those special biscuits for Ayah," Sally decided. For a rupee, that made a very large box. As we were walking away, she asked Baby Ayah to open the box, because Ayah wouldn't miss her having just one.

"No, that's not right," I told her, but she began whimpering and Baby Ayah said Big Ayah would rather have her eat all of them than be unhappy at the bazaar. I stared at Baby Ayah, hating her for spoiling my sister. Sally crunched into a biscuit, giving me a triumphant smile.

The beggars, of course, were all around—and now that Sally had opened the box they coaxed her to give biscuits. "I can't give, it's a present!" Sally said, as if they would understand. They would not stop following so I gave them a coin, realizing the next time I looked in my purse that it had been a whole rupee, when I really meant to hand out a ten-paisa coin. Now all that was left were sixty-one paisa and two rupees.

"She would like a book. And then you will still have some money left," Baby Ayah recommended.

I shook my head. I couldn't make heads or tails of the Bengali books at the booksellers, so how would I know a good book? Baby Ayah couldn't read Bengali, so she couldn't help me either.

"What else, Master Julian?"

I pictured Big Ayah in my mind, always in her plain white sari, so very different than the Indian goddesses with draped in flowers and jewels. How they sparkled! And then I knew that while I could get her flowers from the garden, I could perhaps also buy her some jewelry, so she would look as beautiful on the outside as Veruka, the star we'd seen in the Calcutta cinema hall. I grew warm at the thought of her face when she unwrapped a small box to see jewels. I didn't want to tell Baby Ayah and hear her say my ayah wouldn't like it, so I kept quiet but had my eyes open, searching past all the shops selling spices and kites and metal bowls and saris to find one with jewels. Then, as we turned into the next lane, I caught sight of a jewelry shop with many brilliant colored bangles stacked up against the walls and a glass counter full of necklaces and earrings.

"This shop may be good," I said to Baby Ayah, walking firmly into the place. Two men were inside, both wearing little crocheted caps and Muslim pyjama suits. The first one looked at me and said something to the other. They both laughed, looking pleased.

"Welcome, young master!" said the fatter, older man with a smile so wide his eyes became very small.

"You don't have enough rupees for this shop," Baby Ayah whispered to me.

"Maybe I do. Mummy says jewelry in India is cheap."

"Not cheap—very fine!" the friendly shopkeeper said eagerly. "What can I help you with—Saheb?"

Saheb was what everyone called Father. Did he know I was part of the family—and would he treat me kindly for it? In a clear slow voice, I said, "I am Julian Millings, son of the Commissioner of Burdwan. I'm here to buy a Christmas present for a lady."

The shopkeeper said something to Baby Ayah in Bengali. In the middle of it I made out the word "Commissioner."

Baby Ayah listened anxiously, but at the end, she nodded and said, "ha, ha." I knew by now this did not mean she was laughing. She was saying "yes."

Now the shopkeeper bent down so that his eyes were on the same level as mine. "Sir, I have many fine bangles along the wall. Glass, brass, silver... Please, have a seat while you wait."

There was a white mattress on the floor; I sank down on its cloudy softness, and my sisters and Baby Ayah settled around me. Sally was smiling now and talking about whether there were princess tiaras for sale.

"We look at bangles," Baby Ayah said to me. "Maybe you can pay for that, but not more."

The men looked at each other again, and then back at us. "Please, you must be getting thirsty. I will bring you all tea."

After we had tea and sweet cakes, Sally and Polly became very giggly and were crawling over the white mattress, with Baby Ayah chasing after them. I could not play; I had to find just the right present.

"What is the wrist size for the lucky lady?" The shopkeeper asked me in English.

"I don't know," I admitted. "But her wrists are very nice."

He smiled at this. "Her age?"

"Seventeen. I'm almost seven, you know. There are only about ten years between the two of us!"

This brought some laughter between the two fellows. "Our bracelets have many sizes for many wrists. If you don't know the size exactly, it is better to choose something like necklace or earrings. Please look carefully, Saheb. After you choose your favorites, I will bring them out."

Ayah always wore a necklace; a tarnished silver chain with a cross on it, the kind of Jesus cross they had in the church downtown, only that one sparkled gold. I remembered Nigel yanking hard on Ayah's necklace once, and her yelping in shock. I didn't like that necklace; a new one would be better.

The man used a long key to unlock the jewelry case and lifted up the lid. It was like a pirate's treasure chest full of so many glittering necklaces and earrings and bracelets. I was dazzled, not knowing how I'd ever pick the right one. They all looked so nice.

"Please examine," the man said, lifting up a necklace as carefully as if it were a small bird.

"Red is a good color for Christmas," I said, looking at the one he held.

"Yes indeed—and rubies are the favorite jewel for brides. These rubies were dug up from a mine in Burma."

"I've got some Burma stamps in my collection," I said as he put the necklace in my hands. The shining red stones glimmered like animal eyes set in gold. "How much?"

The salesman smiled so his teeth glittered. "Will you kindly tell me what funds you have? I would like to make it possible."

"Don't show your money!" Baby Ayah cried out as I began to reach in my pocket.

The two men looked at each other and said some quick words to each other. Then one said to me, "If you prefer, you may sign for it; surely your father won't mind. We can send the bill to your house. All that we are needing is your address."

This was the way grownups shopped, without money. I'd seen Mummy just write down her name when she was buying things in Darjeeling or Calcutta. I told him that I could sign very well, which I did, and then he put down some more information on the same piece of paper. I told him how to spell Father's name, and that we lived at Government House on the first private drive going down to the river. I added, "Everyone knows the house," I said, because I'd heard Mummy say that many times.

The shopkeeper placed the necklace inside a box lined with slippery satin in the careful way Baby Ayah used to place Polly in her cradle. He also put next to it a copy of the paper with writing, but told me not to let her see it, or it would spoil her surprise.

As his assistant wrapped up the box in gold paper, Baby Ayah grumbled to me, "I'm surprised they gave you that nice set, with the little money you had!"

I thought of explaining that all they wanted was for me to sign—that they hadn't even taken my rupees—but that was probably too complicated for her brain. She only understood children's English, not big words. But I let her clutch the jewelry store bag after we left the shop to make her feel it was safe from thieves.

After Baby Ayah gave the jewelry box back to me in the nursery, I secreted it in a drawer, feeling the warmth that comes from giving to others, just like the bishop had said once at our church. I couldn't believe I'd thought up exactly the right present for Ayah and had got it so easily. What a wonderful surprise she would have; it wouldn't even matter that it was six days later than Christmas when she got it. I could already guess what she would say when she let me put the rubies around her neck:

Thank you very much, Julian. Nobody has ever given me such a great gift. How I love you!

CHAPTER ELEVEN

MENAKSHI

Midnapore
Winter 1924

The slum area had no sewers, just ditches along either side of the dirt path filled with dark cess and unknown garbage. The only thing cutting this excruciating smell was smoke from cooking fires outside burlap-covered shelters and lean-tos built of scavenged pieces of wood and metal. Motuk brought me to the edge of it and drove straight away, coughing. Holding my breath, I picked my way through the rows of shacks. As I walked, the poor gaped at me—for it was clear that I didn't belong. I was hesitant to look into each of the makeshift homes, so I asked a lady if she knew where my mother stayed.

She shook her head. "I don't know anyone by the name of

Lata Dutt; but we usually just call each other Sister and Aunty and so-on. So many people are coming and going, I cannot meet them all. You should ask Dilip-babu. He collects fees from all who stay here, whether they make the shelter themselves or stay with others."

I felt horrified to learn my mother actually had to pay someone to live in this squalor. I thanked the talkative lady, who was getting on preparing supper and left, carefully double-checking my bag holding the letters, in case it had been touched by one of the many hangers-on listening to our conversation. The letters really were still sealed; Janak had not taken the rupees out. But why hadn't my mother returned to her old house to pick up my letters—or why hadn't she asked the new postmaster to hold mail for her? My pay packet was her chief income. I didn't understand how could she just walk away from it.

• • •

The boss of the slums, Dilip, had a long, gray beard as if he were some kind of holy man. He sat on a cushion in a well-appointed hut, with his daughters coming and going around him, bringing him tea and a plate of sticky orange jelebi sweets.

"Your mother is Lata Dutt. A clean lady. I had trusted her," he said, licking the fingers of his right hand after he popped a sweet into his mouth.

I watched him, thinking that I would not have eaten anything from his place, even if the girls had offered it to me; which they had not. And I wondered too how my mother had kept clean.

Now he pointed the sticky finger at me and said, "Your Ma did not keep her promise to me! She stopped paying rent."

"She did not receive the money I usually provided for her, because she had to leave our house." I tried to keep my voice courteous, although I fantasized spitting at him the way Nigel did when he was upset. "Sir, please tell me where she is in this place. Only when we are together can I fix the financial situation."

"Ah! She didn't receive the letters because she went into hospital." As he spoke, I saw a black gap between his teeth stained red from chewing pan: a hole in which I imagined poor, desperate people vanishing forever.

"Hospital!" I said. He'd said the word in English; it was unmistakable. Anxiety gripped my chest, tying it so hard that I felt breathless.

"You didn't know?" His overgrown eyebrows rose. "She is in the natives' hospital in Midnapore. Your sister took her three weeks ago."

I had lost my father already; I could not bear losing my dear mother. I did not bother asking Dilip what had sickened my mother; not a moment could be wasted. If she'd left three weeks earlier, she might very well be dead.

The hospital's patient ward was almost as squalid as the bustee, filled with desperate-looking people crowded around cots. They had brought their own blankets and pots of food, making me worry all the more for my mother.

"She's still here after three weeks?" I asked the Indian duty nurse who was walking me through the chaos, as if there was nothing unpleasant about the place. "I must see the doctor to speak with him."

"Dr. McCall is busy helping others—it cannot happen today," the nurse said sharply. "Anyway, I will tell you the very same thing he would say. Your mother's body is infected with parasites; the doctors have tried a few medicines, but so far, she is not better."

She had used the English word, parasite. I had learned it in school, and I knew what it meant. Insects that sucked blood, and chewed flesh—just like the rats I'd feared in Darjeeling. We'd never really seen one of the infamous rats—but without a doubt, much tinier beasts were destroying my mother.

The nurse led me to a cot where I saw a gray shell of a woman with watering eyes that stared at nothing. I wanted to say this was not my Ma, but then I recognized the thin ivory bangle with a red strip that she always wore; the best thing she owned, the symbol of her marriage.

"Ma!" I took her hand in mine; it was hot, dry, and all veins.

Slowly, my mother's head rolled toward me. "Menakshi?"

"Yes, yes!" I bent to kiss her, trying to ignore the awful smell. "I'm so sorry, I didn't know what happened. I came for the holiday but now can take care of you. I have money you did not receive. You will not go back to that bustee again."

"No. I am indebted," she rasped. "I cannot afford a house or even a rented room. I am too much of a burden on you. I've asked God to let me die."

"I will go now," the nurse said. "I have brought soap and a bowl, in case you want to wash her. The tap is at the end of the room."

They were not even giving the patients boiled water? Despair swept me, but I smiled at my mother. "You will get better. The medicine takes some time to work."

"By now, the worms have eaten most of me." Ma sighed, shrinking even more into her cot. "I was so hungry, I ate some food in the bustee that was spoiled. So stupid of me—now I have this pain, night and day. You must not drink or eat there."

"I won't," I reassured her. "While you're in here, I'll find a better place for you to live. And we must get Nikhil away from the fields and into the boys' school."

"No," my mother said weakly, "He has food and shelter from Janak-babu. And Renuka is a lady's maid for the Barrister's Memsaheb. All my children are placed, thanks be to God."

It was as if Ma had forgotten whom we had once been. "What about the mission, Ma? Won't they help you?"

"Oh, yes. Because of them, I have this bed and medicine. And they helped Renuka find her job. Surely the doctor does his best."

I wondered if the doctor had more expensive medicines at the white hospital: something that might cure my mother that he couldn't afford to give to charity cases. I would look into that myself. In the meantime, I would reassure her that she wasn't destitute.

"Ma, I sent some letters to the house you did not receive. Janak-babu gave them."

"Read them to me, because my eyes are not working well now. I must know about Julian, Sally and Polly. And what news do you hear of the oldest boy who's in England now?"

So I read. And when I was done, she slept, and I sat with her, crying silently. After the long separation, we were finally together; but it was nothing like the holiday I'd expected.

• • •

Renuka arrived in the evening, after first stopping at the fieldworkers' hut to bring Nikhil. My little brother whooped when he saw me; then threw his arms around me and held tight, as if he never wanted to let go. Renuka wept and apologized for not knowing about my arrival, for she would have brought more food. She only had brought with her a flask of rice gruel given by the cook at the Barrister-saheb's house for Ma.

"The nurses hardly give her any food," Renuka said to me in a low voice. "And when they do come to her, they don't have enough time to sit and slowly spoon it to her."

"What do you know about Ma's condition—these parasites?"

"The doctor told me they are especially thick in privies—and the bustee has a very horrible area," Renuka said with a grimace. "These bugs are very tough, too. The doctor said that, short of extraordinary measures, the only thing that can be done is hoping one of these medicines may work. But she's become weaker since last week."

Extraordinary measures. What might they be? I doubted the nurse would tell me—and clearly, Renuka hadn't thought to ask the doctor. I would have to think about this later. I had other concerns as well.

"How did Ma come to lose the house?" I asked. Ma had taken the food I'd spoon-fed her, and was now half-asleep again.

Renuka said that ruffians had broken into the house one day when Ma was outside. They'd found all the money earned by Ma, Renuka and me kept in a small cooking pot that was Ma's secret bank. Ma had reported the crime to the police, but the criminals had not been found.

"They were very bad men!" Nikhil said, his voice serious.

"Yes, they were bad," I said, hugging my little brother, who had grown taller and thinner, too. "And how is it working in Janak-babu's fields? Are the men decent to you?"

"The big boys are good to me—but Janak-babu is tough. We must dig potatoes just the right size—not too small. I'm not so good at guessing the right size, and sometimes my trowel cuts the potato. I'm in trouble then."

Renuka had done what she could to wash Nikhil before bringing him; but when I looked at my little brother's hands, I was shocked. They were still small but marred by scratches and cuts, with solid red dirt under the fingernails. Julian dug in the earth for fun, so I'd seen his hands dirty—but not like this. I supposed there was little to be gained in cleaning under Nikhil's nails because they would be prying through the earth again by sunrise.

"Are you allowed to come to the hospital every night?" I asked Renuka.

"Of course, and I always bring Nikhil." My sister looked at me with soft eyes. "I'm so glad that you were finally allowed to come. You are so far away, and we know from the letters, it is hard."

I had not meant to complain about anything in my letters; just to paint an amusing picture of the Millings children and exotic, elegant Chinsurah. How had Renuka known, that even with three children around me, I was lonely? I reached into my bag and took out the letter into which I'd put all my cash. "Almost seventy rupees are inside here. I want to spend it to help Ma, if there's anything more the doctor can do. We won't give a paise to that slumlord Dilip."

"Sshh!" Renuka put her fingers to her lips and whispered, "The nurses will not think she is a charity case, if you talk about having such a sum."

I flushed with nervousness, because indeed, a few heads on nearby cots had been turned toward us, during the conversation. I had been thoughtless. Nobody should know I was walking around with money.

"Read the letters again." My mother's voice came quietly from nearly. "Please, Menakshi. I have been missing your writing voice."

So I read that night—all that I'd written. And after we'd kissed Mother, we walked out into the warm evening with Renuka and Nikhil.

"Where are you going to stay tonight?" Renuka asked.

"I'm not sure." With so many shocks hitting me that day, I hadn't even thought about my own sleeping arrangement.

"We will take Nikhil to his place, and then you will come stay with me." But Renuka's tone seemed doubtful.

"Would the Barrister-saheb permit it? My employers would not."

"If you stay in the servants' area, he may never know. I will talk to our bearer about it."

"Perhaps I can stay with Nikhil," I suggested.

My little brother frowned. "Didi, there are only men and boys in the tent. If ladies visit, they stay at the edge of the field, to one hut only—"

Renuka gave me a meaningful glance, and shook her head. In a low voice, she said, "Those women are involved in quite immoral behavior."

"My God!" The exclamation slipped forth from me in English. I decided to stay in that language as I spoke to my sister. "If they are behaving immorally, what kind of men are these to be raising our Nikhil?"

"The usual kind." Renuka's voice was sad. "That is why you cannot go there, Didi."

• • •

It was dark when we arrived at the Barrister-saheb's large white bungalow in the center of Midnapore. I rested underneath a banyan tree so wide it masked my presence, while Renuka went inside to plead her case to the head bearer. She came back dejectedly, saying he'd told her that under no circumstances could servants have guests.

"You have money—go to a hotel. You must be safe!" Renuka said as I bid her goodbye. I had a different idea: visiting the mission. I was very hungry by the time I reached its wrought iron gate that was decorated with a wreath and red balls. Christmas, I remembered.

I recognized the old guard, Mohan-saheb, but because it had been so long, I showed him the cross I wore around my neck and told him I'd been baptized at the Mission. I said that I'd come many miles because of a family emergency.

"Menakshi-didi," he said warmly. "You were the one who always came outside during holiday parties to leave the plum pudding. Old Mohan knows you."

"You really remember?" Tears sprang to my eyes at Mohan's kindness. "You see, I went away a year-and-a-half ago and everything changed. My mother lost possession of our house. She is very ill. Everyone's scattered."

"I keep some pillows and blankets in the gardening cottage back there for situations like this," Mohan said soothingly. "Don't worry—I'm on watch all night. You'll be safe. There is a clean privy across the way. Is there anything else you might need? Food after the journey?"

"I am hungry, but I don't want to get you in trouble—"

"No trouble at all." Mohan told me to go to the kitchen door at the back of the mission and tell cook to give me some leftovers.

I blessed him for his kindness and said I would ask permission for staying longer on the premises from the Mission staff the next morning.

Mrs. Jones, the Padre's wife, received me in her parlor at ten o'clock the next day. Although English, she seemed to come from a different country than Mrs. Millings did: an old-fashioned place where hair was gray, blouses were high-necked and skirts very long. But although the minister's wife looked drab, she always smelled sweetly of flowers. When she was once visiting our Sunday school, I asked her how she could smell of flowers when there were none in her hair. Without cracking a smile, she told me she used something called violet water. At first I thought this meant Mrs. Jones drank it; but when I saw Mrs. Millings' perfume bottles in later years, I understood.

Mrs. Jones had no questions about my ayah job, but she mentioned that she knew my mother, Mrs. Dutt, from the fine embroidery she'd brought to the women's collective. Nervously, I told Mrs. Jones that I had come from my ayah job in Chinsurah to discover that my mother had lost her home and had become ill after shifting to a harsh slum environment.

"Yes, I know. Our junior pastor has already gone," Mrs. Jones said in her strict-sounding voice. "He reported that your mother was asleep when he was visiting, so she could not pray with him. He also reminded the nurse that because she is a parishioner, her expenses are forgiven. Although I must say, we haven't seen your mother bringing in sewing or coming to church for some time."

"She is doing quite poorly. I don't think she could manage attending," I said defensively. So she was like Mrs. Millings—an older, plainer, version.

"But even before the hospitalization, she didn't come. I know she was grieved by the death of your father; prayer would have helped her with that and more."

I thought about my mother taking her children out of school, losing her house and then shifting to the bustee. Perhaps Ma couldn't bear to show her face before others in the Indian Christian community. But I could not say that to Mrs. Jones because pride was considered a sin. I needed to talk about what really mattered.

"Mrs. Jones, my mother doesn't seem to be getting any better, even after some weeks there. I wonder if the English doctor might have some other medicines that could be helpful. I have some money with me; but I've been cautioned not to let anyone know I have it. If you could look into whether I could make things better for her, I'd be so grateful."

"It's a possibility," Mrs. Jones said after a pause. "I will ask my husband if he has time to stop by the ward. He knows the head doctor very well and can get to the bottom of the situation."

"Memsaheb, thank you." Unhappily, I readied myself for the humiliating favor I had to ask. "There is another favor—I'm terribly sorry, but I'm in need of shelter, since the house is gone—"

"I heard you were in the garden shed yesterday," she said. "You mustn't stay there again. It's entirely unsuitable."

Now the degradation was complete. She was only following up on my mother's situation as a religious duty—but she saw me as forgettable as any beggar in the market. My face burned, and I began to turn away.

"Miss Dutt, there's a small bedroom in the building that we keep for visitors. I'll have it prepared—the only question is how long you think you'll need it?"

Now I was overcome. “Mrs. Jones—I don't know what to say—”

“Mary and Joseph were turned away, at this time of year. We certainly won't do the same thing for one of our scholarship girls. How long will you be here?”

“Not more than two weeks. I'm expected back by New Year's Eve.”

“All right then.” Soberly, she added, “You'll be able to join in Christmas Eve services. And perhaps you can help with the holiday party.”

“Of course, Madam.” I would do everything I could—even eat the plum pudding, if I had to.

CHAPTER TWELVE

MENAKSHI

Midnapore
Winter 1924

"Extraordinary measures. What are they?" I asked Dr. McCall.

Thanks to Mrs. Jones, I had an audience with my mother's physician the day after I'd asked for help. When I'd come, the nurse had shown me into a small office crowded with books, where a red-haired man with a tired face brightened slightly when he heard my fluent English.

"It's a figure of English speech," he said, sounding cautious. "It could mean anything. Who specifically are you asking about?"

"Lata Dutt is your patient of three weeks—and my beloved mother," I said with as much force as I could, yet still sound polite.

"Last week you told my sister, Renuka, that the medicines aren't working, but extraordinary measures could save her. I have about seventy rupees here. I know the Mission is paying for standard medical care—" I did not say typical *native* care—"but I'm willing to pay for more. Could there be a special medicine at another hospital?"

"Oh, I remember now. It's actually not a matter of medicine being needed."

"But she's dying!" I was outraged at his callousness.

"Please listen, Miss Dutt. " In a sober voice, the doctor explained that while the latest medicine he'd tried was showing evidence of killing the parasites, it was also reducing red blood cells. This was the reason Ma had become so weak.

"Do you want the medicine to kill the bugs—or to kill her?" Without pausing for my answer, he went on. "It's a miserable situation. But since you've asked, there is one last possibility. It's a modern procedure called a blood transfusion."

Dr McCall explained that blood transfusion was a medical technique that was being used for patients in Britain and Europe and America. This would be his first attempt—he corrected himself quickly to say *procedure*—in India.

"Is it guaranteed to help her?"

He smiled for the first time. "If we can find blood of the same type for her, yes. The best chance would be to test both your blood and your sister's. If one of you matches and is willing to have blood drawn, you will almost certainly ensure your mother's recovery."

I did not know what Renuka would say. But as I was nodding and saying yes, I would have my blood tested that afternoon, I was thinking, *what if something went wrong?* Not just for Ma, but me. If

I died because of this blood coming out of me, my mother would lose her financial support. She would be in a dangerous position.

"It's very safe," Dr McCall said, as if he was hearing my thoughts. "And if this works, just think. You may start others being willing to try. You could lead other families to saving loved ones' lives."

Before I could change my mind, he told me to sit down. The nurse came and wiped my arm with a wet cloth. She told me not to shiver; that I must hold still. The doctor was the one who pricked the needle into my arm. The blood that flowed out through tubing into a glass vial made me feel like I was in the midst of some kind of terrible accident. Through the shock, I tried to remember what he'd said, that my body was very strong and would make new blood to replace what was lost. Afterward he put a small white bandage over it. When I went back into town later, one of our old neighbors asked me what was wrong with my arm, and I told him I'd cut myself. I didn't want anyone knowing that Ma, the penniless widow, was being given a fancy foreign procedure that nobody else had heard of, and that probably wouldn't work.

The next day, I returned to hear about my blood and Renuka's. The doctor said that while Renuka's blood was a different type, mine was called O and just the same as Ma's. With this news, I understood the course that should be followed. And ironically, I wasn't frightened for myself anymore. I would be able to help during this time I wasn't working, and Renuka could continue earning at the Barrister's house and see Nikhil each evening.

The next day was the last one before the transfusion. I went for a final examination by the doctor and to sign a paper agreeing to the treatment. As I sat in his office, I saw the telephone on his desk. It was the perfect chance to ask Dr. McCall to ring the

Millingses and secure permission for me to stay longer, if need be. I'd likely be in hospital for just a day, but as he'd said, sometimes there were complications. But I knew one thing: if Mrs. Millings told him that I couldn't be spared, the Doctor wouldn't go ahead. So I just signed the paper and said nothing about my employers, although I asked Renuka to send a telegram if by some awful chance, I didn't do well. Surely that would explain my absence; though I knew my mistress would be angry when I returned.

On Christmas Eve morning, I made my apologies to Mrs. Jones about not being present for the evening's service and celebration. We prayed together, and then she hugged me goodbye, wishing all the best for the operation. The walk to hospital—just two miles—felt like the longest journey of my life; all the fears I'd pushed down were back. I was terrified because I knew that Dr. McCall had it in his power to kill me, no matter what he had promised. A nurse leaned in and covered me with a sheet, making me feel even closer to death. Then she put the needle inside my left arm, and began to draw blood.

Ma was lying on another table that had wheels, placed alongside mine.

She reached out and grasped my right hand. Under her breath, she told me that I should not be doing this for her. I was just a child, with life ahead of me: she was old and ready to die.

"No, don't say that! I love you, Ma." My heart was breaking at how much her life had changed and her willingness to accept it. If only my fresh blood could renew her spirit, so she could again become the smiling, confident woman I knew.

"Drop hands, please," Dr. McCall said, and then he turned to Ma. "Mrs. Dutt, it is soon your turn."

"Don't be afraid," I said, although that was exactly what I was feeling for her. I had seen my blood filling up a big bag and realized for the first time it was almost a Christmas red. Soon I would be out of hospital, attending the mission party. Plum pudding, and all the rest of it.

How dizzy I felt. The contents of my stomach rose, and I breathed deeply to keep from feeling sick. Then, I must have gone to sleep, because I did not remember anything more.

When I awoke, I was not in pain, but I felt very tired. I noticed straightaway that Ma was gone and my first fear was that she'd died. But a nurse who brought water for me to drink assured me she was doing well resting several rows away from me in the large room. A woman waiting to give birth was in a cot on one side of me, and an old lady who moaned on the other. I didn't feel like talking to either of them. All I could look at was the ceiling: among the water stains and other irregularities were two long, parallel cracks. Between these long lines was a series of short cracks crossing them. Like railway ties, I thought, but the line went only a short way.

When Renuka and Nikhil visited, they went to Ma's bedside first, and then came to mine.

"She's looking rosier than before the operation," Renuka assured me. "Your blood is making her strong. How about you? I'm surprised he hasn't let you out yet. It's been two days!"

"I feel about the same as yesterday." I did not have an appetite, but that was because I was supposed to eat only rice, and the hospital served a very poor quality. "When will they let Ma and me out, Renuka? It's Christmas Day! And did you remember to send Mr. Millings a telegram?"

"You said only to write if you were having a problem," Renuka reminded me.

I lay there, thinking. "I might be having a problem. I don't feel like myself."

"I'm sure you're fine!" Renuka soothed. "Probably best not to send them anything yet."

"I've got a feeling—"

"No, Didi." My sister said that if the Millingses learned where I was, they would be able to trace me and speak to the doctor about sending me home, even if it was too soon. Employers were known to do such things. Renuka reasoned that when I was well enough to travel to Chinsurah, I should give them the news. They might send a tonga to collect me in Midnapore, which would be less tiring than the train.

Not really, I thought, my mind turning to Ram, who was expecting me to come through the station. I would have liked to see him, even for a few moments. I had not wanted to admit it, but his attention had slightly turned my head.

As Renuka chattered on about what Ma could eat, I went back to looking at the railway track-cracks on the ceiling. I blinked, for it seemed that a train was there, on it—a strange train. I was becoming quite warm, feeling the heat break across my skin in little bumps. I remembered when Sally and Polly and Julian had come down with the pox. It was before Darjeeling, wasn't it, when Nigel was getting ready to go to England? By some blessing, he had not caught it, and neither had I. But now...

"Are you feeling all right, Didi?" Renuka put a hand on my forehead.

I whispered, "I think I may have the pox."

"There's not a spot on you. Don't worry—you've only given up some blood, that's all. You're thin. That's why you fainted so easily when you gave the blood."

"Something's wrong—tell Dr. McCall." That was the last thing I remembered saying before the train barreled down from the ceiling into my head, and I couldn't see anything at all.

CHAPTER THIRTEEN

JULIAN

Chinsurah
Winter 1924

I had thought it was going to be a good Christmas, but it really wasn't.

The trouble started Christmas Eve, when Mummy and Daddy had a fight about presents. They always opened theirs the evening before, because Father Christmas didn't bring to them, but they gave to each other. Mummy had got Daddy some golfing clubs, and he thought those were splendid. But when she opened his gifts to her—a bottle of perfume, and a silk cloak to be worn over the shoulders to evening parties—she looked strange.

"It's not really all I'm getting yet—is it?" Mummy yawned. She had been sleepy lately. I was used to this sound.

"Actually, it is." Father's voice had an edge to it that made me a little nervous.

"Are you sure that there isn't just one more thing?" She sipped the last bit of claret in her glass and smiled up at him.

"We're being careful this year," Father said.

"Really." Her voice had a hurt sound to it. "No surprises, under the pillow? Or in my stocking?"

"I didn't know you put out a stocking for Father Christmas!" I said.

Father shook his head. "That's it. I'm sorry if you aren't pleased with your gifts yet again."

Mummy's voice came out like one of those screeching garden animals late at night. "Then you'd better tell me who's getting the ruby necklace and earrings!"

How did Mummy know? I felt a slow burning on my face, and kept my eyes on the floor.

"I don't know what in hell you're talking about," Father said in a gravelly voice. "For *you* to accuse me—"

"A man from a jewelry shop in bazaar delivered the bill two days ago," Mummy snapped. "Rather extravagant, I thought—a Burmese ruby necklace and earrings set in 24-karat gold! The bill states that you took the jewelry set with you and asked them to bring the bill to our residence!"

"Let me see the bill," Father said. "If it's as you say, I'll have these imposters shut down tomorrow. No, tomorrow's Christmas. Day after that."

"You mean—there's nobody who actually received this jewelry?" Mummy still looked angry.

Father grumbled, "Do you think, if I had a mistress, I'd buy something for her right in town and have the bill sent to Government House?"

Sally, who knew perfectly well who the jewelry was for, nudged me. I considered what I should do. If Father tried to shut down the men's shop, they would tell him about me. Also, Ayah would never be able to wear her necklace without Mummy noticing.

"I bought it." My voice squeaked as I said it. I sounded daft, but I must have been loud enough, because Mummy and Daddy stopped looking at the bill Mummy had found in her desk.

"What's that, Julian?" Father asked. "Don't tell stories."

"He did buy it," Sally piped up. "I was in the shop."

"I didn't know I was doing anything wrong," I stammered. "I thought it was all right to sign when you're buying. That's how Mummy does it. And Cook signs too, when he buys wine and food."

"Ah," Father said. "So this scribble here—which I can't make out—is your signature?"

I nodded, unable to look into his face.

"But what on earth were you doing in a jewelry shop in the bazaar?" Mummy asked.

"It was when we were in town with Baby Ayah." I gulped, realizing I was about to get her in trouble, if I didn't explain carefully. "The shopkeepers were speaking English with me, and she didn't understand everything. She was very careful though, carrying the box out herself—"

Father had closed his eyes. "Julian, you will bring the jewelry box to me by the count of ten or I'm sending back every one of your bloody Christmas gifts!"

Shaking, I ran down the long marble corridor to the nursery, where I'd been keeping the gift in my almirah. I hurried back and handed the box to him, but in an instant Mummy had grabbed it and was tearing at the bright gold paper.

"You mustn't open it, it's not for you!" I cried. Now I wished I'd not said anything. I had a bad feeling, whenever Mummy got things in her hands.

She let the slim golden chain dangle from her fingers and asked, "For whom did you buy this?"

"Big Ayah. I'm giving it to her on New Year's Eve. That's when she's coming back and giving us our gifts." Tears were starting, and I wiped fiercely at them. Boys my age were too old to cry.

"Really!" Father's face was more serious than I'd ever seen it. "And did your Ayah tell you this was the kind of gift she wanted?"

"Oh, no. It's because she never got anything except sweets from Father Christmas."

"Sally?" Father asked in the same cold voice. "Did you ever hear either of the ayahs asking Julian to go to a jewelry shop?"

Sally shook her head. "No. And *please* let me give Big Ayah the biscuits I bought. I ate just a few of them, the rest are put safely away—"

Neither of them answered.

Mummy had spread out the necklace to count the rubies. In her white hands, the red stones looked flat and ordinary, not magically glowing like they had in the hands of the shopkeeper. She said, "Tubby, our son's actually got good taste."

"To the tune of four hundred rupees, thank you very much!" Father said.

"I think the set would go well with the red and black I'm wearing on Boxing Day." Mummy smiled up at him the way she looked at her friends in Darjeeling.

"You can't be serious." Father said. "It must go back."

"But Big Ayah will be upset!" I cried. "Her best present taken away!"

"She is not here now. She need never know," Father said. "Julian, this situation is a little like if Mummy went out and bought a Bentley. We can't buy things we don't have money for. It's fair enough to buy a gift for someone, but you must do it with your own money."

"Maybe Father Christmas will bring something to her hut," Mummy said with a half-smile. "She is a Christian."

From that moment, I felt like I was in a tunnel—one of those railway tunnels through the mountains in Darjeeling, where everything was still and muffled and cold. Yes, my stocking was hung at the foot of my bed that night, and in the morning it was filled with chocolate soldiers and a big orange and a real spyglass that could show small things from the verandah all the way down to the river. Sally squealed over her new dollhouse with wooden shingles and a tin roof, and a tiny family to live inside. Polly received new teddies and a plush striped tiger. Everyone had a new suit or dress to wear for the Boxing Day party. In the end, I received what I'd asked Father Christmas for: a clockwork-mechanism moving train set with six passenger compartments and a locomotive engine.

But I couldn't enjoy it, without Ayah getting to play. And knowing that when she came back, only Sally would be able to give her a present, and that would be stale biscuits.

When the jewelry shop men came to the bungalow again with a bill, there was some arguing but they took the necklace away. In exchange, Mummy got another necklace made out of sapphires and gave them some money. She wore the new necklace to the Boxing Day party.

She was getting a little bit fat. I thought the necklace, which so many other ladies were noticing, gave them something they could still praise her about. For the New Year's Eve party, she wore a different new dress that was looser, but kept on the same necklace.

She was already dressed and made up in the late afternoon of New Year's Eve, when she and Father were hosting another party, mostly for friends outside of the district. Some of the Calcutta people were bringing their children with them; Mummy said it was all right, since Big Ayah would be back and able to help mind everyone. It was high time, because Polly had a potty accident every day of Ayah's absence, in difficult places like the drawing and dining rooms, and even on Mummy's special chaise lounge.

But shortly before the guests were to arrive, the postman cycled up with a telegram that Nimu brought quickly to Mummy and Daddy, who were having their get-ready-for-the-guests drink on the veranda. Because I wanted to greet Ayah right away, I had stationed myself on the far edge of the veranda with my train. I stopped playing when I saw Mummy opening the telegram, in case she would read out to Father the news that some unpleasant guest might not be coming to the party after all.

"Damn it! Of all the excuses—doesn't she know I've heard this before?" Mummy exclaimed, and there was a sound of paper crumpling.

"Is it from Ayah?" Father asked, looking up from his eggs.

"Yes, indeed." Mother said. "Our mother very ill in hospital. STOP. Menakshi must stay extra days to recover blood transfusion. STOP. Love to children and please forgive. STOP. Your humble servant's sister Renuka Dutt. Stop, stop, stop!"

"A blood transfusion? Can they do that sort of thing in local hospitals?" Father sounded quite interested.

Mummy banged her fist on the table. "We will call her on this nonsense. Tubby, call to the hospital and see if there's any lady named Dutt as a patient. I'm only sorry we don't have her mother's name. I'd like to catch her out on this one."

"Certainly, but—which hospital would it be?" Father asked. "Honestly, Marjorie, she's got us by the ears. We'll have to wait to find out the truth."

Mummy's voice came fast and angry. "I was far too soft-hearted to allow her to go away. No doubt this fictitious operation will have complications or fail. She'll sneak back after we've left for Camp and enjoy a quiet week here by herself. And if we bring the children to Camp without her, they could die of snakebite or get lost in the jungle. It's overwhelming with three—"

"You're being overdramatic," Father said. "But if you're really concerned about three children being a load, let's send Julian to join Nigel at St Paul's this spring. It may be possible for him to be admitted mid-year."

"No!" I blurted. They had said not until the fall term. They had said!

"Julian, don't tell me you're eavesdropping again," Mummy said. "If you have something to say about school, come before us here and speak properly."

Awkwardly, I got to my feet and looked at my parents. How evil Father looked, puffing on his cigarette and glaring at me. Mummy was looking cross as well; she had crumpled up the telegram so it lay on the middle of her plate of half-eaten papaya. I could see Nimu standing in the back of the veranda, waiting with his head bowed to take away the plate and probably tell all the servants what he'd heard. I hated the thought of not being able to read the telegram for myself, never to know if the words Mummy had spoken aloud were true.

"I won't go away to school! I can learn all I need from Ayah," I said.

Mummy and Father exchanged looks; then Mummy said, "Julian, don't be silly. If it's not St. Paul's, it will be St. Joseph's or another good school in Darjeeling. Of course you can't be educated by a native servant. She's only pretended to believe that you can read and write."

"But I can read!" I snatched the telegram up from the plate before she could stop me. I began parroting back aloud the words she had just read. They were typed in plain black capital letters, looking plain and hard. "The only word I don't know is trans—"

"Not bad reading—and that word is transfusion," Father said. "It means taking blood from one person and putting it into another person whose blood is sick and needs to be changed. Did you know there are different types of blood, Julian? You can only change blood with someone of the same type."

"Oh!" The idea was both frightening and thrilling. I liked it when Father talked to me about things other than school or cricket. "So Ayah's giving her blood to her Mummy? Will there be any left for her?"

"We're not sure," Father said, and I gasped. "No, your Ayah will be fine. We just don't know the specifics of her mother's situation."

"Hush, you're making me sick," Mummy said, standing up. "I've got to feel better before the party starts. I'm going to my room to lie down."

I believed that Mummy was telling the truth. I'd heard her being sick in her bathroom some mornings during the fall. Ayah had heard it, too, and she said to be especially gentle and quiet around Mummy, and then she might start feeling better. Now I wondered if all that had happened during Ayah's absence was making Mummy feel worse. And this only made me more upset about how things would be if Ayah did not come back.

Perhaps it was like I'd heard Mummy say before, that she only took care of us for the money and in her heart was dishonest and unreliable. And now, because there were too many of us for Mummy to manage by herself, I'd be the next one sent away.

As the next week began, Ayah was still missing. Mummy cancelled going to Camp with Father to stay home with us. Each morning after breakfast I began my vigil on the bungalow's veranda, watching for Ayah to come walking up. I pictured her not with the small shoulder bag she'd left with, but a heavy valise full of presents for us; and her bow-shaped pink lips would be whispering apologies. *I'm so sorry, Julian. I was wrong to stay away. I do love you very much; more than your sisters or anyone else in the world.*

On Sunday morning after we'd come back from church, I hurried to my watching post as usual. And after lunch my heart skipped a beat, for a horse-drawn tonga was coming up the drive. I trained my new spyglass on the carriage.

Unfortunately the tonga's passenger was not revealed to be Ayah, but someone unfamiliar wearing a man's straw hat and a khaki suit. I strained to see the passenger as the tonga continued up the drive, passing Sally who was scratching letters in the dirt with sticks.

When the passenger stepped down from the tonga, I saw that he was a light-skinned Indian. His eyes crinkled at the sight of me and he said, "Hey, Julian."

"Who are you?" I demanded, confused because the voice did not sound quite Indian, nor English.

"I'm your old friend from the train, Ram Hollander!"

"Where's your cap and uniform?" I demanded, because I felt annoyed not to have recognized him.

"It's my day off." He grinned at me, and now I remembered the many times he'd given me sweets. "I didn't see your ayah coming back through the station last Wednesday, so I came to pay my respects. She is off duty on Sunday afternoon, isn't it? Do you think your parents will allow me to say a quick hello?"

"Ayah never came back." There was a lump in my throat as I said the words, trying to keep from crying.

The smile was gone from his face—like that. "Do you mean she's not back, even four days later?"

"She sent a telegram, but Mummy thinks it's a lie—"

"Julian, don't talk to strangers!"

It was Mummy, come out with a fresh suit of clothes for me in hand; I imagined she was about to tell me to wash up and get ready for going to somebody's house for tea.

"I'm sorry, Mrs. Millings, but he knows me. I know you all, actually. With all due respect, I'm Ram Hollander from the Bengal-Nagpur Railway—"

"Oh, you're that little ticket inspector."

Ram nodded, and I could tell from his expression that he had not like being called little.

"Has there been a railway accident? Do you need to report to the Commissioner?" Mummy asked.

"No accidents, rest assured. I came because I'm concerned about Miss Dutt. What's this Julian said about her staying on?"

"Master Julian shouldn't have said anything," Mummy said

coldly. "And while you really have no business coming here to see one of our servants, I don't mind informing you that Ayah is no longer working for us."

"Are you saying she resigned? I'm afraid I don't understand. She only said she was going to visit her family through the New Year."

"She didn't return when she was supposed to; that is grounds for dismissal, and she knows it. The telegram allegedly sent by her sister was her false excuse. And now I must ask you to leave. Julian, it's time to go inside. You must have your bath before the Morgans arrive. Baby Ayah is almost finished with Polly; your turn is next."

I looked at Ram Hollander. His color was very high, and his eyes were shining, as if he were about to weep. He didn't even know what the telegram said. Part of me was thrilled that I had read it myself, and knew every word including all the stops. But I couldn't repeat it to him with Mummy glaring at me.

I looked down our long driveway where the hired tonga still waited on the gravel path lined by potted tulips. In my most obedient voice I said, "Yes, Mummy, I will take my bath. But may I first please pick a few tulips for Mrs. Morgan? She does admire the tulips. I could make a bouquet for her."

Mummy smiled faintly. "All right. But only the ones that are very long and leaning to the ground."

Given my release, I began wandering down the driveway. First I went to Sally, who was taking the doll for a ride in her new little red cart. I whispered to her that I'd give her some of my Christmas toffees if she'd tell Mummy I was just on the other side of the house. What I did next was go to the distant side of the tonga, where none of them could see me. As light as a cat, I placed my feet on the edge of the high carriage and climbed over and in. The Bengali driver, who was humming a song, did not hear me as I hid on the floor, covering myself with a wool blanket I found folded on the seat. All the dust made me want to cough, but I breathed carefully, so I did not.

A few moments later I heard footsteps on the gravel, and the tonga lurched as Ram got into it. In the distance was Mummy's voice calling, "Julian? Julian? Where are you?"

"He went round to the other side of the garden for more flowers, Mummy."

As the tonga bumped down the driveway, Ram Hollander said nothing. As the driver turned a corner, he asked in broken English, "Where, Saheb?" In Bengali, Ram Hollander answered something. Then under his breath he said, "Bloody bitch."

Was it Ayah or Mummy whom he was angry with? In any case, it was time for me to reveal myself. I lifted my head out of the blanket and said, "Who are you talking about?"

"Hey! You mustn't come with me!" Ram pulled the blanket off me. In Bengali, he said, "Driver, turn back!"

"Wouldn't you like to hear about the telegram?" I offered.

"Yes—No, Driver, don't turn yet." Ram's strong hands lifted me up and onto the seat next to him. "What is it, lad? Do you know something they didn't tell me?"

"Ayah's sister said she can't come back yet because her mother is in hospital. She is going to have to switch her blood."

"The mother is changing her blood?" Ram paused. "What the hell? I never heard of such a thing."

"It's called transfusing. Do you think Ayah's lying about it, like Mummy believes?"

He shook his head. "If Menakshi allowed her sister to send such a telegram, it must be fact. But where is the hospital? She rode off on the westbound local. Did she ever tell the name of her village to you? Think, Julian. It's very important."

"Ayah's not from a village. She lived in a town where her father was a postman. She went to a girls' school—"

"The Methodist Mission School." Ram snapped his fingers and looked almost cheerful. "I remember her saying this! Perhaps there's a mission hospital in Midnapore. It would likelier be there than in a village."

"Let's go there to find out!" I said. "You must take me. I must see her again!"

Ram laughed, but not in the happy way he had on the train. "And be charged with abduction of the Burdwan Commissioner's son? Sorry, lad. I'm going to have the driver turn around and take you home."

"No, Ram! No!" I broke down in embarrassing tears. I couldn't bear to stay with Mummy and Father, but not Ayah. He only patted me on the back and said, "I'll have something for you the next time you're on the train. In the meantime, if I find Menakshi, I'll give your love."

"Ayah," I corrected in a whisper. She should not be called Menakshi or Miss Dutt or anything else he might want to call her. I imagined him saying *Darling* or *Sweetie* or *Love*, the way Mummy and Father used to, ages ago.

As the driver whipped the horses to hurry faster back to the bungalow, I punched Ram twice in the side. The first hit was for taking me home, and the second was for going after this woman he called Menakshi. He gritted his teeth, caught my hand and held it tightly. I struggled, feeling furious: not just with Ram, but myself. He didn't deserve the information about the telegram. I'd come to realize that if I didn't lose Ayah because of Mummy's anger, I would lose her because of him.

CHAPTER FOURTEEN

MENAKSHI

Midnapore
Winter 1924

I knew that we had reached Chinsurah Station because of Ram Hollander's voice. He was calling, "Menakshi! Time to wake up!"

I had been so tired. Julian's head was on my shoulder, and my own head on top of his. What a small world of warmth and affection, as we nestled in the last moments before Mrs. Millings would return from the dining car.

"Menakshi, I've come all the way for you! Please open your eyes."

I blinked my eyes open, and the first class train compartment vanished. I was in the dingy white hospital room with tracks on the ceiling. Leaning over me, instead of the doctor, was Ram

Hollander, wearing an unfamiliar grey coat with a white shirt and black tie—and also an expression that looked like a combination of eagerness and worry.

"Hello, Mr. Hollander." Still thinking I was dreaming, I glanced on either side of me and saw the same old lady on my left, and a different woman patient on my right. So he really had come all the way to my village and the hospital. "What's happened here?"

"You had a complication: an infection that led to a fever. I spoke to Dr. McCall and he says you're going to be fine. And maybe . . . you could call me Ram again."

"My mother—did she get this fever too?"

"No. She has made an excellent recovery and moved into the mission. She did not want to leave you, but the doctor thought it was a risk for her health to stay overly long in this place full of sick people."

"How can she be staying in the mission?" I asked, feeling a wave of relief wash over me.

"Mrs. Jones gave your room to her—permanently. When she is strong enough, she will take on work stitching the pastor's clothing and all the special cloths used in the church—what are they called?"

"Vestments," I said. "Oh, that is quite a good position for her. She likes to sew. Tell me, what day is it?"

"Wednesday the 8th of January. And it's 1923 now. Happy New Year."

"Goodness, I've been here a long time," I said, feeling my calm slip away. "What will the Millingses say? Probably they've hired somebody to replace me."

"Would that be so awful?" Ram's voice was unexpectedly hard. "They aren't worth half of you."

"When I can leave this hospital?" I said quickly, for Ram's comment flustered me. "I have Christmas presents for the children in my bags which are with my sister. Have you met her, too?"

"Yes. Renuka's very nice, and so is Nikhil. I got him a railway cap, and he says it fits."

"That was very kind of you," I said, thinking suddenly of Julian. How he would have loved such a cap for Christmas.

"What are you thinking, Menakshi? You look sad."

"Oh—just about the children not knowing I'm here. I want to send my own telegram to them telling what's happened, but Renuka's not keen on them knowing."

"Yes. She told me she's worried they'll force you back before you're well. Tell you what: I'm passing through Chinsurah tonight on the northern run. I'll send word to them. But Menakshi, if they don't take you back, you mustn't worry so much."

He did not understand that I'd been everyone's support. Shaking my head, I said, "Of course I must! Ma may have a place at the mission, but Nikhil works too hard for a little boy. He has no education. I cannot help him if I earn nothing—"

"I have savings. Menakshi, you can rely on me."

"I am not a family member of yours. I cannot take your charity!" I said, because that surely was what he was thinking, seeing a poor Indian ayah sick in a hospital bed.

"No, of course not!" Ram's face flushed. "It's not what I meant. Just that— when the doctor tells me you are well enough to travel, I will come here and bring you back to Chinsurah on the train."

"It's not your normal route," I protested.

"No, it isn't. But I can request for leave for family emergencies."

"You know that I'm not family—"

In a soft voice, Ram said, "I hope that will change."

• • •

Four days later I left, wearing Nimu's wife's sari, washed clean and starched by Ma, who was doing well at the mission. Surrounded by my family at Midnapore Station, I wept—but with joy rather than sorrow. Ma was cheerful and living in a safe, clean place; Renuka and Nikhil would continue with their work nearby and visit with her as often as they could. I could go away satisfied, knowing I had shared something with Ma worth more than any amount of rupees.

"Be careful with him," Ma murmured in my ear, as she held me close.

"Little Julian?" I asked. My mind was already turning toward him, Sally and Polly. Despite my anxiety about their parents, I was looking forward to seeing the Millings children.

"No, I mean Ram!" she whispered.

I was exasperated she would speak this way, after all Ram had done. "Ma, he will not take advantage of me. He's a decent and responsible man."

"Yes! That is what I tell you: do not do anything to lose him."

"What?" I was shocked. Surely she could not be speaking favorably of someone who was not purely Indian.

"He cares for you, Menakshi. Even if your father were still alive and looking around in the community, he could not find you a better one."

Ma liked Ram. She was saying this with her careful words, and in the way she smiled especially long at him when he took my elbow carefully as we boarded the train. But she didn't understand that any sort of connection with him would be difficult to maintain. I would probably not be able to ride Ram's train until the annual Darjeeling trip in April. Then it would be another three months until I came back down. I also had a suspicion that Mrs. Millings might revoke my Sunday afternoon breaks. And if that were all she took, I would consider myself lucky.

CHAPTER FIFTEEN

JULIAN

Chinsurah
Winter 1925

I should have been on the veranda when she came back. I could have got to her and stopped everything that came next. But I had spent so many hours waiting in the sun that Mummy said my skin was too burnt. I was no longer allowed outside and had to take buttermilk baths twice daily.

The day that Ayah came home, I was in the tub with my spyglass, leaning back and looking at lizards on the ceiling. On the other side of the bathroom door was Baby Ayah, arguing that I should let her in to make sure I was cleaning myself.

"I can wash myself!" I shouted through the door, although I had no intention of touching my painful peeling skin. All I wanted to do was lie with my head on the towel rest on the back of the tub, watching two lizards. They were just like Father and Mummy: moving, watching, never touching.

Through the door I heard Baby Ayah exclaim. In Bengali, she said to someone, "She came back?"

"Who came back?" I called out, because I suddenly had a prickling feeling that had nothing to do with the sunburn. "Baby Ayah, tell me!"

She called through the door to me, "Julian, your favorite is finally here."

I rose up so fast that I sent a wave of water onto the floor. I slipped getting out and landed on my hands and knees. I struggled up and realized I couldn't go to see her undressed. Grudgingly, I unlocked the door and Baby Ayah came in, wrapping me up in white cotton. I held still as she put on my underclothing, short pants, and a shirt, because she could do it faster and better than I. Then I'd rushed out of the bathroom, passing my sisters who were playing jacks in the long marble hallway. I was glad they hadn't heard Ayah was back yet; I wanted to be the first one to greet her.

When I reached the veranda, I was surprised to see Ram the trainman. He wasn't in uniform and had sweated so much in his white shirt that there were giant gray circles under his arms.

"Where is she?" I demanded. Had Baby Ayah tricked me?

"Miss Menakshi is inside with your mother. How did you burn your face, kid?"

Relief flowed through me, and I flung my arms around his waist. "You brought her home, then. Thank you, Ram. Thank you so much."

"It's nothing to thank for. Miss Menakshi had to wait until the doctor thought it was all right. You won't believe what suffering she went through." Ram talked on a bit about something called a medical operation. "You be gentle when you say hello. You mustn't grab her as fiercely as you did me."

It struck me then that he did not need to be still waiting. He had brought her home. That was well and good, but now he should go away. I asked, "Why are you still here?"

He shrugged. "Just making sure everything is all right. When's your next Darjeeling trip? I'm looking forward to seeing you in the usual compartment."

I made a face and said, "I'm going early. They're sending me up to St. Joseph's School."

"At least they're not packing you off to England like they did your brother." Ram winked. "Maybe they'll send Ayah with you for the school journey, to keep you safe."

I knew why he wanted Ayah riding on the train with me. I could not forget he was my rival.

"Bye!" I spun around and walked back into the house, not rushing this time because I didn't want to be heard. Mummy might be talking to Ayah in one her bedroom or one of the parlors. It was too late to get a hiding spot under a table, but I meant to fit myself in the shadows somewhere and hear whatever was going to be said.

• • •

The afternoon sun had washed the pale blue walls of Mummy's bedroom into an even lighter color, the way that heaven looked in religious pictures. Mummy sat at the stool before her dressing table, wrapped up in her silk robe. Facing toward her was Ayah, wearing the same sari with small flowers that she'd worn when she'd gone away. But instead of a braid, she had put her hair into in a high, shining bun that made her look like a strange person. And her arms seemed thinner, just like her face.

"Memsaheb, I apologize. I tried to explain about the hospital in the telegram." Ayah's voice was very low.

"What I remember is you left this house giving me your promise that you'd be back on a specific day." She pointed her finger fiercely at Ayah. "You were not the one who fell ill and went to hospital; your mother was. Staying with her to undertake a risky operation was your own decision."

I had felt so lonely while Ayah was gone. Now that she was back, I wished Mummy wouldn't speak in that way. She should just be glad, like I was, that we could go on.

"It wasn't a risky operation. My blood donation saved my mother's life." Ayah's voice didn't sound right; it was trembling. "The doctor could not release me until he was sure I was strong enough to come back. I feel dreadful about it. I missed the children."

"They once were your priority. Apparently not anymore."

"Mrs. Millings, I don't know what you want in order to make up for my absence. Perhaps you would like to take away my Sunday afternoons, or count the extra week and a half as part of next year's leave?"

"Next year's leave?" Mummy laughed in a broken-sounding way. "Do you think I would ever let you go off again? No, that won't do at all."

From the way that Ayah's shoulders had gone up, I knew that she was as tense as Mummy. Still, her voice remained polite. "I imagine it may take you and the Saheb some time to think about this. May I go to the children now? I am concerned about them—"

"I don't need help deciding anything." Mummy's voice was sour as the lemon juice she painted her freckles with. "You shall work for the next three months without any pay. Or complaints."

Ayah was quiet for a long moment. Then she said, "I cannot work without pay. It's not a matter of my doing without luxuries: I must support my family with my earnings."

Although she saved her pay, I had never believed Ayah really worked for the money. I thought it was because she wanted nothing more than to care for me and my sisters. Now, I felt worried that it was something different.

"No," Mummy said. 'There are limits to my tolerance. You must work off your debt."

"I—" Ayah turned away from Mummy, and I saw her face was crumpled like one of the tulips after the sun had gotten to it. Ayah wiped her hand across her eyes, and just stood there, shaking. I willed her to look at me through the crack in the door, to see me. I would make her feel better, once Mummy was through.

"If you won't pay wages, I must end my service to your household." Ayah sounded like she was trying not to cry.

At that, Mummy rose up. "You won't! You will not walk out on me and my children!"

Now I was shaking. Hadn't Mummy said several times that she was sacking Ayah for not coming back on time? Her turnabout was confusing me.

Ayah's head shook slowly. "I am decided. After I see the children, I should go. And as you've never liked me, I think this would be a relief."

"You're right that I don't like you." Mummy's voice was fierce. "I hired you for your English, and that was a mistake. But if you're so intelligent, why don't you understand about giving notice? Who will be here for the children you love?"

I hated the words Mummy was saying, but I did agree with the last point. She should not leave us.

"You still have Baby Ayah. And I believe you might send Julian to school this year—so it will be just the two girls, won't it?"

The way Ayah said it made me shiver; as if she thought that my going away was all right, that she didn't care about what happened.

"I don't give a damn about Baby Ayah. I am telling you not to go." Mummy shook her head, and the little golden curls bobbed, just like one of Sally and Polly's dolls.

"I said I would be happy to stay, but I must have my weekly wage. As I said before, I'll give up my Sundays—five months of them, I believe, will erase my debt—"

"Who are you to give me a schedule?" Mummy snapped. "I set the rules of this house."

"Of course." Ayah turned toward the door.

"I am the one who gives you permission to do things!" Mummy's voice rose. "If you attempt to leave this property, the darwans will stop you!"

In a shaking voice, Ayah replied, "I am not a slave. And in truth you should be thankful for everything I've done for your children, including protecting them from you!"

"What nonsense!" Mummy shot back, but I knew that it was true. I remembered how Ayah always managed to pull us away to a different place when Father was angry; how she'd kept Sally from falling in the river; how she had gently lured away the monkey who climbed inside Polly's pram. Mummy never would have noticed any of these things happening or known how to take care of us.

"How many times have I steered them away from noticing your special gentlemen friends?" Ayah went on, her voice growing stronger. "I see you're getting big now, aren't you? Has Mr. Millings noticed?"

And at these words—which were utterly confusing to me—then Mummy sprang up from her stool and lunged at Ayah. As her hand went toward Ayah's face, Ayah caught her outstretched hand and held it high; I knew that with a twist of her hand she could have broken her. Mummy's face was still, as if she feared for herself. And I knew what Mummy saw: a strong brown woman who could tear her apart, destroy everything about the way we lived.

Ayah dropped Mummy's hand and swung around, crossing to the door in wide strides. As she pulled the door open she saw me huddled in my hiding place against the wall.

"Julian! Did you hear us?" And she reached down to embrace me, but I rolled away on the floor. I got to my feet some distance from her. "Darling, come with me. I'll explain."

"Come with you?" I skipped after her, my spirits rising. Ayah would take me away, and I wouldn't have to go to school in Darjeeling! That was why Ram was waiting on the veranda; to take us both away!

Ayah was already a hall's length away, going straight for the nursery; she broke into a run when Mummy came out of her bedroom. But Mummy did not chase her; instead she rushed to the front of the house, calling for Nimu.

I ran after Ayah and into the nursery, where she was gathering up her things. "She's called for Nimu. I think she's going to get him to stop us!"

"She can't possibly." Ayah had taken the laundry basket and tossed out our soiled clothing and towels. Inside she was putting the little things from her special drawer; the framed picture of her father, her books, some clothing and a silver-backed brush. "I'm sorry, Julian, but I don't have enough room in my valise. That's why I'm using the laundry basket."

"I need you to pack my valise," I said, waiting for her to go into the almirah's top shelf and get it down for me. But she didn't.

"Ayah, I said I need my valise. I'm packing, too."

"It's not yet time for going off to school, is it?" Then Ayah stopped packing the laundry basket and looked at me. "Oh, dear. Did you want to leave the bungalow with me?"

"Yes. We always travel together! I'm good on trains, you've always said."

"Dear Julian." Ayah squatted down in her old, comfortable way, and drew me into her arms. "I don't know how much you overheard. I can't work here anymore, unfortunately. And as much as I'd like it, I can't bring you."

"You're lying! Mummy wants you to stay caring for us. You are the one who decided to go. I heard it!" And now the tears I'd held back began squeezing out of the corners of my eyes, and I felt a familiar ache in my chest.

There was a clattering sound, and then one of the bearers and Nimu were in the room. The men's faces were worried; they spoke such fast Bengali with Ayah that I could not understand, except for *acha, acha* at the end. *Yes*, Ayah was saying. They all agreed on something.

"Are you staying?" I asked hopefully, as Nimu picked up Ayah's laundry basket, threw a towel over the top and left the nursery.

"I hope that I can always stay here." Ayah put her hand on my chest, and I felt the warmth through the thin cotton I wore. "If you keep your heart open, a part of me will never leave you. And Julian, please tell your sisters goodbye from me. There is no time for me to see them."

"It's not fair," I cried. "I loved you. I waited for you—"

But Ayah had already picked herself up and was running toward the kitchen. Inside were all the servants; some were weeping along with Ayah.

"Quickly!" Nimu said in Bengali, pointing out the back door. A hired tonga was there, and I could guess who was inside. And I knew then what they were going to do; go out the broken back gate and through rough pasture to avoid being stopped by the property guards.

I could not understand what Ayah said to Nimu, but I heard Sally and Polly asking Mummy where Ayah was. And then Nimu was pushing Ayah out the door, and she was running fast to the tonga and taking Ram's hand as he lifted her up.

"Where is that wretch?" I heard Mummy shouting from deep in the house. "Where has she gone?"

•••

Soon after that, I found out that I was not going to school in Darjeeling but would join Nigel after all at St. Paul's. Mummy and my sisters would travel with me on the steamer *Percival*. Then Mummy and Sally and Polly were going to live with Mummy's parents, my Grandparents Ainsley, in Devizes. How many tears

Mummy had cried, for she did not want to leave India or Father. He would stay in our bungalow alone and continue working as the Commissioner of Burdwan. I did not care if I never saw him again; what hurt was that I would leave India with Ayah still in it.

To catch the steamer *Percival*, we took the Down train to Calcutta, which meant we would see Ram Hollander. When he came to look at our train pass, I would shout at him for what he'd done. If he hadn't stayed waiting with the tonga that afternoon, Ayah would have had no choice but to stay working for us. And after a day or so, Mummy would have stopped being cross, and Father would not have gotten the idea that all of us except him should move to England. All these things I wanted to tell; but instead of Ram walking through the hallways, an Indian ticket taker was there, taller and with spotty skin.

"Where's Ram Hollander?" I asked when he came to take our tickets.

His eyebrows shot up at that and he said, "Not working today, young Master."

"Is he on holiday?" It frustrated me that I would not be able to tell him what he needed to hear before I was gone for good.

"He is not employed with Bengal-Nagpur Railways anymore."

"As well he shouldn't be!" Mummy said from her place in the bench across from me.

The new ticket inspector's eyes widened, and I realized he might think our mother, the Commissioner's wife, might have had something to do with Ram Hollander's disappearance. The fellow bobbed his head and blurted he would send porters upon arrival in Calcutta to help us. And then, with a clatter of the door, he was out.

"What did you do to Ram Hollander?" I asked Mummy, who was once again reading her magazine.

"Absolutely nothing. Your father was the one who made the telephone call. He agreed with me that it isn't safe to have the railway operated by people causing mischief." Mummy gave me a close-mouthed smile.

I thought about everything that had happened since Ayah's Christmas holiday. I wanted to tell Ram how angry I was; but since he was sacked I would never have that chance. "He was only helping Ayah. And now—now we don't know where either of them went off! I won't know where to send letters from school to Ayah."

"She doesn't want letters from a little brat," Mummy said. "It's time for you to grow up into a mature boy, Julian. You don't need your ayah anymore."

But I didn't want to grow up. I wanted things to be the way they were before Christmas. But there was no point in telling Mummy.

Without saying anything to her, I stood up from my seat and carefully walked out into the train corridor. Through the wide-open windows, I felt the air rushing and saw ponds and banana trees and rice fields click, click clicking away. Soon I would be far away from Ayah—wherever she had gone—and Father in his bungalow with tulips on the drive.

But I knew that I would find her. I would finish school and come back to India and train for the railways. I might be the first white ticket taker for the Bengal Nagpur Line in the new independent India—but why not? Ayah had told me that I could do things nobody would ever expect.

I could imagine how we would meet. She would be riding on a train; never third class, but maybe second or interclass. Whether she was wearing her white sari or the one with flowers, I would know her; and although I would be a tall young man, she would look into my eyes.

"Julian," she would whisper. "I never meant to leave you."

And I would tell her the same.

EPILOGUE

MENAKSHI

Penang, Republic of Malaya

1952

Closing the book, I shook myself back to my real life. Mrs. Abbot had a handkerchief pressed against her unseeing eyes, and I realized that although her eyes don't work to see, they still could weep.

Julian's stories had lasted much longer than two cups of tea. They'd involved almost a fortnight's worth of reading, time that went so swiftly that I could hardly stand to stop to take the last afternoon ferry back. I kept the book at Mrs. Abbot's place because I did not trust myself to read the stories alone without collapsing. But on the ferry rides to and from Georgetown, I tried something I'd never done before. I took one of my children's old, half-used school notebooks—the ones I couldn't bear to throw away. And on those clean lined pages, I wrote out my own stories in response to each one of Julian's. In bed at night, after Ram slept, I went over them with a pencil and crossed out the wrong words. Then I slipped out of bed to my daughter's old room, where we kept the typewriter she used for schoolwork on a stand, and I tapped out my handwritten stories onto crisp white stock.

Mrs. Abbot never knew that every few afternoons, I was reading her my own tales. I could never have spoken spontaneously about my ties to J. Winslett and his book, but I wanted her to know the full story.

Julian had been honest about almost everything. He had changed the family's surname and first names, except for his own. For some reason, and kept all the house staff names true, including mine. Was it because he thought I'd never come to read the story? He might imagine me still in India caring for little children, no longer running but walking slowly, my braid turned gray and thin. Even after Independence; because what else was I trained to do, except raise children?

He didn't know that after leaving the Winsletts' home, I had a miserable two months with Ram's sister and her husband, who insisted that a cross-race engagement would only bring us woe. When Ram was sacked from the Bengal-Nagpur Railways, their prediction seemed to be coming true.

But Ram's supervisor, Mr. Green, hadn't really wanted to dismiss him; he'd been forced to carry out the Commissioner's request. Privately, Mr. Green gave Ram an excellent letter of reference to use for an application to the Malaya Railways; and within days a telegram came offering Ram and any dependents sea passage to Penang, and a job on the newest line. After our wedding at the Midnapore Mission, with all of my family and some of his around, we shipped off to Malaya, bringing Nikhil with us.

The new railway line boomed, and within five years, Ram had become a station master. By then we had a three-year-old daughter and a newborn son, and Nikhil was preparing for the entrance examinations for university in Kuala Lumpur, where he would eventually study dentistry. We had enough money to send for Ma and Renuka to visit, which they did about once every decade. Ma had remarried a nice gentleman—an Indian deacon within the Mission—and was busy with social life in the town and caring for Renuka's two daughters. My sister married a shy, very scholarly court reporter who'd fallen for her when he'd come round the barrister's bungalow on business. I missed them, but tried not to think about the great distance between us. Both of my own children had married and their own offspring; being a grandmother suited me. Outside of the frightening war years, I'd had a very good experience. A life of looking forward, not back.

But now Julian had reminded me of the life that I had almost forgot. And I grieved at my shortness with the boy as I rushed to free myself from his house.

"I wish you could find another book like that," Mrs. Abbot said after we'd finished. "It's been ages since I had an ayah of my own. I never thought about how I spoke to her. I'm sure I was rude."

"You are nothing like Mrs. Millings. I would say you have a generous heart like the Mrs. Jones character."

"Maybe, maybe not. I should like to write a fan letter to the author. May I dictate it to you?"

"Yes, and I'll be happy to type it, if you like that." For along with Mrs. Abbot's letter, I resolved that I should handwrite one of my own. I would tell Julian that although his story made me cry, I liked it. And if Julian wrote back, and if Ram thought my stories were good enough—I might send them to him to read.

I can't guess what could happen next. All I know is that I'm no longer trapped in silence of the past. Through the decades, I've felt a small hand reach out and tug on my braid. Now I can reach back and finally pull the boy close.

India Gray

INDIA GRAY

Assam, India, 1945

As the C-45 descended, I wanted to look away, but I couldn't.

Just underneath, abandoned shops and houses were missing their roofs, offering a view straight into ruin. Along a splintered railway track, train cars had fallen on their sides like overripe fruit. The town of Jorhat had been thoroughly pummeled.

Such graphic pictures of the Japanese bombings hadn't made it into the newspapers; too demoralizing, I imagined. Surveying the devastation, I reminded myself that I'd wanted to come here. I'd spent days convincing Simon that I'd be a strong volunteer, and then he in turn had convinced the hospital.

I flinched as a horrible grating noise began.

"It's only the wheels," Simon yelled cheerfully, his Oxbridge accent causing some American soldiers to turn around. "Your first aeroplane flight is almost over. It's better to keep breathing."

I hadn't realized that I'd been holding my breath. I exhaled, praying for a safe landing. I felt the dampness of my hand evaporate inside my husband's warm grip.

For a moment, the plane was still and quiet. Then it nose-dived, and my stomach rose into my throat. The plane's front wheels hit the ground hard enough that I bounced up out of the seat. The C-45 careened forward, continuing along the runway as the passengers applauded.

"Gentlemen, welcome to Jorhat!" the pilot called over a crackling loudspeaker.

"We're safe," I murmured, still trying to convince myself.

• • •

A young American sergeant met us on the runway and we spent the next hour in a military car traveling on through the wreckage. The car groaned its way up into the foothills of the great mountains we'd flown over. At last, we reached our private quarters: a small timbered cottage inside an abandoned tea estate. The house reminded me of a fairy-tale cottage, perhaps the one that belonged to the three bears who'd gone away, leaving it to Goldilocks.

After throwing open windows in rooms that reeked of mildew, I got a better sense of the place. The cottage's small rooms were furnished in simple Indian-made rattan pieces suitable for Europeans. A row of gilt-edged family pictures was placed along the stairway. From the dark hair and eyes of the tea planter's wife and two young daughters, I guessed that this had recently been the home of Anglo-Indians.

I knew without asking that we'd been billeted in such a spacious home only because we were married, and because Simon was on loan from the Indian Civil Service. Exactly what my husband would do with the Allied military forces, he hadn't yet said. I knew not to ask: secrets were par for the course in his work.

Within a few hours of our arrival, an American officer stopped in to welcome us with a bottle of brandy. Major Chris Jones, a smiling blond man in his late thirties, shared what he knew about the home's prior residents. When the bombing had commenced, Mr. Peter Lindsay, the tea plantation manager, had taken his family to safety at another tea plantation in the South Indian hill station of Ooty. The tea plantation and cottages had been left to the protection and use of the military.

"Many locals have fled, but not all," Major Jones said. "Now that you've arrived, Mrs. Lewes, there should be quite a few locals coming to beg for work."

"Actually, I think I'm set. I've hired two women already." I described how two bright-faced sisters, Bindu and Araj, had arrived within the first hour of our opening up the house. Bindu wanted to cook, and Araj said she had cleaned for another British family in the area. After the government had canceled tea harvesting in Assam two years earlier, they'd not had regular work.

Our conversation had been conducted in a mix of my Bengali and their Assamese, with Simon chipping in a few words of English. After we'd come to terms on a weekly wage, I gave the women money for shopping. They left with a plan to return the next day with brooms, dusters, soap and whatever food they could gather from the local market.

After hearing our report on Bindu and Araj, Major Jones nodded. "You can trust the people here—they're mighty glad for some company and aid after the bombings. Still, you might find the best provisions are in the commissary."

"We'll have to get Kamala some kind of official identification," Simon said. "I just hope that volunteers will receive the same kind of ration card as the rest of us."

"I'll make sure of it." Major Jones gave me a long look. "I must admit it's a surprise meeting you, Mrs. Lewes. I hadn't known what Simon had up his sleeve."

"You didn't think he'd bring a full-time hospital volunteer?" I asked.

"No, I mean—you're Indian, aren't you? Full-blooded or half-caste?"

For an Indian living inside India, it felt insulting to have to define myself to the man who truly didn't belong. With a laugh, I said, "I was just wondering the same about you, Mr. Jones."

"My wife isn't half anything," Simon said smoothly. "She's got twice the intelligence, charm and heart of any woman I've known."

"And twice the sex appeal." Christopher Jones gave a low laugh. "I'd think carefully about allowing her to volunteer in a hospital filled to bursting with men. There's no telling if you'll get her back."

I gave him a cynical smile, and Simon must have been disturbed, because the next day, he returned from a morning visit to the hospital with a plain white sari with a Red Cross insignia and a dowdy, long-waisted blouse.

"I don't know if this would make me look more like a ghost or a nun," I said, handing him back the garments. "Do you mind terribly if I dress the way I'd like for the volunteer interview?"

"Of course not. I was only trying to help you fit in," he said.

"Well, the Red Cross hasn't actually approved me. I'll wait to hear what they say before I put on a uniform!"

For the interview, I chose a practical, dull green cotton sari that I'd had for several years. It was a comfortable fabric for the humid atmosphere. Cotton was not something an Indian lady would typically wear for a professional interview, but there hadn't been any silk saris to buy for the last few years; India's whole silk harvest was going to military parachutes.

Miss Allen, the American nursing volunteer administrator, looked a few years older than me—thirty, I guessed. Her hands didn't show an engagement or wedding ring, but they did sport nails that were painted the same red-orange as her lips. My first American lady. I gazed at her, wondering what she would wear if not the tailored gray suit with the Red Cross patch.

She was looking me over too. "I think your sari is impractical for hospital work. I don't know if you wear it for, uh, religious reasons—"

"I do not."

"We do have some official Red Cross saris—your husband asked me for one—but I'll give you a regular uniform. What size are you?"

"I'm afraid I don't know European sizes." I felt light-headed with the thought of wearing a garment that ended at my knees.

"American sizes are different. You're probably an eight."

She went into a cupboard and came back with two uniforms folded within paper bags—ensembles of a jacket just like her own to be worn with either a matching skirt or trousers. She also slapped two small plastic-wrapped packages on top. "Nylons. You don't have any, do you?"

Inspecting them, I said, "Are these the famous nylon stockings that are in shortage everywhere?"

"Yes, indeed. You'll have to take good care of them, because they're rationed. Now, about the slacks: they're new to you also, I'm sure. They are mandatory wear during monsoon months, as the mosquitoes are so terrible. Slacks are also key when bicycling. Your quarters are a little bit distant, I heard."

"Yes. We're staying in a cottage within a tea plantation." I felt another flutter. I'd seen British women war volunteers cycling in Calcutta, but never Indian women or girls. I had not come to Assam to change myself at all, but it looked unavoidable.

I sat in a camp chair across from Miss Allen's desk while she recorded details of my clerical skills and languages. When she heard that I knew Hindustani, Bengali, Oriya and a bit of Urdu, she turned from her typewriter.

"You'll be a real asset to the nurses; most of them only speak English. You'll be able to talk with almost all the patients—excepting the South Indians. They mostly speak Tamil."

The sincere warmth, and the challenge she'd posed, made me immediately want to learn Tamil. "About how many South Indian troops are being cared for here?"

"We have a Madras regiment that served at Imphal and a handful of others who arrived from Singapore and Malaya. I'd say we have fifteen Tamil speakers at the moment, but it's always changing."

I held up a finger to halt the quick-talking lady. "Sorry, I don't understand. If they're foreigners, how did they become part of the Indian Army?"

"It's not been reported in the papers—censored," she said,

holding a finger in front of her glossy lips. "When the Japanese gained control of Southeast Asia, they promised any captured soldiers of Indian descent serving with British colonial armies that they could go free if they'd join a new army: the Indian National Army. We've got a large number of INA prisoners of war recovering in the wards."

"I see. So they're Indian National Army—not Indian Army, who are part of Allied forces, along with Britain, China and the United States."

I wouldn't tell her that my good friend Supriya Sen had slipped across the Indian border to join up with the INA. Supriya believed that, despite its sponsorship by Japan, the INA were the only force that could free India. After all, this army was headed by Subhas Chandra Bose, the valiant nationalist nicknamed "Netaji," which meant "honored leader."

"Last July, hundreds of prisoners surrendered or were captured at Imphal. Many of them were suffering from wounds and other injuries and diseases. So they're being treated here. Some people don't like us doing anything for them, but taking care of political prisoners is part of the laws of war. We treat patients to the best of our ability, without discrimination."

"I agree with that," I said, liking Miss Allen's forthrightness. But at the same time, I had a new worry. Simon had worked on propaganda to counter the INA from his office in Calcutta. Perhaps his work assignment here had something to do with the INA patients.

After filling out all the necessary papers, Miss Allen gave me a tour of the recently built single-story hospital and outbuildings. Each ward held a field of iron cots with a few electric fans whirring overhead. Nurses wearing the khaki uniforms of the Women's

Army Corps, or Red Cross gray, moved between the cots, their slow, quiet movements reminding me of peasant women tending to delicate young rice.

As we stepped into the trauma recovery ward, one man's ragged sobs cut the air. He cried on, and I was dismayed to see nurses moving past, behaving as if they hadn't heard.

"Mother, Mother," he cried. "My foot. It hurts. . ."

"He's in such pain!" I said to Miss Allen. "Isn't there something the doctors can do?"

"No, because it's a ghost pain. Lieutenant White had to have an amputation due to a snakebite. It will take time for his nerves to adjust."

"Are you a nurse, Miss Allen?"

"By training, yes; now I've moved into management. But whenever patients fly in, I look at their background and the medical report."

I hoped against hope Supriya hadn't been admitted. Although if she had, it would mean she would not return to the war. Hesitantly, I asked, "Have you had any women patients?"

Miss Smith raised her eyebrows at me. "Not here. But a lot of Australian nurses died after Singapore fell. It was a horrible situation—you don't want to know, dear."

In the malaria ward, Miss Allen explained that almost eighty percent of the hospital staff had caught malaria at least one time. She said that Simon and I should burn oil torches inside our quarters at night and never forget to use a mosquito net. Trousers were required daily wear for both genders during monsoon season. She advised that tall boots with high socks underneath were the best guard against leeches, which were very active in damp, forested areas. A broken-off leech head could live, burying itself and creating a devastating infection that went through tissue and down to the bone.

"For every man who dies from battle trauma, twenty-two more perish from diseases. We're going to bypass the wards for infectious diseases—dysentery, cholera and such. But in the next building we have men recovering from typical war injuries—grenades, bombs, bullets and knives. They've been airlifted here from Burma and most are eager for company."

As we continued our tour, Miss Allen described the horrors of jungle life: the heat, rain, venomous snakes and insects, and appalling shortages of food, water and shelter. By the time the walk-through was done, I wondered whether these patients would ever be brought back to normal conditions.

"I hope I can help distract them from what they've been through," I confessed to Miss Allen. "But it sounds like they've been left in a terrible state."

"You'll be fine, Mrs. Lewes," Miss Allen said. "I've heard about how you've worked with famine victims back in Calcutta. Your husband said you've got nerves of steel. You'll find yourself in good company here."

• • •

When I returned with Simon to the cottage that evening, we found that Bindu made a fine dinner of steamed brown rice, wild greens and potatoes. She also asked if we wanted the two small river fish that her brother had caught. I said yes, indeed, and cooked them myself with mustard oil and onions.

"Did you know this hospital is treating prisoners of war?" I asked Simon after he'd told me about his day.

"Yes, mostly survivors picked up in Burma. That's why I came."

This was more information than I expected. Cautiously, I ventured, "But I thought your office was not on the hospital grounds."

"It's in the brig—that's the military term for prison. As they recover, they'll be interviewed there."

"Who does those interviews?" I sipped my tea, trying to seem like I was only casually interested.

"I'm in charge." There was a hint of pride in Simon's voice. "They called me in because the previous fellow in charge had some trouble with malaria. He's been taken off duty."

"How will you conduct such interviews? You barely speak Hindi," I teased.

"Thankfully, there are interpreters for almost every language spoken by Indian troops," Simon said. "My main responsibility is reviewing the transcripts, checking with the Indian Imperial Police about past crime records, and then choosing their colors."

I pondered the strange term he'd just used. "Choosing colors. Is that racial?"

"Not at all. These men may be from Malaya or Singapore, but they're all subjects of the Crown and treated as such." He paused. "If an English officer walked away and joined the Japanese, he'd also be charged."

As I separated fish meat from the tiny, bony skeleton, I thought about leeches burying themselves into men. It seemed cruel that people had survived such pain only to face military charges. "Then what does it mean to choose colors?"

"After their interviews, each of the former INA men is classified as white, gray or black. Those we call 'white' joined up to avoid torture or death at the hands of the Japanese. I'll recommend charges be dropped."

"And what of the 'grays' and 'blacks'?"

"Gray is a designation for those who genuinely wanted to aid the Japanese in their invasion of India. After hospital treatment, they may have plans to disrupt the government and work in the Axis' interest. They aren't necessarily going free."

"Do you think it's right to hold someone in prison based on their political beliefs?"

Simon poured milk into his tea. Stirring, he said, "Believing is different when it involves action. For example, back in Calcutta freedom fighters were arrested for cutting telegraph wires and causing disruptions at British-owned businesses."

"Yes, I know." What he didn't know was that I'd sat in a North Calcutta coffeehouse and listened to students talk about the necessity of these maneuvers. Young, politically active Bengalis revered Mohandas Gandhi, but most of them worried that a passive approach to freedom would never bring change.

Simon tasted his tea and frowned. "It's very difficult, working in the gray area. Many law-abiding Indians naturally wish for independence. There's no law against such a desire. But for men in the military, making a choice to abandon their comrades to help the enemy . . . it's more complicated."

"How does a soldier become classified as 'black'?"

"They're 'black' if they actually accomplished meaningful harm to our troops, or behaved cruelly to the men serving under them. At war's end, they'll face the same legal action as any soldier or officer who committed treason."

"You mean, if the Allies prevail."

"Kamala!" Simon's fork clattered on his plate. "Do you think we won't?"

I pushed the rice to one side of my plate, and the greens and potatoes to the other, making a map. Using my fork as a pointer, I said, "Our men are slipping into Burma, but the Japanese are prepared for their arrival. They've got the guns and bombs and minefields. The killing goes on and on. Who really wins?"

"Nobody will win if we don't get far enough before the monsoon," Simon said. "Six months of high rivers and jungles of mud means nobody can go in either direction."

"I heard a bit about that from Miss Allen," I said. "The patients here are proof of what happens during months spent in the jungles without real shelter. They're wet most of the time and subsist on whatever plants and river creatures they can get. Insects and snakes are all too ready to make work of them—"

"My goodness, you heard a lot of horror stories in the hospital today," Simon interrupted. "Are you sure you want to volunteer?"

"Of course." I took a deep breath. "I'm only telling you this because I loathe hearing you talk about sorting the prisoners as if they're books. They're men who've gone from hell to a miserable purgatory where their future is decided by one very powerful Englishman who's never been to war."

The color rose in Simon's cheeks, and I regretted my words instantly. It had been my mother-in-law's heartfelt wish that Simon never join the army because her husband had died on the battlefield in France.

"I'm sorry, Simon," I said, stretching out a hand to touch his arm. "My words flew out before I thought them through. I don't want you to be a soldier. You're no less of a man for what you do with the civil service."

Simon ignored my touch; he laid his cutlery on the plate as if we were in a restaurant, waiting for a waiter to whisk everything away. Then he pulled a package of Lucky Strikes from his shirt pocket, something he never did at our home table because of my dislike of smoke.

Lighting a cigarette, he said, "When you've been here longer, you'll understand that for these fellows, the hospital is a sanctuary. They aren't hostile to us. These lost souls are very grateful to be back in a clean, warm place with food and water, treated according to the laws of war."

"You may be right." The fact was, I didn't yet know. I sensed that my work would give me a chance to decide for myself.

• • •

The next morning, I rode along in the car that came for Simon. I could see the American driver straighten a bit as he took in Simon's tall frame, the finely chiseled head with close-cropped dark brown hair and piercing blue eyes. Simon's light wool suit was three years old, but his Oxbridge intonations seemed to give him several stars' worth of rank.

I wore my Red Cross uniform with the skirt and the nylon stockings. I told myself that I was covered up because my legs were covered in fabric, but I still felt vulnerable. The chauffeur who drove us avoided looking at me: perhaps he sensed my discomfort, or Major Jones had spread the word about the humorless nature of Simon's one hundred percent Indian wife.

Miss Allen made no comments on my appearance but presented me with a small portable typewriter and a basket that contained paper and pens, novels, and playing cards. An orderly followed with another basket holding freshly made American pastries called doughnuts. The scent of sugar mixed with hospital antiseptic and sickness as I set out on the designated route.

My first visit was a sapper from Yorkshire whose legs had been blown off in a minefield. As I read aloud the stack of letters from his parents and fiancée, his face remained a gaunt, unseeing mask. The nurses assured me that he still had vision and the use of his hands, but he didn't show any interest in writing a letter, nor did he want a book or a doughnut. Miss Allen had prepared me for reticent patients. Later on, I would be tasked with writing to his family on his behalf.

The next British soldier was recovering from a bullet wound to the stomach. He had no letters waiting for him, nor did he want to write. All he wanted was a companion for cards. I played for half an hour, enjoying his smile when he won twice.

And so it went. By one o'clock, I'd finished in the trauma ward and used my ration coupons for a dull lunch of bread and beans. I next visited a ward where patients were recovering from environmental troubles: malaria, snake and insect bites, and various skin diseases.

It was also the day I met my first Indians.

I began my rounds with a Madrasi who'd fought for the Indian Army during the long siege of Imphal. He was recovering from malaria. In English, I apologized for not knowing Tamil. He smiled weakly and answered me in the same language.

"That is all right. These foods you carry, Memsahib: what are they?"

"They're called doughnuts and are like your South Indian snack called *vada*, but quite sweet. And please don't call me Memsahib—my name is Kamala."

"Very well, Kamala-*akka*. That is what we call older sisters in my native language. Call me Swaroop."

Swaroop enjoyed the doughnuts and followed them up with long, enthusiastic sips of tea. He was a cheerful soul who already had a long letter written in his mind. I gave him paper and pen and returned in a while to place his letter in a stamped, addressed envelope.

After Swaroop, I spoke in Hindi with a group of Punjabis whose charts were all stamped in red with POW. They all had the same problems: starvation and Naga sores, the ulcers that grew and destroyed skin after entry was made by sand flies or mountain leeches.

Major Harunjit Singh, a gray-bearded Sikh, was the chief spokesman for the Punjabi contingent. Together we decided how to explain the men's medical diagnoses to their families without causing worry. I would write for those whose hands were bandaged.

"And Kamala-*behen*—please tell them the British are not hurting us."

I thought about what Miss Allen had said about not letting political sympathies become part of my dealings with patients. But like Swaroop, he was calling me by the endearing phrase that meant "sister," and I wanted to help. "Tell me. I don't understand."

His hooded eyes regarded me gravely. "Our families should know that the Britishers haven't put us in chains, denied us food, or beaten us. But we also must not allow them to believe we might travel home soon."

"I know you're all prisoners. I want to help write the exact messages you need to send your families." I looked straight into his eyes, willing him to understand that I held sympathy, not distaste.

"The letters will be in Hindi?" asked his friend, Captain Devgun, in a hopeful tone.

"Of course. I shall handwrite everything in Hindi, if you wish."

• • •

Five hours later, my shift was done, and I reported to Miss Allen. Putting down the typewriter I'd carried through many corridors, I suddenly felt an ache in my shoulders. I rubbed them, watching her leaf through the finished letters.

"Let's see what you've got for me, Mrs. Lewes. Twelve handwritten letters from our patients is excellent for one day."

"Most were glad for the chance to write," I said, feeling warmly toward her. "And I've got seven letters that I typed."

"You're a good typist." Mrs. Allen sifted through the papers; she had instructed me to leave envelope addressing to her office. "They'll go out on tomorrow morning's cargo plane to Calcutta."

I watched her separate out the three letters I'd written for the Punjabi patients. These she slid into a drawer.

Looking at her inquiringly, I said, "Those are also finished and stamped, and I've got the addresses on the corner."

"The investigators have us hold on to the POW letters."

"What does that mean?"

"This is a military operation. The commanding officers are reviewing prisoner communications."

Simon's words came back to me. White. Gray. Black.

"Is something wrong, Mrs. Lewes?"

I'd worked so hard on these letters, telling the suspenseful stories of the men, letting them speak of their fears and also their hopes for the future. Forcing a smile, I said, "No, not at all. I can't believe the first day went so quickly."

"By the way, you were asking yesterday about other women?" Miss Allen said. "Tonight seventeen hundred there will be a hen party in the canteen for nurses and other female staff. If you join us, you'll be able to start making friends."

She didn't know that I'd been asking about women only because I was concerned about Supriya—someone I never wanted her to know about.

Reluctantly, I attended the canteen gathering, where the nurses came mostly from the United States and the remainder from Britain and Australia. There were also two nurses from Bombay who were Anglo-Indian. I was the brief object of curiosity as I introduced myself, but it was clear that my position as a married Indian lady put me in the realm of uninteresting.

That night, I arrived home on foot to find Simon eating biscuits and drinking tea.

"I was worried," he said, getting to his feet. "I stopped by the volunteer ward, and you were nowhere to be found. All those things Major Jones said about men staying in hospital . . ."

"No need to worry at all. I had a busy first day, and Miss Allen encouraged me to attend a hen party. Sorry, I should have sent a message to your office about my plans."

"Hen party?" Simon's eyebrows rose. "Don't tell me you found a chicken for supper."

I laughed. "No. Just a flock of nurses eating crisps and drinking beer."

"Sounds delightful," he said, smiling and coming over to me.

His arms went around my waist, and he kissed me. "Yes, you're telling the truth."

"What do you mean?"

"I taste Pabst. Shall we?" He inclined his head toward upstairs, where the bedroom lay.

I adored Simon, but that night I simply couldn't bear to be intimate. And I couldn't joke anymore either. So I played the dutiful wife. "You haven't had a proper dinner. What did Bindu leave?"

"Not sure. The house was empty when I arrived."

I looked under the lid of the pot on the hob. "Just brown rice. There must not have been anything in the market. Let me look in the larder—I think there's some potato and onion. I'll make a quick *sabzi*."

• • •

The next morning, I caught sight of several Indian patients sitting in a row of garden chairs behind the main hospital building. A familiar rose-colored turban made me pause. Major Harunjit Singh, Captain Devgun, and Sergeant Gondal of the INA were taking in some damp, fresh air. Their ward nurse, an Anglo-Indian named Nora, was wheeling out more patients.

"Good morning, Kamala-*behen*," said Major Singh, nodding at me as I came forward. "Thank you very much for your kindness yesterday."

I spoke quietly to them in Hindi. "There's nothing to thank me for. I just learned that someone shall review your letters before they're mailed. I also don't know when the letters will reach your families. I'm sorry."

There was a moment of silence. Then Captain Devgun, the younger officer, spoke.

"So you are saying the writing of letters home is useless?"

"They might be mailed. It's not clear. But what you say in the letters could be used when the government decides where you go next. You may be questioned about it." I explained about the classifications based on the POWs' feelings about the freedom struggle and the specific acts they'd committed during the war. I also explained that soldiers who'd joined up only because of the threats of death or abuse would be labeled as "white."

"Oh, an Englishman already questioned the circumstances of how we came to join Netaji's army," Major Singh said. "A tall, thin fellow. Not army."

The major must not have caught his surname during the interview—or he would have suspected a link between us. Or did he? I felt myself begin to sweat, aware of the badge on my jacket that said *K. Lewes.*

"He had a translator ask many questions, trying to get us to say which location Netaji might have gone," Captain Devgun added. "Of course, we did not reveal anything that could compromise him."

"We would sooner die than sacrifice Netaji," Major Singh said.

Out of the corner of my eye, I saw Nora heading toward us.

"They're just giving me some extra information for letters," I called out cheerfully to their nurse. "I will bring them back to the ward when you want."

"Thanks, Kamala! By noon, if you don't mind!" She moved on to another patient.

I returned my attention to the men and whispered, "Don't you think that you were dying for the Japanese? When you were found, you had no weapons or food or supplies. The Japanese did not furnish you with proper uniforms to protect you against winter in these mountains."

Major Singh shook his head. "They had nothing for themselves, either, because they did not understand the nature of Burma and Assam. In these mountains, one can only fight for six months a year. The rainy season is dead time."

I was on the verge of tears. "Please do not speak so strongly of your allegiance. If you do, you're in danger of imprisonment."

Major Singh replied, "I will speak my heart about what happened, and why we turned to Netaji as a way to win India's freedom."

"To live truthfully is the responsibility of our faith," said Sergeant Gondal.

"Do not worry for us," Major Singh reassured me. "It was good of you to speak. We will make sure the other prisoners learn about the color classification. Every man will decide for himself what to do with such knowledge."

• • •

As I'd hoped, the information spread from one prisoner to the next about the color classifications. Many veterans were so upset about the intrusion that they declined to write or dictate letters. Following Miss Allen's orders, I wrote letters to their families under my own signature about the patients' medical conditions, their emotional spirit, and the likely timetable before discharge. A few INA veterans still wrote letters, but these communications were all about inquiries into their families' well-being—and the bad news that the Indian Army would not be providing them with pensions, due to their desertion.

• • •

Simon noticed that I had become quiet and brooding and sought out ways to distract me. One Saturday morning, he found a key to the locked shed behind the cottage and wheeled out two bicycles. From the kitchen window, I watched him fill the tires with air and oil the chains. There was nothing to do but try, and as I wavered, falling again and again, I found I really wanted to learn. Cycling was something that children could do, and it would give me more independence.

It took a week of practice before I could balance myself without him running behind as my protector. I reached the hospital in half the time now, and I had the choice to return home on the cycle whenever my work was done, instead of waiting for Simon.

But the rutted paths and obstacles of the countryside made it easy to tip over. And sometimes, when I pulled my bicycle free from roots and stones, I saw things that didn't belong. The tarnished silver bracelet. The tin ration can stuffed with an INA leaflet. And worst were the small, slender bones that Simon agreed were probably the remnants of human feet.

Logically, I knew that this section of Assam was safe, hundreds of miles from the fighting in Burma. But the land told me that somebody—perhaps an INA scout—had already been through. Or were the renegade warriors still around?

It made me think more about Supriya.

I quietly brought up her name with some of the INA veterans, but nobody knew her. And then I learned to stop asking.

"I hear you're looking for someone," Miss Allen said one evening when I came in with my usual raft of letters. "Why is that?"

"What do you mean?"

Unsmilingly, she said, "You're asking the POWs about someone in particular."

Who had told Miss Allen, when she rarely entered the wards? It had to be someone who understood Hindi, Oriya, Bengali or Urdu, the languages I spoke with Indian patients. I thought about the Anglo-Indian nurse who was usually in the ward with soldiers recovering from skin infections and wounds. While Nora barely spoke Hindi, her understanding could be better than I'd realized.

"I ask about many missing soldiers," I said, looking Miss Allen straight in the eye. "So many of the patients have brothers and cousins enlisted in the Indian Army and hope to learn if they survived, perhaps by going with the INA."

"Really. I thought you were asking about someone named Supriya Sen?"

I thought fast. "Actually, Priyom is the correct pronunciation of that name. Priyom Sen is a soldier taken by the Japanese whose cousin was a patient here and died yesterday. His last wish was to know if his cousin survived. Sorry, did I do wrong by asking?"

Miss Allen paused, and her round blue eyes looked at me seriously through the thick lenses of her glasses. "You can speak their language, and that makes closeness come easy. I know you mean only the best. But we cannot forget that the patients who are war prisoners have reason to manipulate our behavior."

"Of course they can, Miss Allen." I paused. "I've heard that often from my husband. He's leading the investigations in the brig."

"Oh, really. You're telling people that?"

"Not often, but . . ." I had thought it would make me seem irreproachable.

"What those men do is classified, Mrs. Lewes. Please remember."

• • •

March turned to April, and Simon's colleagues asked him to stay on. The Calcutta office agreed. Everyone talked about victory being near.

But the pending monsoon would not wait for the Allies. As Simon had said, once the rain fell, tanks and jeeps would become mired in mud, jungles would flood and rivers would rise too high. Soldiers wouldn't be able to move forward, and perhaps not retreat. Supplies couldn't reach them. For vast numbers of men to be trapped away from their bases during monsoon would almost certainly mean death.

But for now, we had no rain, and Saturdays were still for cycling.

One weekend, Simon suggested an excursion uphill. The route wouldn't be easy, but he'd heard from some officers that the views were well worth it. I dressed in my uniform trousers anyway, and loaded the bicycle baskets with a picnic lunch: hard-boiled egg sandwiches, tea and unnamed wild berries that Bindu assured us were edible.

"We won't be able to do this in a few weeks when monsoon hits," I said, huffing a bit as we climbed the rough earthen path.

Simon slowed to a stop and hopped off his Raleigh. Wheeling the bicycle along, he said, "Imagine all this covered in water."

I slipped off my cycle to take the last bit with less exertion. "Yes. No cycling then."

"It feels to me that by the time the rains come, you and I will be moving on."

"Home to Calcutta?"

He gave me a long look. "Perhaps only to clear out the flat. Independence is right around the corner, and there will be no place for an Englishman in the ICS."

The prospect he held out made me pause. "But that could be several more years. Freedom's been held out as a promise since this century began."

Simon unloaded the picnic blanket tied to the back of his cycle and carried it over to a mossy area. Shaking it out, he said, "After what the Indian soldiers have done, laying down their lives for a country that has considered them incapable of government . . . Everyone knows it's time. Not just for India, but the other Crown colonies, too."

"I'm glad that you say that," I answered, taking over the tiffin boxes from my bicycle basket. "But really, we shouldn't have had to lose thousands in order for this to happen. If only freedom for India had come years ago; perhaps there wouldn't have even been a war in Asia."

"I disagree," Simon said. "Don't believe the Japanese would have changed their feeling about expansion. They might have gone after India much earlier—and been successful."

"But India would have been an immense, Asian-controlled power. Diplomatically, things might have been stopped. Now we have a wretched situation for people everywhere. Including the men you are interviewing in the brig."

Simon paused again. When his words came, they were strained.

"I know you think I'm condemning them. But it's been just the opposite."

"How so?"

"I was brought here to uncover scheming renegades. But I've come to believe that most of those men have perished."

I shook my head, not understanding.

"The INA officers whom one would expect to be gray or black . . . I can't label them that." Simon looked out at the horizon. "They'll soon be released to détenu camps for out-processing and release."

"Do you mean you haven't found any grays or blacks?"

"No. For these survivors, it seems clear that joining up was a punishment in itself."

What had changed Simon? Was it the testimonies of the men, or the horror of their physical condition? Surely, his decision couldn't have been influenced by me.

"It will be very good for them to get home." There were many other things I wished to say: that I admired him for going against expectations, for his compassion, for the way he'd grown from being a stereotyped civil service officer to someone who really understood people.

"Bittersweet," Simon said. "Just as it will be for us. I truly loved our Calcutta flat. Those lovely, high-ceilinged rooms. The view to the gardens. Our very own mango tree."

Wrapping my arms around his waist, I said, "We could stay. Together, we could start our own business—perhaps a bookshop? You already own thousands of very special volumes."

"Who would buy books from an Englishman? I'm sorry, Kamala. You married the wrong man, if you meant to stay in India."

"That's not true," I said, meaning it.

• • •

In late April, the air grew heavier than I'd ever felt it in Calcutta. The American and British pilots departed daily, dropping supplies to the Allied units that had already landed in Burma. The code name was Operation Dracula, but so much blood had already flowed in the Asian war theatre that it was hard to imagine there was anything left to suck.

Inside the wards, it was quiet, and the patient load was decreasing. On an afternoon when the sky was especially gray-black, a sense of energy hung overhead.

"I also heard that the rains could come today," Miss Allen agreed when I told her my prediction that the monsoon was imminent. "I don't have far to go, but you do, honey. Go on home now—those letters can wait till tomorrow."

As I hurried home, lightning zipped and thunder rumbled, telling me of strikes. Still, no rain. But the winds were fierce. As I entered the cottage garden, I pulled the cycle under the shelter of the veranda and turned the key to go inside the house.

A giant wind rushed through the bungalow, banging every opened door closed, and open once more. And then the rains hit the ground outside: a barrage that turned the view beyond the windows into an utterly watery blur.

Bindu and Araj and I rushed to close the windows, but only in areas where rain might cause damage. Otherwise, the cool air was a very welcome invasion. My spirits rose, as they always had from childhood, whenever this most welcome season came. But then I remembered what the rain meant and wondered how soon it would be flooding Burma.

I thought of Simon, too, and the difficulty he'd have coming home, now the storm was on. Looking out the window, I saw that the dirt road I'd cycled home on had turned into a thick slick of mud. Children from the nearby hamlet sloshed through it, laughing, turning their faces up to the rain.

The rain was steady and hard. I lit a lamp and made some tea, but I waited to cook dinner. At nine o'clock, I sent my helpers home; they only had to run a few hundred yards. Now, what to do?

The house had no telephone, so I couldn't call the brig's head office and ask whether Simon was still there. Briefly, I considered going out in the rain to see if I could trace him. I imagined an accident, Simon and the bicycle sliding into a swelling stream. Or perhaps the water had come up too high over the bridge for him to safely cross. And thunder was so loud and near—where exactly had the lightning struck?

I doubted that Simon would gaze out a window with a cup of tea, were I missing in a storm. Hurrying upstairs, I unpacked the rubberized canvas raincoat and helmet that the hospital had issued me months earlier. There were also rubber Wellingtons, so ugly and oversized I told Simon I'd sooner get soaked than wear them anywhere. But now I put them on.

Outside, I was quickly soaked. Water seemed to enter every pore and to fill my eyes. I sloshed away from the cottage and onto the gravel road that had transformed into mud. The Wellingtons sank, and I had to pull with tremendous force to raise each foot for another step.

A solitary figure was moving through the countryside: a soldier, judging from the Indian Army raincoat. But the man had no official hat, nor an umbrella. He seemed too tall to be Indian, unless he was Punjabi.

One of the prisoners of war might have mounted an escape. Perhaps he had waited for monsoon, reasoning that the heavy rain would deter searchers from looking for him. Any I.N.A. veteran would understand how to survive the jungle in rough weather.

I could have told the POWs that they wouldn't be thrown into prison, after all was said and done. I'd stayed quiet, realizing that betraying Simon's confidence could be dangerous for him and me. *All will come out well enough in the end*, I'd thought.

But now I wasn't sure.

I kept my eyes on the figure, whose head stayed down as he plodded on. He didn't see me. But fifteen feet away, I recognized the manner in which he moved. It was Simon.

He recognized me in the same instant and rushed forward to grab hold of me. "For God's sake, what are you doing outside?"

"I was worried. And look, you have no umbrella, and your cycle is gone—"

"No umbrella because of caution about lightning! And I was fool enough not to keep a raincoat in the office—one of the captains lent this to me."

• • •

We left a wet trail from the front door up the stairs and into the bathroom, where we pulled off our soaked garments and threw them in the zinc tub.

Simon began drying himself with a towel. Grinning at me, he said, "Actually, I'm late because there was a celebration."

"But the monsoon means another stalemate," I said.

"We just found out the Indian Twenty-Sixth Division took Rangoon yesterday!"

"Are you sure?" There had been so many rumors.

"The Japanese had already left, so nobody even had to fire a pistol. There was a bit of a party in my office. I wasn't in a hurry to leave, but as the rain increased, we all got orders to go home."

"Did you walk the whole way?"

"No, I left the cycle under cover in the building and got a ride on the metal road. Just had to slog for the last half mile."

"If the Japanese are gone, what about the INA?"

"Five hundred INA remained behind to prevent violence and looting among the local people. Apparently the women's regiment traveled to safety in Singapore by lorry, and the men's unit went on foot. Nobody could say where Bose went."

"Of course not," I said. They were no longer going to fight, but they would not give up their leader.

• • •

Inside the hospital, the mood was cheerful, although the Indian National Army survivors were even quieter than before. Their gamble for freedom had failed; they'd seen their friends die, suffered severe injuries, and now would return to India still under British control.

In early May, shortly after we'd learned that Adolf Hitler and Eva Braun committed suicide, the Punjabi officers were judged well enough to be discharged. Miss Allen had the address of the détenu camp in Bengal ready for me to give to them and also provided paper and pens for letters to their families.

"These letters will be posted right away," I said to Sergeant Gondal, Captain Devgun and Major Singh when I came upon them. The three were dressed for departure later that day in simple civilian shirts and trousers. The major's hands had never recovered from their injuries, so I told him I would write to his wife, if he gave me permission.

"Are you sure?" Major Singh looked hard at me.

"I'll put them in the mailbag myself. It's such a relief to me that you're almost home."

"If I do reach home, I will ask my wife to write a letter from me to you," Major Singh said.

"I hope families will be able to visit the détenu camps," I said. "These camps are just a short stop before your release back to freedom."

"We didn't know you had an English husband," Captain Devgun said.

I nodded, waiting for accusations of betrayal. The men had every reason to despise me.

"He mentioned you to us," Captain Devgun continued. "He asked whether you had written letters for us."

"You said yes, didn't you?" As he nodded, I said, "It's the truth."

"He said that you were a beautiful writer," Major Singh said. "Or he said you were beautiful, and a writer. It was difficult to understand all of his words. He is learning."

And so was I.

Bitter Tea

BITTER TEA

The Americans were the ones who sent the *maulana* to Shazia's hometown.

Not on purpose, though. Baba had explained that that it was all because of the war in Afghanistan. On the day the Stars and Stripes rose in Kabul, *Maulana* Ghulam Ali Qadir crossed the Khyber Pass into Pakistan. The tall, thin cleric arrived in Shazia's family's village with a dusty, hard-eyed entourage: Afghanis with Kalishnikov rifles, Arabs with their checked *hijab* head coverings, and the rest wearing army fatigues, mercenaries from countries that nobody dared ask about. People called them *talibs*, but it was hard for Shazia to understand how anyone could call these fearsome men scholars of religion.

The *maulana* had been invited to stay in their town by Abdul Khan, the *malik* who owned most of the area's poppy fields. Ammi said it was a blessing that none of Shazia's grandparents were alive. They didn't see the long-beards exile Mustafa Khattak, the town's popular deputy commissioner, shouting to everyone that they'd come as liberators. *Liberate us from what,* Baba had grumbled—*the right to electricity?* The load-shedding and resulting blackouts were worse than they'd ever been, due to the fighting between these newcomers and the Pakistani Army. Though it seemed that the Army wasn't fighting very hard against them. Shazia kept her ears open, and she'd heard rumors this was also because of the Americans, which didn't make sense at all.

Hush-hush, Baba had murmured in response to her questions, lying back on the cushions after a skimpy dinner of rice, a *sabzi* of greens and potatoes, and watery lentils. *Hush!* her father repeated, adding, *even the walls have ears.* Shazia's younger sister Zara had looked around then, eyes wide, as if the mud walls of the house had suddenly sprung to life.

"I will call him Gaq," Shazia said, using the initials of his name, which when pronounced the English way, made a sound like the ugly black crows who pecked through garbage.

Zara had giggled, and Baba raised his eyebrows. But instead of reproving his daughters, he said, "Gaq it is, then. Still, be careful."

When the sisters lay under thick, hand-sewn quilts in bed at night, Shazia and her sister had concluded that Baba meant to warn them that life in town was dangerous in a way that it hadn't been before. When Shazia was Zara's age, girls covered their hair with loose scarves and dressed modestly in *shalwar kameez* suits, but they'd been allowed to walk freely outside and even play cricket. Shazia had attended a girls' school and shopped with her mother at the village market. But two years ago, when she was twelve, the girls' school was closed upon the *maulana's* order. Now females couldn't leave their houses without a male relative. This was highly inconvenient, because Shazia had no brothers, and Baba worked ten hours a day overseeing the farm fields he owned.

And farming was tough these days, with many of his workers succumbing to pressure to sign up as *jihadis*. The onions and mustard greens that Baba did grow often rotted before reaching market, and he lived in fear of the roadside bandits, who'd taken from him before, and were now rumored to be delivering goods to newcomers.

Things had changed slowly for the worse, ever since Gaq had made himself the village's de-facto mayor. One of the first laws he'd enforced was that all females leaving their house must have their ordinary clothes covered by a dark blue or black *burka*. The first few times Shazia had worn her *burka* she'd felt like an awkward, life-sized badminton shuttlecock. The *burka* was so awful that it made going out something she no longer enjoyed. And many forms of movement were forbidden; women couldn't play ball, dance, or even ride on the backs of their fathers' or brothers' bicycles. Not that there were many cycles left. Asif Rashid, the town's chief constable, had taken almost everyone's bicycles away, because boys in outlying districts needed a way to reach the *madrassa*, the religious school the *maulana* had established in the hopes of creating more young male *jihadis*.

Shazia knew that both her parents were unhappy that the school she and Zara had attended had been closed, but the few in town who'd complained had been the victims of verbal abuse and even beatings. Baba was away from home for long working days and compulsory prayers at the mosque. When he came home, he had little to say. Ammi was in the house more than she wanted and seemed to have grown into herself, the fear curving her back prematurely. They were all trying to look smaller, less likely to be noticed. Her 32-year-old mother's face was becoming pinched and dry, and not just because the Zadeh family's shop no longer carried Pond's Cold Cream.

• • •

Still, when Baba was away, Ammi didn't seem to worry much about whether the walls were listening. One Monday morning, she kept up a grumbling commentary to her younger sister Roshmal, who had come to borrow some sugar. Roshmal-*khala* lived near enough that she could usually scurry across the lane without being noticed, just as Shazia did when she was visiting her cousin Wasila, who had not come with her mother because she'd been tasked with finishing up some ironing.

"Do you remember what you were doing at school at our daughters' age?" Ammi asked Roshmal-*khala* as she stirred a pot of hot, milky tea. "Studying. All these girls are learning is to cook and clean. I tell you—we're training them to be maids!"

Roshmal's nose wrinkled. "Yes, if they don't get husbands, at least they could get positions working in the household of That One. Like Yasmin."

"Yasmin's working?" Shazia looked up at her aunt's revelation about the mother of her old school friend, Farida. Of course, the whole town had heard about their bad luck six months earlier, when Yasmin's husband had died in a car accident on the way to Peshawar. Gaq's men had presented Yasmin and her children with food and money, since there were no nearby relatives to take them in. The *talibs* often did things like that, but now the town was so exhausted from their presence that it didn't gain them any praise.

"Yes, Yasmin moved into the household with her daughter,

Farida, a few months ago. He has a large staff there, just for one person."

"It's one thing to cook and clean for your own family, but can you imagine washing his clothes? Cleaning his cups and bowls? Why, I couldn't trust myself," Ammi said archly.

Roshmal-*khala's* round face flushed pink. "If you poisoned That One, you'd hang within the day. Don't even joke!"

"Of course I don't mean it," Ammi said sharply. "I only wish there were a way to encourage him to move away from our town."

"If he wasn't in charge any more, he'd go," Shazia piped up. "Baba was saying that Gaq was requested to formally run for deputy commander, if he wants to stay in the house."

"Your father said this?" Roshmal-*khala's* voice was surprised. "It's news to me."

"In a few weeks it's happening. And according to Pakistani law, women can still vote. You don't have to vote for *him*."

"Even if there were a local man foolhardy enough to go against That One, who would be brave enough to cast a vote for him?" Roshmal-*khala* asked, looking with concern at Shazia.

"Me, if I were eighteen." Shazia pictured herself at this age and wondered—would school for girls have started up again? Would she be a real graduate, or still in middle school?

"But who do you think counts the votes, checks the papers right after you drop them in the box? Asif Rashid!" Ammi answered her own question without hesitation.

Shazia imagined she was right. The town's chief constable had been eager to curry favor with the outsiders, since many policemen in other towns had been beheaded for trying to hold out against them. It wasn't like Asif Rashid was so religious, either; everyone knew he used to drink *sharab* in the old days.

But he didn't anymore, just as he turned a blind eye on the often-violent behavior of the newcomers arriving in town.

"If Asif Rashid is involved, the whole town could vote against That One and he would still rule the man a winner," Roshmal said with a delicate raise of her eyebrows. Unlike Ammi, she'd kept her eyebrows plucked, even though so few people ever saw her uncovered face.

"Let's not talk of this anymore," Ammi put down the teapot with thud. "The situation is hopeless. We should just be glad we have homes and each other."

"I'd really like to see Farida again," Shazia said. "She was in fifth standard when they closed the school. I talked about lending her my sixth class books... do you think we could invite her for tea one day?"

"She's got no time for books, since she has a job now, Shazia-*jaani*." Ammi's voice, as she called her daughter *darling*, softened slightly. "At least you have Wasila nearby."

"Amir could take us us to ask if there's a time we may visit Farida." Shazia knew her eldest male cousin had plenty of spare time: his market for pirated Bollywood films had evaporated because of the new laws.

"I don't want you at that house." Ammi put down her steel tea cup with a powerful thud. "You are too outspoken! I can only imagine you saying the wrong thing, and being overheard. Next thing, your father and I will be in prison or worse."

"But I learned everything from you," Shazia said and earned a light cuff on her ear. But Shazia had such a good idea, she didn't mind.

In the evening, Shazia sent the flashing-torch-signal from her window to Wasila. It was a method of communication they'd created as small children. Two flashes meant it was time to talk; one cousin would patiently repeat the signal until it was answered. Whoever had the first opportunity would watch for an all-clear—no morality police on the street—and bolt across to the other's home, where the door would be unlatched. Often they'd scamper back before the parents even noticed anything had happened.

Shazia didn't have any time to send a signal until after the evening meal so it was dark, and her light bounced clearly to Wasila's room. Wasila signaled back after a minute—Shazia imagined her groping for the flashlight under a large pile of the illicit, old Indian movie magazines. Wasila's signal of five flashes to Shazia meant she was free to go, and would be the one to travel.

"Wasila is coming now," Shazia casually announced to her parents, who were watching the news on television in the large, open room that served as their dining and living room. It was nine-thirty; the lights would probably last another twenty minutes before shutting off. At this time, village-wide, almost everyone was watching television, reading or doing handwork, because once the darkness came, there was very little to do until dawn's call to prayer.

"I didn't hear the mobile phone ring." Baba looked puzzled, when he opened the door a few moments later to his niece, after her light tap on it.

"The girls persist in signaling each other with lights," Ammi said. "They're very mysterious, cloak-and-dagger sorts."

"Sherlock and Watson," Baba said with a laugh, referring to the old British detective novels that Shazia and Wasila had read before the morality police had ordered them burned. Shazia didn't dignify her father's weak joke by answering. She just ushered Wasila into the closet-like room she shared with Zara, who hung onto their every word, once they'd sworn her to secrecy.

"Do you remember Farida, from school?" Shazia began.

"Sure!" Wasila answered. "She's the shy girl from the class below. Her father died—"

"Yes. And because of it, our cook said that Farida and Yasmin have become servants at Gaq's place." Shazia lowered her voice so any parents who might pass by the room wouldn't hear. "I think we should visit. It will cheer her up, and we might get some information our parents should know.

"Yes," said Wasila, who was always game for adventure. "Farida's sweet—and I'd certainly be interested in hearing about what That One is really like. But what could we bring her?"

"How about my old schoolbooks?" Shazia suggested the same thing she'd said to Ammi.

Wasila shook her head. "No, that could be dangerous if they're found. Something ordinary..."

"There's always tea," Shazia said. "But I can't go to the market by myself to buy a new package. If I went with Baba, he'd ask why I was buying it."

"I could probably take a small amount from our house," Wasila offered. "It's that cheap bitter stuff, unfortunately."

"At least it's something. Would Amir walk with us to the house, tomorrow following afternoon prayers?"

"I'm sure he will. And if anybody stops us on the street, he'll say you're Sharifa." Wasila was talking about her older sister, who was married and living nearby. This was the one advantage of the shuttlecock robes. *Burkas* covered so much, you couldn't really tell who was inside.

• • •

The next afternoon, Amir and Wasila came to the door and requested that Ammi let Shazia accompany them on a walk to gather mushrooms. A walk was more or less the truth, since they were going about three kilometers, some of it through forest. After a long argument Ammi let Shazia go, adjusting her daughter's *burka* and checking that her fingernails were short and free of polish. Nail polish was a vanity that Wasila and Shazia indulged in constantly. When life was so boring, changing one's nail color was the least that could be done, although there were no replacement bottles left to buy in Zadeh's Goods Shop.

"So, this Farida, is she pretty?" Amir asked, between puffs of his Goldleaf cigarette. Ever since Gaq had established a rule against watching films, Amir's business had evolved from film to what he called "number data"—gathering the names and account numbers of people with credit cards and using them to untoward ends. *Such a waste*, Baba had said to Ammi; if Amir had been admitted to university, he would have learned ways to use computers for good. But now Amir was his family's biggest earner, and the thought of him leaving to attend university in Peshawar seemed impossible.

"She was quite pretty back in school—how old were we then, though, twelve?" Wasila said.

"Yes, and Farida was eleven, which would make her thirteen now. She's too young and don't try your *filmi* lines on her, not with That One in the house." Shazia felt vaguely excited to be coming close to the architect of her family's misery, but she was not suicidal.

Throughout the Northwest Frontier, telephone service was spotty, so people communicated primarily with mobile phones, although that was problematic given the towering mountains that rose between villages. The deputy commissioner's home that the *maulana* now occupied had a land line, but few others did.

Shazia couldn't imagine Yasmin had a private telephone, so the three cousins walked four miles to stand before a buzzer that had been set into the great stucco wall surrounding the grand old deputy commissioner's bungalow. The home surrounded by a high wall was built during British times and was comprised of a main house with a great room, parlors, and three bedrooms. There was a separate house where she imagined Yasmin and Farida slept with any other female servants, and an extra guesthouse for male visitors. Shazia had been inside once, for an Eid celebration when she was much younger. The old Deputy Commissioner, Mustafa Khattack, had given out candy to all the children.

Shortly after the buzzer sounded, Yasmin's voice came tinnily over the intercom, asking who was there. When Amir gave all of their names, she buzzed them through the high iron gate to the main building.

"What a surprise!" Yasmin said. She wore a *burka,* even though she was inside the house, but the slit revealing her eyes showed that they were bright with happiness at their visit. Shazia wondered how long it had been since she and Farida had seen old neighbors from the village.

Yasmin at first refused the gift of tea, then accepted it with many thanks. She explained all the other female servants had left and offered to take the girls *burkas*, which they gave up with pleasure.

"The *maulana* is at Dr. Khan's home, attending an election planning meeting. You two go can go through the hall and join Farida in the kitchen. Sir, I'll bring you tea, but please wait in the side garden," she added to Amir.

"Thank you, Yasmin-*khala*," the girls chorused. Holding shoes in hands, so as not to leave anything incriminating at the entry, they walked along the cool marble floors that were so clean their bare feet squeaked. At the end of the front hall was an arched open doorway that led to a garden. There, amid a struggling array of small palm trees not suitable for the northern climate, they left Amir to wait. He took out his mobile phone and started to play a game, looking up once at Shazia with an expression that seemed to say, *don't take too long.*

Inside the main house they located the kitchen and Farida, who was squatting on the floor. She was sorting lentils, carefully placing the perfect ones in a bowl and the inferior ones on a cloth on the floor. Farida may have been thirteen, with her long, silky black hair worn in braids just like their own, but there was an exhausted sorrow in her face that drew down her bow-shaped lips Shazia. She was not wearing a *burka,* but a gray *hijab* covered her hair and the top of the black *shalwar kameez* suit that she wore.

"Farida! It's been too long," Shazia said, getting on her knees to join her. The girls clasped hands, and Shazia was surprised to feel how rough Farida's palms were; like those of a mother, not a girl. Wasila, too, moved closer to greet their old schoolmate.

"Sorry, I need to get this finished before *Maulana* returns," Farida said, dropping her hands and sitting down again with the lentils. "Such a pretty *hijab* you're wearing, Wasila. It's not from a local shop, is it?"

"No, my brother brought it from Peshawar. It's not new,"

Wasila answered, slipping the grape-colored head-and-shoulders scarf off her shoulders and over Farida's. Amir had business dealings that sometimes resulted in gifts. In the old days Amir had given both girls movie magazines and CDs, but that was too risky now. "You take it. It's nicer than the tea."

Farida shook her head. "Please take it back. I couldn't risk having anything pretty and new like that noticed. I think some of his men have been in my room, looking. Or maybe he's done it himself."

Shazia exchanged glances with Farida; this didn't sound good at all.

• • •

Yasmin brewed the cheap black tea that they'd brought, mixing in cloves, ginger and cinnamon.

"I'm sorry I can't give you sugar—the *maulana* believes it causes excitability in women," Yasmin apologized.

"The tea, as you've made it, is very delicious!" Shazia assured her, although without sugar, it was even more bitter than it had been at home.

Yasmin smiled sadly and melted away to the scullery area where the sounds of vigorous washing commenced. The girls chatted leisurely, giving Farida the town's gossip, and when the tea was finished Farida said she would show them around.

"Just so you know—I have a special place," Farida said, leading them through the marble halls and toward the sunlight of the garden. Under scrubby weeds circling a walnut tree, she found a flat stone and lifted it. Underneath lay the flat top of a brass box. Farida took a key attached to the string of her *shalwar* trousers to open the box. Inside were banknotes bundled together with rubber bands, identity papers, and a mobile phone. "You can text me if you like. It's always on silent mode."

"I can't believe you're showing us this," Wasila said. "Your secret treasure box!"

"I want you to know where it is. "Just in case anything happens to us."

"What could happen?" Shazia asked, feeling a tightness in her chest.

In a small voice, Farida said, "I'm—I'm not sure I want to stay here."

"Yes," Wasila said sympathetically. "The work seems very hard—"

"No, it's not the work. It's the *maulana*."

"Is he cruel?" Shazia's heart was beating more rapidly.

Farida gave a shudder that was so delicate her *hijab* barely moved, but Shazia noticed it.

"What is it, Farida?"

"He—he's begun asking me to be the one to always bring him things and serve his meals. If my mother was there I wouldn't mind but he stares at me so that it frightens me. I don't know what he's thinking; anyway, I cannot say no to him. If I did—can you imagine?"

Shazia and Wasila exchanged glances, and then Wasila said, "Amir has his own cell phone. You must call us on that, right away, if you need help. That mobile phone—does it still work?"

"Yes. We recharge it when we have a chance, and check messages every day, when the men are gone. If you want to meet again, call me at this number." She wrote it down on a corner of one of the notebook pages the girls had given her, and tore it off and gave it to Wasila.

"What's his daily schedule?" Shazia was thinking about returning to see Farida, but she certainly didn't want to run into the imam.

"He goes out by late morning to the mosque or the *madrassa*, but he's home most evenings. Except Wednesdays for the political meeting."

"Who's at those meetings?" Shazia realized it would be useful to know exactly who in the village couldn't be trusted.

Farida named Constable Asif Rashid, which was no surprise, and several clerics who had lived in the town for years, and a representative of the district council who lived in the next town, and the town's physician, Dr. Hussein. Shazia was mulling over the significance of these men when a rattling sound came from the house.

The three girls turned to see Amir standing in the doorway. As Shazia's heartbeat returned to a relieved, normal pace, her male cousin nodded awkwardly toward them, then stared with interest at Farida.

"You fool!" Wasila screeched at her brother, as Farida turned to fling the scarf that had fallen to her shoulders over her head.

"Sorry!" Amir croaked, disappearing from the room just as the sound of Yasmin's voice rose from the side garden, asking him if he would try a few sweets.

"I'm sorry for my brother's boldness," Wasila apologized. "He must have come to tell us we'd stayed too long!"

"Yes," Shazia said. "We still have to find mushrooms before it gets dark."

The girls were subdued on their walk home, though Amir was

full of commentary. While the girls had been with Farida, Amir had sneaked around a bit and seen something you wouldn't expect a *maulana* to have: a big-screen television with a satellite channel box.

"The television was off, but the name of the channel he'd been watching was on the box. It's the adult channel," Amir said. "What a hypocrite! And how does he get it? That stuff is prohibited by our government. He must have some very strong satellite getting shows from abroad..."

"There are all kinds of satellites around," Wasila agreed. "American ones, Indian..."

Shazia typically would have enjoyed this kind of speculation, but she was more concerned about what it meant for the women in the house. "Now I know why Farida's so worried about Gaq asking her to serve him alone."

"Serve him alone?" Amir suddenly seemed less jovial. "But that's against the rules!"

"He makes rules for everyone else," Wasila said. "But not himself."

The next day it rained, but the town punishments were still on schedule for three o'clock in the afternoon. Everyone over the age of twelve was expected to fill the stands of the soccer stadium. On a platform set up in the field's center, two unlucky people awaited their respective punishments. There was a man who'd stolen bread—"for his children," Ammi had murmured under her breath—and a shrouded woman.

The girls shut their eyes tightly while the man lost his hand with an anguished scream that never seemed to stop. But when the shrouded woman's name was pronounced aloud, Shazia's eyes flew open and she gasped. She was Miss Shireen, their old teacher from the girls' school. Another lady sitting near them murmured that Miss Shireen had run out of her house without a *burka* when her toddler son had wandered out the door and into the road. Unfortunately, the *talibs* were passing by.

The sound of the blows, and the teacher's choked cries, made Shazia writhe. She wanted to run away to a world where this wasn't happening: anywhere, even India, Pakistan's big enemy. But to move would attract notice. She remained as trapped as all of them.

When all the punishments were finished, the *maulana* took center stage. Gaq stood in all his glory, long scraggly silver beard hanging over his black robe, his hair hidden in his large, twisted, gray-red turban. The passages he was reciting went unabsorbed by Shazia. She was thinking about what he had ordered done to the man and woman; what he was doing to all of them. Two years he'd been in power, and all this had happened; if he stayed, what would life be like in ten years?

That night, what Gaq's big screen television nagged at her as she tossed and turned. Such hypocrisy. But then she had a strange dream—and by the time she'd woken up, a really good idea.

• • •

"Amir, what do you know about bad movies?" Shazia asked. She was visiting Wasila and Amir's house later that morning; the mothers, covered by their *burkas* despite the midsummer heat, were in the garden hanging laundry.

The girls were rolling chapattis for lunch, and Amir, who was supposed to be downloading virus protection on his computer, had come in to badger them to make him a cup of tea.

"Bad movies? You mean, where the acting's terrible... or the story is immoral? There's plenty of both, often in the same film." Amir took his cup of tea and after sipping, groaned. "That's almost as bitter as the tea Yasmin-*khala* gave! Are you also denying me sugar?"

"Sugar's in short supply for everyone," Wasila replied with a sneer.

"Amir, can a person buy bad movies through mail order, just like you did all those Bollywood films when you were running that business?" Shazia continued.

"Yes, of course. Not that I'll buy one for you! Even if there weren't rules against it, you shouldn't be thinking about things like that."

"Amir, since you know so much... what do you think might happen if That One were discovered to have ordered such type of films?" Wasila asked on cue.

Amir made a *you're-crazy* circle with his finger. "He watches that filth on his TV already. He doesn't need to order anything."

"But if a package addressed to him came from India to Pakistan...customs might open it, and then the government would charge him with a crime!" Wasila said.

"Or the postmaster would not say anything but demand some kind of pay off," Amir countered. "I sometimes had to pay bribes when I was pirating CDs and DVDs. I budgeted for it!"

"That kind of trouble could hurt his campaign, couldn't it?" Shazia asked. "Even if the package made it to his house, he could have trouble."

"Not really. If he opened the package in his home, nobody would see," Amir said.

Shazia sighed. Her elder cousin was so slow. "If he opens it at home, he'll surely take the time to view it before he throws it away. And I'm not sure he'd want to throw it away. And that could be his undoing."

"Somebody from the outside would have to see the film." From Amir's pensive tone, it seemed he finally understood—and was becoming interested—in Shazia's scheme.

"Yes. How about his election committee?" Shazia said to him. "We've got Farida living inside his house, with her own mobile and a land-line. She can tell us what he's doing when. And then it's just up to us to get the men of the town over to the house to catch him."

"If Farida's caught, she would receive a lot more than a caning," Amir said.

They all would. That was left unspoken.

• • •

The details were simple. First, Shazia and Wasila looked at one of Amir's old catalogs to choose a film, judging strictly by title and cover. Amir pulled up numbers data on a Visa cardholder in California. A few strokes of the keyboard brought a pleasant confirmation email that the goods had been purchased and would immediately ship to one of Amir's old black market contacts in India. Because of the challenges in cross-border smuggling, Amir's contact thought the venture might take two weeks. The election was two-and-a-half weeks away, which meant that the timing was close, but Shazia was hopeful. She'd been in telephone contact with Farida, who assured her that she would keep a close eye on Gaq's behavior and the location of any packages he might bring into the house.

Gaq's assistant, Iqbal Shad, made a sweep of the post office several times a week, and with the election coming up, he went daily. Sixteen days after the order was placed, Iqbal Shad picked up a flat, plastic-wrapped package for the *maulana.*

"Probably a campaign contribution," he'd reportedly said to the postmaster, who'd naturally commented on the India postmark. When Iqbal Shad had gone to pick up his boss in the center of town, he'd handed him the package with a flourish that had been noticed by two shopkeepers, six children and even Ammi, who was with Baba on one of her rare trips outside the house.

"That One was strange today, opening a parcel and then quickly shoving it into his clothes," Ammi recounted as she was peeling potatoes. "I wonder if it's bad news from the government?"

"Not likely," Baba said glumly. "More likely it's seeds. He wants more of the farmers to start growing poppies. I don't know how long I can hold out against him."

Shazia could hardly bear until the meal was finished, and she'd have a chance to get over to her cousins' house to use Amir's cell phone to call Farida. But finally, it happened. To her surprise, the call didn't ring into Farida's voicemail, but was picked up by the girl herself.

"I saw the package arrive!" Farida said by way of greeting.

"Does he—has he thrown it away?" That was Shazia's secret fear, that all would be wasted.

"I'm not certain—he doesn't seem any different in demeanor. He came in, said he didn't want to eat anything, and asked Iqbal Shad to drive his whole entourage to Shangla look at some weapons."

"Tomorrow?"

"No. He sent Iqbal Shad right away. Iqbal grumbled to the others about it, because who wants to drive in the dark just to go somewhere and look, not buy?"

"So Gaq is home alone with the film." Shazia pondered the significance of this.

"Yes. He went into his study with the DVD player straightaway. He forgot his five o'clock prayers, can you imagine that? Mother said he must not be feeling right."

"Really?" Things were moving almost too fast. "Farida, go about your normal business. But can you keep the telephone close?"

"Yes. It will stay in the inside pocket of my *burka*."

• • •

Dr. Hussein was not at his surgery office nor his home—but at an election committee meeting at the mosque. Amir, posing as one of the *talibs*, reached the physician on his mobile phone. "The *maulana* not well," he intoned, speaking in Urdu, not Pashto, so he sounded more foreign. "Please come to the house to see what you can do."

Dr. Hussein had asked for Gaq to come to the phone, but Amir pleaded that the religious leader had lost consciousness. "Please, Doctor, just come to the house and see for yourself!"

There was no ambulance in the village, so the vehicle that rushed up to the house was Dr. Khan's Land Cruiser. Out of it sprang not only the town doctor with his bag, but all the others on the committee including Chief Constable Asif Rashid. After buzzing open the gate, Yasmin and Farida melted away, leaving Yusuf, the sweeper who was half-blind and senile, opened the door to the visitors. He stammered out that he had heard nothing about an illness. When Dr. Hossein demanded to see the housekeeper, Yasmin was brought forward. In a frightened voice, she told the doctor she had not seen the *maulana* in the past two hours because he'd refused an evening meal and told her to take her daughter to the women's quarters. All the servants had been sent out of the house to their quarters, so nobody had heard about the health emergency one of the *talibs* had called the doctor about.

"Know-nothing woman!" Constable Asif Rashid scolded and pushed past her toward the *maulana's* room. The other men thundered past, kicking off their sandals behind them, raising a tiny cloud of dust that made Farida cough. Still, she followed, a tiny black shadow that nobody noticed.

As everyone drew closer to the *maulana's* room, strange sounds came faintly through the door: a kind of frenzied breathing, and the most peculiar groans Farida had ever heard, as she later narrated to her friends. Asif Rashid broke open the locked door with the key he'd taken from Yasmin. As the policeman, the doctor and all the companions entered the room, the grunts turned to shouts: first from the imam, and then from Constable Rashid.

From her hiding place, Farida saw the big-screen television filled with a glowing image of a bare golden body. Gaq lay sprawled on cushions very close to the screen, seemingly oblivious to his visitors until the last minute. The DVD package was on the prayer rug, and Farida could clearly see the picture of half-naked women and the film's title: *Hot Girls in the City.*

Farida fled the room and out to the hall, where her mother was waiting. Holding hands, the two rushed out to the garden to scoop up their hidden possessions. They then crept under the cover of darkness across the fields and forests to Shazia's house.

The ladies' knocking on the backdoor awoke Shazia and her parents. The guests, in hushed voices, told about what had transpired at the great house. Ammi and Baba were shocked, but said that Yasmin and Farida must certainly take shelter and be moved to a safer location outside the village the next day.

Shazia could barely sleep that night, but this time it was because she was excited. All had gone according to plan. But what might come next? Would news get out and spoil Gaq's chances in the election?

The answer came the next afternoon, when Baba came in with something he'd heard at the mosque. Just before prayers, the old Imam in charge of the place had come forward and made a startling announcement. Ghulam Ali Qadir had been relieved of his duties. He no longer had authority over the village.

"Why is this?"

"What about the election?"

The crowd of male worshippers, at first shocked into silence, had many questions.

"The *maulana* will not run for deputy commissioner," the Imam intoned. "It's not my decision, but a matter of abiding by *sharia* law. You will learn more after the trial."

"What trial?" Baba had called out, one voice among many.

"The *maulana's trial.* He will be tried privately by the *jirga* and then have his sentence carried out at three o'clock this afternoon."

• • •

The stadium was full that afternoon, but it seemed to Shazia that the townspeople seemed to be hiding smiles. And though the *maulana* sputtered and blustered, the case against him was short and sweet. Representatives of the *jirga* recounted the details of the package that had arrived, what had been found at the home. Although he had proclaimed innocence, the fact that he had a television with stored pornographic materials belied his words. The sentence was severe: stoning to death. Now the morals police were tasked with doing away the *maulana*.

When the sentencing was carried out, Shazia kept her eyes tightly shut as usual, and her hands clamped on her ears. But after the broken body had been carried away and everyone rose up to leave, there was a roaring sound in the street. She opened her eyes to see a small convoy of jeeps, SUVs and trucks leaving town. Gaq's old assistant Iqbal Shad and Constable Ali Rashid ran after the vehicles, and someone reached down from a jeep to pull them up.

A cloud of dust hung on the street after the vehicles had groaned their way out of the village. But as the dust dispersed, a cheering began. The men hurried off to the teashops to find out who wanted to run for mayor. Inside the houses, women put kettles on and called for friends to come over. Boys and even a few girls took their cricket bats and ball and set up in the park. Little ones everywhere shrieked with laughter and played tag.

"This is not what I expected," Shazia said, when she, Farida and Wasila had finally settled down after the revelry to very sugary tea and biscuits. "I never intended to *kill* anyone."

"You didn't kill him. Their laws made it happen," Wasila pointed out.

"Be quiet; we must never speak of it again," said Farida with a warning look toward the garden, where all the mothers were gossiping. "More sugar, please!"

The next morning, all three girls took turns riding on the back of one of the many bicycles that Amir and his friends brought back from the *madrassa*. Shazia's balance was off after two years of inactivity and the burden of her *burka*. Amir grumbled until Shazia gained her confidence and was sitting in a secure sidesaddle position. Then, as he picked up speed, Shazia felt a laugh start inside her, something crazy and deep that she wasn't afraid to let out, for once.

More About This Book

Some of the works within *India Gray: Historical Fiction* are very recent. Others were previously published. Here's the background:

The Ayah's Tale is a stand-alone novella that I wrote following a few interesting months that I had in India with my own baby daughter and an ayah that relatives felt certain I needed. After the experience, I realized how difficult such relationships are. Imagine throwing colonialism on top of the ordinary tensions between mother, caregiver and children! If you'd like to read more about children and ayahs in British Colonial India, I recommend *Two Under The Indian Sun* by Jon and Rumer Godden, and *Plain Tales From The Raj* edited by Charles Allen.

I wrote *Bitter Tea* in 2007 for a mystery anthology because I was concerned about the growing subjugation of women in rural parts of South Asia. Then, in 2012, 15-year-old Malala Yousafzai was shot for disobeying the school restrictions put on girls by the Taliban invaders of her town in Pakistan's Northwest Frontier. She reminded me so much of a more serious version of Shazia. I recommend Malala's memoir, *I Am Malala: The Girl Who Stood Up For Education And Was Shot By the Taliban.* She's also published a young reader's edition that's suitable for elementary and middle-school students.

If you were intrigued the World War II Indian setting of "*India Gray*," you will probably like *The Sleeping Dictionary*, a novel spanning 1930-1947 featuring Kamala. *The Sleeping Dictionary* was published in 2013 by Simon & Schuster and is available as a trade paperback, ebook and audiobook. In India, it's published under the title *The City of Palaces*. It's also published in Italy and Turkey.

I became interested in the history of Indian students within Britain after reading Antoinette Burton's *The Heart of the Empire: the Colonial Encounter in Victorian Britain*. For fascinating details on St. Hilda's College and the lives of women students, I'm indebted to the St. Hilda's Emeritus Fellow Margaret C. Rayner, a retired Tutor in mathematics at St. Hilda's and author of *The Centenary History of St. Hilda's College, Oxford*. Any mistakes about St. Hilda's or Oxford's complicated structure and history are all my own!

I enjoyed the characters of Perveen and Alice so much that my next full-length novel will be a legal mystery set in 1920s India. Perveen and Alice will find themselves embroiled in a complex case that exposes the plight of wealthy, secluded women. Look for it in 2017.

Sujata

About the Author

Sujata Massey is the author of twelve novels, two novellas, and numerous short stories. Her work is published in seventeen countries. Her novels have won the Agatha and Macavity awards and been finalists for the Edgar, Anthony, and Mary Higgins Clark prizes. Sujata writes a modern mystery series set in Japan starring the young female amateur sleuth Rei Shimura, and suspense and mystery fiction set in late British colonial India featuring different heroines.

Sujata was born in England to parents from India and Germany, and was raised mostly in St. Paul, Minnesota, although her home for more than a quarter century has been Baltimore, Maryland. She holds a B.A. in the Writing Seminars from the Johns Hopkins University and was a features reporter for the Baltimore *Evening Sun* newspaper before becoming a fulltime novelist.

Sujata welcomes correspondence from readers. For an answer to a specific question, contact her via her website (sujatamassey.com) or visit Sujata Massey Author on Facebook. She also sends a free newsletter, *AsiaFile,* to super-fans interested in book news, Asian recipes, and giveaways. For a free email subscription to *AsiaFile,* sign up at her website.

Made in the USA
Middletown, DE
25 February 2024

Praise for Sujata Massey's Historical Fiction

"Massey deftly plays with several strong threads, each of which gives a certain heft to the story. She explores the relationship between parents and children, Indians and British, upper and lower classes, hope and hopelessness, India and abroad, stories and reality. Read it to find out what speaks to you most."
—*South of the Border, West of the Sun*

"Sujata Massey beautifully depicts the life of an Indian ayah and the complicated relationships that people in the employ of their colonial masters had to deal with. Even though Menakshi endures great hardships in her life, she feels love in these pages and the prospect of a more hopeful future."
—*Marie's Book Garden*

"Evocative descriptions of the late Raj period's Indian cultures, customs, cuisine, flora and fauna are narrated delightfully. Although this is essentially a story of love and human endurance, Massey, an award-winning author, has admirably woven event of the Indian independence movement into her plot . . . this is an informative and entertaining historical novel."
—*The Historical Novel Society*

"Historical fiction at its best."
—*Booklist* (starred review)

Other Books by Sujata Massey

India Books

The Sleeping Dictionary (2013)
The Ayah's Tale (2013)
India Gray: Historical Fiction (2015)

Japan Books

The Salaryman's Wife (1997)
Zen Attitude (1998)
The Flower Master (2000)
The Floating Girl (2001)
The Bride's Kimono (2002)
The Samurai's Daughter (2003)
The Pearl Diver (2004)
The Typhoon Lover (2005)
Girl In A Box (2006)
Shimura Trouble (2008)
The Kizuna Coast (2014)